Titles by Sofie Kelly

A CASE OF CAT
AND MOUSE

A MAGICAL CATS MYSTERY

SOFIE KELLY

BERKLEY PRIME CRIME
New York

BERKLEY PRIME CRIME
Published by Berkley
An imprint of Penguin Random House LLC
penguinrandomhouse.com

ISBN: 9780440001195

Berkley Prime Crime hardcover edition / September 2020
Berkley Prime Crime mass-market edition / August 2021

Printed in the United States of America
1   3   5   7   9   10   8   6   4   2

Book design by Kelly Lipovich

1

"Dead?" Rebecca asked.

I sighed. "I'm sorry. Yes."

"That's what I was afraid of." She looked glum, which was surprising because Rebecca was a very positive person in general, and the dead thing we were looking at was a glass bowl filled with an inactive sourdough starter.

"How long have you had it?" I asked. Rebecca had been baking since she was a girl, so her starter was likely years old.

Two splotches of pink appeared on her cheeks and she ducked her head. "Less than a month."

"Oh," I said. That was a surprise.

Her blue eyes met mine. "Kathleen, when it comes to starters, I have to confess that I'm the kiss of death."

I smiled. "I find that hard to believe. You're a very good cook. No one makes piecrust as flaky as yours."

"Well, I do like to feed people," she said.

I glanced over my shoulder at my two cats, Owen

and Hercules, sitting by the chrome kitchen table, their gaze fixed on Rebecca. "And cats," I teased.

Rebecca smiled. She kept Owen supplied with yellow catnip chickens and Hercules with tiny organic kitty crackers. They both adored her. "It seems feeding is the problem. According to Eric, I've been over-feeding my starter."

Eric was Eric Cullen. He owned a diner downtown, near the waterfront.

"Where did this one come from?" I picked up the bowl and gave the contents a swirl. It was an odd, unappetizing shade of pink and it had a funky smell of decay that just confirmed what my eyes were telling me.

"Eric gave it to me," Rebecca said. She took the dish out of my hands and poured it down the sink.

"Well, I'm sure he would be happy to get you started again," I said.

Eric wasn't just a great cook, he was also a very generous person, quick to offer his time and talents to his friends and to the community.

Color flooded Rebecca's face a second time. "I really don't feel I can ask him again. The third time may be the charm, as my mother used to say, but I think the fourth time would be just making a pest of myself." She rinsed the bowl and set it on the counter. Then she dried her hands and turned to face me. "I don't just need a bit of starter to get one of my own growing again. I need a lot. I need enough to bake with. I may have inherited my mother's love of feeding people, but I didn't get her way with a sourdough loaf. I need to practice my bread at least a couple more times. And I have to leave some free time because we're filming promos this afternoon."

Rebecca was one of the contestants on the revival of the television show *The Great Northern Baking Showdown*. Filming for the first season had begun here in town in April. Six episodes had been completed and there were just four more left to film. Mayville Heights had been chosen, among other reasons, because the show's executive producer, Elias Braeden, who had bought the rights to the show, was from this part of Minnesota. And he knew it would be very affordable to film here. Rumor had it that a major network and at least one streaming service were interested in the show, but as far as I knew it hadn't been sold to any outlet yet, so the filming budget was tight. Participants on the show came from Minnesota, Wisconsin and Illinois. Rebecca and artist Ray Nightingale were the only local contestants. They had won their places in a regional event.

No one had been surprised when Rebecca was among the top three in the area competition. Anyone who had ever had a slice of one of her blueberry pies or a bite of her pumpkin spice donuts—which was pretty much everyone in town—knew she was a talented baker.

Ray Nightingale also making it onto the show was much more unexpected. Ray was an artist who created elaborate ink drawings that were a cross between a mosaic and a Where's Waldo? illustration. They featured a small rubber duck named Bo who always wore a fedora and black-framed sunglasses. No one had had any hint that Ray even knew the difference between shortbread and puff pastry or how to make a croquembouche. He and Rebecca had become fast friends once they'd won their places on the show.

"Well, what about Ray? He might have some starter," I suggested.

Rebecca made a face. "I'm sure he'd want to help," she said. "But he needs to practice just as much as I do. He'll need every bit of his own starter."

Rebecca's goal was to finish in the top three once again. There would be a three-minute profile on each of the finalists at the beginning of the finale episode of the show. She was hoping to focus as much attention as she could on Mayville Heights during her segment.

Like a lot of small places, the town's economy depended on tourists who enjoyed our quieter pace of life and the gorgeous scenery. In some ways the town hadn't changed that much in the past hundred years or so. That was part of its charm. From the St. James Hotel you could still watch the boats and barges go by the way they had a century ago. You could still climb to the top of Wild Rose Bluff for a spectacular view of the water.

Aside from some shots of the Riverwalk, the Stratton Theatre and the gazebo at the back of the library that were used in the opening credits, Mayville Heights hadn't been mentioned much at all in the show up to now. The spotlight was on the competition and the bakers.

Ray was easygoing and affable but he had admitted to me that he wanted to win the competition. Like Rebecca, he wanted the opportunity to bring some attention to everything Mayville Heights had to offer. I suspected in his case it was more about redemption than his love for the town. In the past Ray had helped fudge some artistic credentials for another artist and had come within a hairsbreadth of being kicked out of the local artists' co-operative. To his credit, he had worked hard to get back in his fellow artists' good graces—not just apologizing but working to promote both the artists' co-op store and its website as well as volunteering his talents with the rescue group Cat People.

Rebecca was staring at a point somewhere over my left shoulder, probably trying to think of anyone she knew who could help her. Who did I know who made sourdough bread? I couldn't think of a single person, although I had had sourdough pancakes just last weekend at my friends Eddie and Roma's house.

"Eddie," I said, holding out both hands as though the answer was obvious—which it suddenly was.

Rebecca gave her head a little shake and focused on me again. "Excuse me, what did you say?" she asked.

"Eddie," I repeated. "He doesn't make bread, at least as far as I know, but sourdough pumpkin pancakes are his specialty. Roma said when he was still playing hockey it was tradition for him to make them before every Saturday home game. And I've had them. They're really good." My stomach suddenly rumbled as if to give more credence to my words.

"I suppose it wouldn't hurt to ask," Rebecca said, a smile starting to pull at the corners of her mouth.

Her phone was lying on the kitchen table and I gestured at it. "Call him," I urged. "I'll drive you out there. I don't have to be at the library until twelve thirty and I already have all the information ready to drop off to Eugenie and Russell."

The Baking Showdown was being hosted by cookbook author Eugenie Bowles-Hamilton, along with musician Russell Perry. Two weeks ago I had been hired to replace the show's researcher, who had broken both of his arms trying to vault over a sofa to win a bet. Football and a large amount of beer had been involved, I'd been told.

I'd gotten to know Eugenie when she'd come into the library a few days after she'd arrived in town, looking for more information about Minnesota than the show was supplying her with. She wanted to work in regional references whenever she could during the filming of each episode.

"I want more than just the usual drivel about which is the best choice for pastry: butter or lard," she'd told me. I'd taken that as a criticism of the information she'd been getting from the show's researcher. "I want Minnesota color and flavor." The animation in her voice and her gesturing hands were a contrast to her cool and elegant appearance.

"Did you know the Bundt pan was invented here?" I'd asked. "So was the pop-up toaster. And some people believe that airplane hijacker D. B. Cooper was a Minnesotan."

Eugenie had smiled then. "That's the kind of thing I'm looking for."

I'd answered her questions, found her a couple of reference books and then dropped off another book and a magazine to her the next day. When the research job had become vacant Eugenie had lobbied hard for me to take it.

It was only part-time, providing background information that dovetailed with whatever each week's focus was. So far I'd been able to juggle it with my work at the library. Like most librarians, I have good research skills. In any given day I might be asked what time the recycling center closes, how many wives Ben Cartwright had on *Bonanza* and what color puce actually is—four thirty, three and purplish brown, respectively.

However, I was fairly certain that Elias had offered me the job as much because of the show's tight filming schedule and financial constraints as for my expertise and Eugenie's support. Although there seemed to be a lot of people connected to the Baking Showdown, I knew that keeping costs down was important, given that the show had not been sold yet.

Rebecca's smile grew wider as she considered my suggestion. "Having you drive would be a big help. I don't think it would be a good idea for me to be behind the wheel and holding on to a bowl full of starter at the same time."

At her feet Owen suddenly meowed loudly.

"Good point, Owen," Rebecca said to the cat. "I should call Eddie first before I start making any plans.

I'm getting a little ahead of myself, counting my chickens before they're hatched, so to speak." She reached for her phone while Owen looked around the room. As far as he was concerned there was only one type of chicken he cared about.

I leaned toward him. "Rebecca's not talking about your kind of chicken," I said softly.

"Mrrr," he muttered, wrinkling his nose in annoyance. With a flick of his tail he headed for the living room. If we weren't talking about a yellow catnip Fred the Funky Chicken, Owen didn't seem to see the point of the conversation.

Hercules watched his brother go and then looked up at me. He almost seemed to shrug. The charm of catnip was lost on the little black-and-white tuxedo cat. I reached over and gave him a scratch on the top of his head before I straightened up.

Rebecca was just ending her phone call. I was pretty sure by the wide smile on her face that Eddie had agreed to help her.

"He said yes?" I asked.

She nodded. "I explained my predicament and Eddie said he would be happy to give me the lion's share of his starter. We can drive out to Wisteria Hill right now, if that will work for you. He's out there working on the new home for the cats."

"I'm ready," I said. "All I need are my shoes and my bag." I picked my mug up off the table and drank the last mouthful of coffee. It was cold but I didn't really mind.

"Are you sure I'm not taking you from anything

important?" Rebecca asked. She brushed a bit of flour off the front of her long-sleeved pink T-shirt.

"I'm positive." I set the cup in the sink and crossed the kitchen to get my shoes. The only plans I'd had before she'd shown up at my back door with a troubled expression and the rank-smelling bowl of starter was to scrub the kitchen floor, and that could wait for another day.

"You're in charge," I said to Hercules. He immediately sat up straighter as if he had understood my words. Given that Herc—and Owen—weren't exactly ordinary cats, I was fairly certain he had.

Rebecca didn't think it was the slightest bit odd that I talked to the boys pretty much as though they were people. She talked to Owen and Hercules all the time as well, and as she'd said more than once, with just the slightest edge of indignation in her voice, "Cats are people, too!" Now she leaned forward and smiled at Hercules. "There's a little something special in your future," she said in a low voice.

"No, there is not," I said firmly, shaking my head for emphasis. "Hercules does *not* need a treat and neither does Owen. You spoil them." We had had this conversation several times before. I had no illusions that anything I said would dissuade Rebecca, but I still felt I should make the argument.

"I didn't say I was going to give him a treat," she said. "This is just something to help with his recuperation."

Apparently, Hercules knew what the word "recuperation" meant. He immediately looked at his back right leg where a patch of black fur was beginning to regrow. He'd had to have stitches there after catching his leg on some old wire fencing buried in the bushes between my house and the one next door belonging to the Justasons. Mike Justason had immediately cleared out all the rusted wire and trimmed back the bushes. He had a dog that often nosed around in the same spot. Hercules was still giving the area a wide berth.

Neither Hercules nor Owen liked to be touched by anyone other than me, probably because they had been feral early in their lives. That made visits to the vet traumatic for everyone, but Roma had managed to sedate Hercules so she could clean and stitch his wound and give him a shot. She'd been watching him carefully for any signs of infection since then.

The cat had suffered through the indignity of wearing a cone for several days and was still trying to convince me to wait on him every chance he got.

"He's already recuperated," I said as I pulled on my dark gray hoodie. It was cooler than usual for late May. I fished the keys to my truck out of my right pocket. "I'm ready."

Hercules followed us out into the sun porch and hopped up onto the bench by the side window. "We'll be back soon," I said.

Out of the corner of my eye I saw Rebecca wink at him. I was pretty sure that like every other conversation I had had with Rebecca—or really anyone else—about treats for Owen and Hercules I was going to be roundly ignored.

We climbed into my truck and I headed up Mountain Road. Until recently, Wisteria Hill, where Roma and Eddie lived, had belonged to Rebecca's husband, Everett Henderson. He'd sold it to Roma. Now Roma and Eddie were married and they were working on the property, turning it back into the much-loved home it had been when Everett was young. It was Everett who had brought me from Boston to Mayville Heights to oversee the renovations to the library for its centennial—his gift to the town. I had originally come to town on a two-year contract to supervise the project. I hadn't expected to stay. I hadn't expected that I would ever want to stay.

Back then I'd wanted to shake up my life for a number of reasons, not the least of which was the fact that my boyfriend, who had gone to Maine on a two-week fishing trip after we had had a major fight, had come back married. And not to me. (For the record: friendly diner, even friendlier waitress, lots of alcohol.)

I loved my wacky family—Mom and Dad, and Ethan and Sara. And I missed them like crazy. They were all artistic; impetuous and unpredictable. Mom and Dad were actors. Ethan was a musician. Sara was a makeup artist and filmmaker. The artistic temperament had somehow skipped me. I was organized, responsible, pragmatic. Someone had to run the washing machine. Someone had to keep us in Band-Aids, ice packs and aspirin.

I had been the practical person in the family as far back as I could remember. Coming to Mayville Heights, coming halfway across the country to Minnesota, had been the most impulsive thing I'd ever done. I hadn't expected to make friends, to make a whole new life.

So many things had changed for me in the last four years. I'd made friends who felt like family, fallen in love with the incredibly handsome and equally stubborn Detective Marcus Gordon and I'd found Owen and Hercules—or, closer to the truth, they had found me.

"Do you remember the first time you saw Wisteria Hill?" Rebecca asked as though she had somehow known what I was thinking.

I shot her a quick sideways glance. "Yes, I do." For a long time Everett had had complicated feelings about his family homestead. He didn't want to live there, but he wouldn't sell the property, either. It had been overgrown and neglected when I discovered the old farmhouse one late winter day just after I'd arrived in town.

"Hercules and Owen were just kittens then," Rebecca said. "I have a photograph somewhere of them sitting on your back steps."

I grinned. "They were so tiny the first time I saw them, but they were determined to come home with me. I had no idea I was going to end up with two opinionated, furry roommates." I had actually carried the kittens back up the long driveway a couple of times when they'd followed me, but they would not be dissuaded.

I glanced at Rebecca again as the road curved uphill. "Do you ever regret Everett selling the property to Roma?" I asked.

Rebecca's mother had kept house for the Hendersons as well as using her herbal remedies as a kind of unofficial nurse to most of the townspeople. Rebecca had basically grown up at Wisteria Hill and she and Everett had loved each other all their lives.

Out of the corner of my eye I saw her smile as she shook her head. "No, I don't. I've seen what can happen when you live in the past. I have so many happy memories of the place as a child, picking blueberries in the back field and blackberries on Mulberry Hill, climbing trees, swimming in the stream. But I don't want to go backward. I like where we are now."

"So do I," I said. Rebecca and I were backyard neighbors. She was the one who had first taken me to tai chi class and to Meatloaf Tuesday at Fern's Diner.

"I'm happy that Roma and Eddie are building their life out at Wisteria Hill. That's how it should be."

When we got to the top of the long driveway we spotted Eddie up on a ladder in a clearing back away from the driveway, working on one of the small outbuildings on the property that had been moved up closer to the old carriage house. The farmhouse was to the right of the driveway. It was white with dark blue shutters and yellow doors. Roma had done a lot of work on the house even before she and Eddie had gotten married—which had taken place in their living room.

"One thing I most certainly do not miss is that bumpy old driveway," Rebecca said.

I nodded in agreement. For a long time the driveway had been nothing more than two ruts cutting through an overgrown field. In the winter it was icy. In the spring it was more like a mud hole. I thought about all the times I had bounced my way to the top, on my way to feed the feral cat colony, fingers crossed that I'd make it safely up and then back down again.

I parked and we got out of the truck. Rebecca looked down the driveway. "I remember one time being in the backseat of Everett's old Impala. About halfway up that hill we hit a pothole that must have been six inches deep. My head smacked the roof of the car and I said a rather unladylike word."

I put my arm around her shoulders. "And exactly what were you doing in the backseat of Everett's Impala?" I teased.

"A lady doesn't kiss and tell," she said with a sly smile. "But I do miss that old car sometimes. I wish Everett still owned it. It had a lovely backseat." She bumped me with her hip. "I would have loaned it to Marcus. You two would probably be married by now."

With that Rebecca walked over to greet Eddie. I just shook my head and followed her. Marcus and I had met because of one of his cases. For a while he'd actually considered me a person of interest. It wasn't the best way to start a relationship, which didn't stop what felt at times like the entire town from trying to play matchmaker.

As I got close to the old carriage house I was hit with the memory of Eddie's daughter, Sydney, getting stuck up in the hayloft. When her soon-to-be-stepsister—Roma's grown daughter, Olivia—had tried to reach Sydney she had gotten trapped on the shaky platform as well. I'd been able to use a little physics along with a lot of luck, a coil of rope and a rusted chain to get them both down.

Eddie followed my gaze as I joined him and Rebecca and I saw him swallow hard. "I'm so glad you were here that day," he said.

My chest got tight for a moment. I nodded. "Me too."

Rebecca gave my arm a squeeze. She tipped her head in the direction of the shed that Eddie was shingling. "When do you expect to be done?" she asked.

"A few more days," he said. "Assuming the weather cooperates."

Eddie was six foot four inches of muscled ex–hockey player. He still had all his own teeth and his nose had never been broken, unlike a lot of other players. He cooked, he could refinish furniture and renovate a house to put it all in. He was a romantic husband and with his sandy hair, brown eyes and wide smile he looked like he belonged on the cover of *GQ* as much as *Sports Illustrated*. I knew this small outbuilding he was fixing up as a new home for the cats would be done on time and done well.

Rebecca glanced over at the carriage house again. "Selfishly, I'm happy that you and Roma decided not to tear that building down."

Eddie swiped a hand over his close-cropped hair. "It is structurally sound, at least as far as the framing and the roof trusses go."

"So what are you going to do with the space?" I asked.

He grinned. "Let's just say Roma and I haven't reached a consensus yet."

I laughed.

"Does Roma think the cats will accept the move into their new home?"

Eddie rubbed his stubbled chin. "I hope so. There are only five cats left now and Roma has been talking about moving Smokey down to the clinic full-time."

"I didn't know that," I said.

"She's just had the thought in the last couple of days. She said she was going to ask you what you thought."

Smokey was the oldest cat in the feral cat family. He had gotten his name from his smoke-gray fur. Desmond, another Wisteria Hill cat who had lived at Roma's animal clinic since Marcus discovered him and the previously unknown colony, had seemed to tolerate the old tomcat when Smokey had spent an extended visit there. It might work.

"Maybe," I said.

Eddie smiled at Rebecca and at the same time tipped his head toward me. "If our cat whisperer here can convince Lucy to accept the new space, I think we'll be okay. Where Lucy goes the others will follow."

Since Lucy was feral, too, I could never get too close to her, let alone touch her. But I had some sort of connection with the little cat, the same way I did with Owen and Hercules and with Marcus's ginger tabby, Micah, who had also come from Wisteria Hill. Lucy seemed to somehow know I had her best interests at heart. And I wasn't going to forget that it had been

Lucy's insistent meowing that had brought Marcus into the carriage house just before the hayloft had collapsed.

I smiled. "I'll do my best."

"You know, she's been coming out to watch me the past couple of days," Eddie said.

"That's a good sign," Rebecca said.

I'd been so busy at the library and working on the show that I hadn't seen much of Roma or Eddie, or anyone else for that matter, for the past couple of weeks. "When are they going to start working on the warehouse?" I asked.

One of the empty warehouses at the far end of the waterfront downtown was eventually going to be the home of Eddie's hockey training center. The project had been stalled multiple times but now that Everett had gotten involved, things were finally going well.

Eddie grinned. It was impossible to miss his enthusiasm—or to not catch a little of it. "Three weeks. Assuming there are no last-minute problems." He gestured toward the house. "But you didn't come here to talk hockey. C'mon. My starter is in the fridge."

We headed across the yard. Rebecca seemed so tiny walking next to Eddie. She was more than a foot shorter and with her layered silvery hair she reminded me of a tiny forest fairy.

"I want to hear all about the show," Eddie said. "What's it like cooking on the set?"

"Hot," Rebecca said, raising her eyebrows for emphasis. "And steamy. Last week when we got those two unseasonably warm days I thought I was going to melt and run down a crack. Plus, the space is a lot smaller than it looks and sometimes it's hard not to get in each other's way." She smiled then. "And it's lots of fun. I never thought I would be on TV."

Even though the show hadn't aired yet, Rebecca had already developed a fan base online. That hadn't surprised me at all.

"Do you all get along?" Eddie asked. "Or is it more cutthroat?"

"Cutthroat? Heavens no!" she said. "When I broke my rolling pin Ray loaned me his. And when Caroline upended a bowl of flour on Kassie we all helped clean it up."

"The guys used to watch the original version of the Baking Showdown all the time," Eddie said. I knew he was referring to his former teammates. "I'm glad Ruby's friend revived the show. And by the way, Sydney wants your autograph the next time she sees you."

"I'm honored," Rebecca said.

Eddie looked at me. "What about you, Kathleen? How do you like working behind the scenes?"

"I like it," I said. "It's not that time-consuming. Basically, my job is to find interesting facts for Eugenie, and sometimes Russell, to use in conversation with the contestants. I'm trying to work in references to Mayville Heights any chance I get. I've had to research some pretty obscure things, so it doesn't always work."

The original *Great Northern Baking Showdown* had aired on network TV and ended twelve years ago. The premise was simple. A dozen amateur bakers competed for the top prize, fifty thousand dollars and a top-of-the-line double oven, six-burner gas range. In Elias's remake the winner still received fifty thousand dollars, along with a chance to study at the Culinary Institute of America in New York.

Each of the ten episodes had a different theme: bread, pastry, dessert, etc. However, at any time the judges could add a complication, such as a mystery ingredient or a mandatory baking technique. They could also take away any tool, from the bakers' stand mixers to the parchment paper they used to line cookie sheets. The competition wasn't just a measure of the contestants' baking skills. It was also a test of their flexibility in the kitchen.

At first I'd hesitated when I was approached by Elias Braeden himself to take the researcher job. I'd met him the previous winter. The man was an intriguing mix of bluntness and charm, qualities he had honed while working for my friend Ruby Blackthorne's grandfather. Idris Blackthorne had been the town bootlegger and had run a very lucrative regular poker game, among other enterprises.

Elias's interests included a casino. While I had no reason to think he was anything other than an honest businessman, he had worked for Idris, which meant he wasn't someone to turn your back on. But Ruby was very close to Elias. He'd known her from the time she was five days old and he was one of the few people she'd been able to count on as a mixed-up kid. So when he'd asked me to step in to avoid a delay in production it was partly my loyalty to her and partly my loyalty to the town that had made me say yes.

"I think just having the production here overall is good for the town," Rebecca said as we stepped into the side porch. "The production crew is staying here. So are the bakers. Maggie is helping the illustrator. You're doing research. Eric is catering. Harry and Oren have worked on the sets. And I know they've had inquiries at the St. James and several of the bed-and-breakfasts from people interested in trying to get a glimpse of filming. Everything's going perfectly!"

As soon as the words were out of Rebecca's mouth I had the urge to knock on wood. I wasn't generally a superstitious person but I had grown up around theater people and they were. "Knock on wood" was one of my actor mother's superstitions, a way to avoid tempting fate.

I felt silly but I tapped softly on one of the kitchen chairs.

Just in case.

2

Eddie kept a small amount of the sourdough starter for himself and sent Rebecca home with the rest, along with a detailed list of instructions for its care and feeding. Rebecca held the glass bowl securely on her lap and smiled all the way down the hill. Whatever uncertainty she'd had before seemed to be gone.

"Thank you for everything, Kathleen," she said as I pulled into the driveway at her house. "I'll bring some bread over for you to try this evening."

"I'm looking forward to that," I said with a smile. All the contestants practiced their recipes multiple times before an episode was filmed.

Rebecca pulled a small brown paper bag out of her pocket and handed it to me.

I shook my head as I unfolded the top to look inside. I knew exactly what I was going to find. Kitty treats: big surprise. They were tiny crackers shaped like little birds.

"Roasted chicken," Rebecca said helpfully. "It's a new flavor Roma's friend is testing."

Roma had a veterinarian colleague who also owned a small organic pet food company. Owen and Hercules had been his eager taste testers in the past. I hadn't even noticed Eddie slip Rebecca the bag while we were at the house. Clearly it was something the two of them had planned, probably when they'd talked on the phone.

"What am I going to do with you?" I asked.

"Wish me luck with my bread-making," she said with a completely straight face.

I laughed and leaned across the seat to hug her. "Good luck," I said. "I can't wait to try the results."

Rebecca headed for her back door, carefully carrying the bowl of starter. I headed home.

I found Hercules was still sitting on the bench in the sun porch looking out the side window. It wasn't that he didn't like the outdoors; it was more that he didn't like wet grass under his feet, or mud between his toes or grackles dive-bombing his head. He liked Mother Nature from a distance.

He turned to look at me, a questioning look in his green eyes.

"Yes, Rebecca sent you a treat," I said, holding up the small paper bag.

"Mrrr," he said. Then he jumped down and went through the door to the kitchen. *Through the door* as in he passed directly to the other side of the solid wooden door without even pausing and without waiting for me to unlock and open it.

Hercules had the ability to pass through solid objects. It seemed impossible. It seemed to defy the laws of physics that I had studied in high school but it still happened. I had yet to come across any wall or door that was too dense for the little tuxedo cat to pass through to the other side.

I pulled out my keys and heard a faint but clearly impatient meow from the kitchen. As I turned the doorknob he meowed once again.

"Excuse me, some of us have to actually stop and open the door," I said as I stepped into the kitchen.

His whiskers twitched as though he was making a face at me. Which he was.

Owen then appeared in the living room doorway. Literally appeared. Unlike Hercules, Owen couldn't pass through solid objects, but he could make himself invisible—also equally unexplainable.

The first time I had seen Owen's ability was in the backyard while he was chasing a bird. It was easy to dismiss what I'd seen—or more accurately what I hadn't seen—as a trick of the light. The first time I had been confronted with what Hercules could do was at the library. *That* had been harder to explain away.

At the time a section of the library had been cordoned off. One of our meeting rooms had been part of a police investigation. Hercules had slipped nonchalantly under the yellow crime scene tape. I had scrambled after him, but he had just walked out of my reach, through the closed door in front of us, and disappeared.

I remembered how my knees had started to shake.

I'd closed my eyes and taken a couple of deep breaths. "Be there," I'd whispered. I'd opened my eyes again. There was no cat.

I had kept the secret about Owen and Hercules for years. I was too afraid of what might happen to them if anyone found out, even though there had been some close encounters during that time. Finally, a couple of months ago, I'd told Marcus. He had had trouble accepting what I was saying, even when Hercules walked through the kitchen door and Owen sat on a chair and then vanished right before our eyes. Marcus was even more shocked to learn that his own cat, Micah, shared Owen's gift. Weeks later he was still looking for a rational explanation when I wasn't sure there was one. Sometimes I had the feeling that all three cats were getting a little tired of it.

I saw Owen and Hercules exchange a look. More than once I'd wondered if telepathy could also be one of their special skills. Owen came purposefully across the floor, stopped at my feet and fixed his golden eyes on the bag in my hand.

"Merow," he said sharply.

"Is there any point at all in having our usual conversation about how spoiled you both are?" I asked, one hand propped on my hip.

Once again they exchanged a look.

"Mrr," Hercules said and he almost seemed to give an indifferent shrug.

I took that as a no.

I gave them each three of the crackers. The tiny

birds did smell like roast chicken and gravy. I had no doubt they were going to be a hit.

I went upstairs to get ready to head to the library. I needed to leave a bit early because I wanted to stop and see Eugenie. I was on tiptoe trying to reach my favorite sweater at the back of one of the shelves in the closet when I heard a meow behind me.

"No," I said without turning around. Just as I managed to snag my sweater with two fingers Owen wrapped himself around my right ankle. I looked down at him. "No," I repeated.

He cocked his gray tabby head to one side and gave me his cutest face.

I crouched down so my face was close to his. "I love you, too, but no more treats." I stroked the fur on the top of his head. "You should know by now that all of this 'I'm so adorable' stuff isn't going to work."

He sighed—at least that's how it sounded to me—and looked at the sweater in my other hand. Then he wrinkled his nose.

I stood up, shook out the sweater and held it against me, but Owen continued to make the face. I set the sweater back on the shelf and pulled out a blue, fitted, three-quarter-sleeved shirt that Maggie had convinced me to buy because she insisted it flattered my brown hair and eyes. Maggie Adams was one of my closest friends in Mayville Heights. She was a mixed-media collage artist and past president of the artists' co-op. She had short blond curls, green eyes and aside from small furry rodents, nothing rattled her. She was also the most creative person I had ever met. If she suggested I try a certain color combination, I generally listened to her.

Owen seemed to consider the shirt for a moment and then gave me a mrr of approval. I held it up, checked my reflection in the mirror and decided the cat was right.

Owen had already disappeared, maybe literally, maybe figuratively.

"Thank you," I called. I received an answering murp from the hall.

Once I was dressed for work, I grabbed lunch from the refrigerator—a container of chicken soup and a cheese and bacon biscuit. I pulled on my jacket, picked up my messenger bag and called, "Good-bye."

There was an answering good-bye from upstairs—Hercules. I waited another minute and Owen meowed from the living room. I knew what he was doing in there. He was stretched out in my big wing chair with his hind feet propped against the chair back and his head almost hanging over the edge of the seat. I decided to pretend I didn't know that.

I drove down Mountain Road and parked in the community center's parking lot, turning down my driver's-side visor to display my show parking pass. The building where the actual filming took place was set up beside the boardwalk running along the waterfront. It was a temporary structure that Burtis Chapman and his crew had assembled with a PVC roof, steel cladding and two steel roller doors. There was no other place in town large enough to work. The building looked very utilitarian on the outside. On the inside the space had been set up to resemble a cozy country kitchen with (faux) exposed wooden ceiling beams, retro-look appliances and white Shaker-style cabinets.

The walking trail that the boardwalk was part of was one of the highlights of the downtown area for me. It curved its way from the old warehouses down by the point, went past the downtown shops and businesses, including the library, and continued all the way out beyond the marina, past Wild Rose Bluff. The path was shaded most of the way with tall elm and black walnut trees. I'd walked it a lot when I had first arrived in town.

While filming of each episode took place on the kitchen set, a practice continued from the original Baking Showdown, the community center was where everything else was happening for the duration of the production.

I was just about to step in the back door when someone breezed by me without speaking. Kassie Tremayne, one of the show's judges. She wore a pale mint-colored dress with short sleeves and a triangle cutout at her midsection. Her ankle-strapped, stiletto-heeled pumps had to add close to four inches to her height, which still put her below my five foot six. Her blond hair was pulled into a sleek, low ponytail. She looked so elegant and pulled together. I took a quick glance down at my gray trousers to see if there was any cat hair stuck to them.

Kassie was beautiful. Or she would have been if she hadn't had a slightly dissatisfied expression on her face all the time. She scrawled her signature in the sign-in log and swept up the stairs without even acknowledging that I—or anyone else—was there.

To my surprise Harry Taylor was at the security desk just inside the back door. "What are you doing here?" I asked as I signed in.

"I'm filling in for Thorsten," he said. "He had to go rescue the camera crew that went to film some background shots over by the marina and somehow managed to get their van stuck." Harry smiled. "What are you doing here?"

"I came to bring some information to Eugenie," I said, patting my messenger bag. "She is here, isn't she?"

He nodded and gestured to the cup and saucer on the desktop. "She brought me tea and a cookie about five minutes ago."

Harry had helped set up the cooking stations and he had built a set of cupboards when the ones that had been shipped in from Chicago had been deemed to be too small for the back wall of the set. He had also unearthed a cabinet for Eugenie's office since she was very particular about keeping her research organized. She in turn had been sharing her tea with him. For her there was none of the pop-a-teabag-in-a-cup-of-microwaved-hot-water stuff that the crew drank. Eugenie had her own kettle and a china teapot complete with quilted cozy.

Rebecca and I had watched the two of them talking on set one day. "I think she likes the cut of Harry's trousers," Rebecca had whispered. Based on the gleam

I'd noticed in Eugenie's eyes when she talked to Harry, I had a feeling Rebecca might be right.

I went up the stairs and headed toward Eugenie's office. Kassie was several steps ahead of me.

Kate Westin, one of the contestants on the show, came around the corner, wrapped up, as usual, in one of her long sweaters, her hands jammed in her pockets. She pulled a hand out and held out something to Kassie. It looked like a gold cell phone case. "I found this on the set," she said. "Norman said he thought it was yours."

Kassie took the phone from her. "Where did you find it?" she asked.

"It was on the floor by the ovens," Kate said.

"It must have fallen out of my bag." Kassie swept a finger across the screen and seemed satisfied with what she saw. Still looking at the phone, she moved around Kate and disappeared around the corner. It didn't seem to occur to her to say thank you.

Kate stood there for a moment and then she turned and went the same way.

I didn't think either one of them had noticed me.

I found Eugenie in her office.

In my opinion she'd been an excellent choice to host the show. Eugenie Bowles-Hamilton was not just an acclaimed cookbook author, she also owned a very successful bakery in Vancouver, Canada. As one of the two co-hosts of *The Great Northern Baking Showdown*, she was the straight woman to musician Russell Perry. The lead singer for The Flying Wallbangers was a lot funnier than I'd expected.

Eugenie was tall, easily two or three inches above my five six. I'd guessed that she was in her fifties but I wasn't really sure. She wore her silver hair in a short bob with bangs. She tended to dress in gray or navy and she always wore a pair of oversized earrings and a Cartier Tank watch with a black leather strap. She reminded me of actress Helen Mirren.

"My face just disappears in the crowd without my earrings," she had told me when we first met and I had complimented her on the blue baroque crystal dangling earrings she'd been wearing.

Eugenie had an impeccable British accent, even though she'd lived on the Canadian west coast for the past twenty years. It added a level of credence to everything she said. I loved listening to her read out loud whatever notes I brought her.

I found her sitting behind the wood and metal desk that Harry had managed to shoehorn into her office. Her co-host, Russell, was perched on the left front corner of the desk. If he had an office of his own, he was never in it. He was almost always in Eugenie's. The singer was dressed in his ubiquitous black skinny jeans and one of his many pairs of Vans shoes—red-and-black plaid this time. He wore a black, short-sleeved T-shirt that showed off the muscles in his arms. His spiked blond hair and the mischievous smile on his face made him look more like a teenager than a grown man. "Hey, Kathleen," he said.

I smiled back. It was impossible not to. Russell just had that kind of personality. Being a co-host on the show was a chance for him to clean up his image a little. This past winter a video clip of him had shown up online and gone viral. Russell was dancing to Taylor Swift. It wasn't the dancing or his choice of music that was the problem. Although it was a surprise to most people that the alt-rocker was a Swiftie, it was the fact that he was wearing nothing but a red beanie and a pair of Sorels as he danced, back to the camera, to "Shake It Off." According to Ruby, Russell's arms weren't the only muscular part of his body.

"Hi, Russell," I said.

Eugenie looked up and smiled. "Hello, Kathleen. Thank you for bringing next week's notes on such short notice."

"It wasn't a problem," I said. "I had everything ready. All I needed to do was print out a copy for you." I pulled a brown envelope out of my bag and handed it over the desk.

Eugenie undid the flap. "Do you have time to wait while I skim the material to be certain there's nothing else I need? Not that I believe I will. You're always so thorough."

"I have time," I said.

Eugenie indicated the lone chair in front of her desk. Before I could sit down Russell frowned and leaned toward me. "You have something caught in your hair," he said.

It was likely a clump of cat hair or some part of a yellow catnip chicken. I lifted a hand but before I could run my fingers though my hair Russell reached over and pulled a cherry—complete with the stem still attached—from behind my ear. He immediately looked at Eugenie.

"Better, but I could still see a bit of the stem when you palmed it," she said without actually looking up from the notes she was reading.

"I need longer fingers," Russell said, shaking the cherry as though it were a tiny bell.

"No, you just need a little more practice," Eugenie countered.

"I didn't see anything, if that matters," I said.

"No offense, but the camera is more observant." Russell slid off the edge of the desk. "I'll go work on it in front of the mirror." He smiled. "Later, Kathleen." With a wave of the cherry he was gone.

Now I understood why Eugenie had asked me to find out if the fruit grew in Minnesota.

I sat down as she glanced up from the papers in front of her. "I had tea with your friend Maggie last evening at her flat. You have a pair of very photogenic cats."

I smiled. "Owen and Hercules do love the camera."

"Maggie told me the calendar is a promotional tool for the town."

I nodded. "It is. The first printing sold out and we had to do a second one, and people are already asking if there's going to be a follow-up calendar."

"What a smashing idea," Eugenie said. "How did your cats end up being the models?"

I explained how Ruby had worked with the boys

before, painting both of their portraits to be auctioned to benefit the charity Cat People.

"Both Owen and Hercules are feral. They came from a property just outside of town. They won't let anyone aside from me touch them, but they do like Ruby." I smiled. "Probably because she gives them treats."

"They're clearly very intelligent and talented creatures."

You don't know the half of it, I thought.

"Would it be possible to obtain a copy of the calendar?" Eugenie asked. "I'd like to hang it on the set. I don't think Elias would object."

Since Elias Braeden was a big supporter of promoting Mayville Heights, I didn't think he would mind, either.

"If the former version of the show is any indication, after each episode we'll hear from viewers looking for more information about something they've noticed on the set—everything from our vintage refrigerators to that intricate metalwork sun hanging above the cabinets on the rear wall. In the past they even had inquiries about the aprons the contestants wore." She adjusted her glasses again. "The cameras are always panning around the kitchen so it's quite possible your calendar will attract some attention. Owen and Hercules are very striking."

"Yes, I can get you a copy of the calendar," I said. "And thank you for thinking of displaying it on the set."

Eugenie smiled. "You're most welcome."

I decided to check with Lita over at Henderson Holdings. Everett and Rebecca had bankrolled the calendar project and Lita, who was Everett's assistant, might still have a copy or two. If she didn't, I would give Eugenie the one I had hanging in my office at the library. "The library closes at eight. I could leave the calendar at the security desk on my way home tonight," I offered.

"I'll likely be here at that time," she said. "We have a production meeting and Russell and I are going to work on another magic trick."

Over the two weeks I'd been working with her I had noticed how Eugenie always made an effort, in her understated way, to work references to Minnesota in general and Mayville Heights in particular into the show. She had already managed to get both the library gazebo and the Stratton Theatre in the opening credits.

Before she went back to scanning her notes, Eugenie handed me a piece of paper. "I thought perhaps you would like to see this. It's a mock-up for an advertisement that will be running in *People* magazine."

"So the show's been picked up by someone?" I asked.

She shook her head. "Not as far as I know. Elias is just trying to generate some interest."

I studied the ad. It featured Eugenie and Russell on the Riverwalk. Russell was sitting in a tree with what looked to be a tiny paper bird on his shoulder. They were joined by Kassie and the other judge, Richard Kent. Richard was leaning against the tree with one hand on the trunk. There were no paper birds on his shoulder, just his black Longines diving watch on his right wrist.

"I like this," I said. The boardwalk and the shore-line were highlighted by the new leaves on the trees, and the cloudless, deep blue sky seemed to go on forever.

"We all do look rather attractive," Eugenie said. She bent her head over the notes again and went back to reading, one finger making its way rapidly down the page.

I made a mental note to send my mom a quick e-mail—she wasn't much for texting—to tell her to watch for the ad. Mom and Richard Kent had worked together recently. My mother played a recurring character on the daytime drama *The Wild and Wonderful*. She was immensely popular with fans and the soap would have happily signed her to a long-term contract. A standing offer was on the table. But Mom's heart belonged to the stage. She wasn't willing to make a commitment to television. Still, she was happy to stop in for a short stint on the show two or three times a year.

"All those fans that are clamoring for me to join the show permanently would probably get tired of my face if they saw it all the time," she had said to me after the last offer from *The Wild and Wonderful* producers.

Given her popularity, I doubted that was true. My mother had that undefinable quality that drew people to her. It was more than charm, more than the fact that

she was beautiful and funny. There was just something about her that made people want to be around
her. I was a little biased because she was my mother,
but I had always thought it was her genuine interest
in people that made her so compelling.

Richard Kent had guested on *The Wild and Wonderful* just over a year ago, playing himself in a short
scene set at an extravagant gala in which an evil twin
came back from the dead with a new face. Mom and
the celebrity chef had had the briefest of encounters
in the scene. Richard and her character had bumped
into each other on the fictional gala's red carpet and
exchanged quick apologies with each one going in the
opposite direction. Then they had both turned back
to take a second look.

Their chemistry was electric: my mother's character smiling over her shoulder and Richard looking at
her like he had just seen the woman of his dreams.
Their pairing had fans before the one-hour episode
was over. The fact that Richard was about half Mom's
age bothered no one. As Maggie—who was a big fan
of the show—had explained, "They almost shorted
out my TV."

Not something you really want to hear about your
mother and a man who isn't your father but *is* a couple
of years younger than you are.

But Mom had that effect on people—men and
women—and I could see why viewers of the show had
liked Richard. He was the most popular member of
The Great Northern Baking Showdown at least as far as

online, preshow buzz went. Eugenie came a close second. Richard had gone to study at Le Cordon Bleu in Paris when he was just sixteen. He'd gone from pastry chef to head chef at a popular New York City restaurant in less than five years. He was tall and lean and he didn't look like he indulged in any of his decadent desserts very often. He wore his short dark hair trimmed close on the sides, longer on the top. His most striking feature was his deep brown eyes.

Maggie had told me that a group of fans had started a petition to get Mom and Richard together on the show once again. I had a feeling that he might be open to the idea. When I'd been introduced to him the very first thing he'd said to me was, "You're Thea's daughter, aren't you?" If he thought that anything other than a fictional relationship would ever happen with Mom, he was going to be disappointed. My father was the only man for my mother. They were crazy about each other, and sometimes they were just plain crazy, which was why they had been married, divorced and then married again.

Like my mother, Richard also had the reputation for having chemistry with just about everyone he worked with—at least the women. He was also reputed to have a bit of a short temper, although I hadn't seen or heard any evidence of that so far. However, the chemistry between him and Kassie Tremayne seemed to be lacking. The two of them got along well enough on camera to make the show work, but I had noticed that they ignored each other the rest of the time. There was none of the easy rapport Richard had shared with his co-host on another cooking show, a chef named Camilla Flores.

Camilla, who owned two restaurants, was quiet and elegant, but quick with a smile and a word of encouragement for the contestants on her show. Richard could sometimes be a bit cutting with his criticism but somehow she had brought out his gentler side.

Kassie seemed . . . pricklier.

Eugenie had confided that Elias had wanted Camilla as a judge for the Baking Showdown but she'd just had a baby and had turned down his offer.

Kassie was a popular food blogger and social media influencer, but Rebecca had confided that none of the crew liked working with her. "She would do a lot better if she remembered how to say please and thank you," Rebecca had commented. I had also heard that several crew members were quietly pushing for someone, anyone, to replace Kassie.

There was always a sharp barb, it seemed, under any of her words of praise. For instance, she had told Ray Nightingale that she had expected him to fail spectacularly at the patisserie challenge and she was surprised to see he hadn't. When Kate Westin, who was the youngest of the contestants, had paired banana and bacon in her open-faced sandwich, Richard had expressed his admiration for the way the sweetness of the banana cut through the fatty saltiness of the thick-cut bacon. Kassie had nodded her agreement while at the same time making a bit of a face as she took a bite. My father would have said she gave back-handed compliments.

Eugenie scanned the last page of the notes I had given to her and then looked up at me and smiled. "The information is on point and well organized," she said. "Not that I had expected anything less from you."

"Thank you," I said. I got to my feet. "I'll see you later tonight with the calendar."

"I'm not putting you out, now, am I?" she asked.

I shook my head. "Not at all. As I said, it'll be some-time after eight."

"I'll see you then," Eugenie said.

As I headed back down the hallway I could hear voices arguing. They were coming from one of the offices that I thought was being used by an associate producer. As I got closer I realized that the voices were those of Richard and Kassie, but I couldn't make out their actual words until I was just about level with the half-open door. Richard had his back to it. I didn't see Kassie but I did hear her.

"Don't play games with me, Dickie," she said in a voice laced with equal parts honey and venom. "Or I promise, I will end you and your career!"

3

I thought about what I had overheard Kassie saying to Richard as I drove over to Fern's Diner. Her words just seemed to confirm what I'd observed and the rumors I had heard about her. Whatever Kassie's issues were with Richard, whether they were justified or not, people liked him, and when it came to taking sides they were all going to be lined up on his.

I was going to Fern's to pick up an order of cupcakes—devil's food chocolate with mint-chocolate-chip buttercream. Usage numbers were up again at the library and I thought we should celebrate. Georgia Tepper, who owned Sweet Thing bakery, had made them for me. She had been doing all of her baking for the last two days in the diner's kitchen after a small fire on top of a power pole on her street had caused more damage than anyone had realized.

"Hi, Kathleen," Peggy Sue said when I walked in. She was wearing hot-pink pedal pushers and a pink-and-white short-sleeved polka-dot blouse with the collar turned up, along with her retro cat's-eye glasses. With her bouffant hair and a hot-pink scarf tied at her neck she looked like everyone's idea of a 1950s diner waitress. She even had a pair of roller skates that she would put on for special occasions. Peggy was co-owner of the diner and a very savvy businesswoman.

She reached down behind the counter. "I have your cupcakes," she said. "They smell terrific."

"Thanks," I said, taking the cardboard box with the Sweet Thing logo on the top from her. "Is Georgia here?"

Peggy shook her head. "The power is back on in her kitchen. She left about an hour ago."

"I'm glad to hear that," I said. "Thanks for hanging on to these for me."

"Anytime," she said with a smile.

It was a quiet Friday afternoon and evening at the library. I put the box of cupcakes in our staff room—minus the one I took for myself. I knew they would be gone by the end of the day. I set our newest student employee to work cleaning gum from under the table and chairs in the children's department. It was a tedious, neck-knotting job but Levi had actually offered to take it on.

Levi Ericson had worked part-time as a waiter at the St. James Hotel before I'd hired him. He was a voracious reader, at the library at least once and often twice a week. When he had applied for the part-time job I'd had a good feeling that he might be the person we had been looking for.

We all missed our former student staff member, Mia Janes, who had left to attend college. We'd had a couple of students since then but neither of them had the rapport with the rest of the staff or our patrons that Mia had had. It was looking like Levi was going to be a good fit. The quilters and the members of the seniors' book club were already trying to fatten up the lanky teenager. The little ones crawled all over him at story time and he didn't seem to mind. And he read everything from graphic novels to *War and Peace*, which meant he could suggest a book for pretty much any reader who came in. I was hoping he would stay with us for a while.

Marcus called during my supper break. "How's the paperwork coming?" I asked. The Mayville Heights Police Department along with the police in Red Wing had broken up a group smuggling counterfeit blood-sugar-monitoring devices.

"I swear someone is rearranging it all whenever I get up for a cup of coffee." He raised his voice and I knew the words were being directed at someone besides me.

I pictured him standing at his desk, his tie loosened, his dark hair mussed because he'd been running his hands back through it.

"I have to drop something off to Eugenie after the library closes but it shouldn't take long." I broke a bite off my biscuit. "Any chance you'll be done by then? We could go to Eric's for chocolate pudding cake or just sit in the truck and make out like a couple of teenagers."

"I thought you loved me for my sharp intellect," he teased.

"Nope," I said. "Turns out I'm way more shallow than that."

Marcus laughed. "You're many things, Kathleen, but shallow is not one of them."

We agreed I'd call him when I finished with Eugenie and we said good-bye.

I was just bringing one of the book carts back to the front desk after my supper break when Kate Westin and another contestant from the show came in through the front doors. They both looked around in surprise. We often got that reaction from first-time visitors. The building, a Carnegie library, was more than a hundred years old. It had been restored to its original glory in time for its centennial, and I still took pride in showing off the mosaic tile floor, the refinished trim, the huge windows and the beautiful carved sun with the inscription *Let There Be Light* over the main doors, reminiscent of the original Carnegie library in Dunfermline, Scotland.

I walked over to say hello. "Kathleen, this is a beautiful place," Kate said with a shy smile.

"Thank you," I said. "A lot of people put in a lot of work to restore the building."

"That railing outside on the steps, is it original?"

I shook my head. "No. It's actually a reproduction. The original had deteriorated so much it had been replaced with a wooden railing about ten years before we started the restoration of the building." It had been one of the things that had struck me as "wrong" the first time that I saw the building

Oren Kenyon had installed the new railings and had done a lot of other work inside including making several pieces of trim to match the original woodwork. The metalwork had been done by a blacksmith in Red Wing with a lot of help from Oren on the design. Wrought-iron spindles supported the flat handrail. The center spindle on each side split apart into a perfect oval and then re-formed again. The letters M, H, F, P and L for Mayville Heights Free Public Library were intertwined and seemed suspended in the middle of the iron circles.

"It's beautiful work," Kate said, glancing back over her shoulder at the front doors.

Kate made me think of a princess from a child's picture book. She was tall and slight and her dark blond curls were loose around her shoulders instead of pulled back in the tight braid she wore on the show. She had pale blue eyes, very fair skin and a perfect oval face. And she was smart as well. The former model was working on a graduate degree in psychology, I'd learned. We had started talking after a production meeting when she had noticed I had Ernest Jones's biography of Sigmund Freud poking out of my bag.

"I've always been fascinated by what makes people behave the way they do," she'd explained in her soft voice. "When my modeling career ended I wasn't sure what I was going to do. I had already taken a couple of psychology courses in high school and I'd done well in both of them. So I enrolled in university. I did think about cooking school, but I had only really ever cooked for myself—just for fun. But now, if I could just make it into the top three, maybe . . ." She hadn't finished the sentence. She hadn't had to. It had been written all over her face how desperately she wanted to do well.

Kate had gone on to very matter-of-factly explain that her promising modeling career, along with a lucrative contract with an exclusive line of makeup, had disappeared when five years ago—at twenty-one—she'd had an allergic reaction to a facial mask that had been marketed as being "natural."

"I didn't know the word was meaningless when it comes to skincare," she explained, her voice laced with bitterness. "Anyone can just use one or two natural ingredients in a product and call it natural. I wasn't the only person who had a reaction, but by the time we all connected with each other and thought about hiring a lawyer, the owner of the company, Monique Le Clair, had left the country. Some people think she might be in Asia somewhere or maybe Mexico. No one has been able to find her."

After the allergic reaction Kate had developed a skin infection that had left her with scars on her face that both the modeling and cosmetics industries couldn't seem to see past. I looked at her now and all I could see was how beautiful she was.

Caroline Peters was with Kate. Caroline was old enough to be Kate's mother but the two of them had connected the same way Rebecca and I had. Caroline was a stay-at-home mother, I knew. She was short and round with a head full of black curls and deep blue eyes. She was wearing a blue flowered wrap dress with a jean jacket and white Adidas Superstars with black stripes. She turned in a slow circle to take in the main floor of the building. "What an incredible building," she said. She gestured to the words over the front door. "This is a Carnegie library, then?"

I nodded.

"So is my library at home. These are great pieces of history. I'm glad this one was restored."

"A lot of the buildings aren't libraries anymore," I said. "I'm glad this one still is."

Caroline smiled at me. The mom of five was a perpetually happy person. "Right now, we're looking for a place to hide out for a little while," she said. "It seemed like a perfect evening for a walk but sadly that means we might possibly be missing a quick get-together for the contestants."

I laid a hand on my chest. "Your secret is safe with me," I said. "Librarian's honor."

"Is that a real thing?" Caroline asked with a teasing smile.

"As real as wishing on a star," I said. "How's the baking going for this week?"

"We're just baked out," Caroline confided. "I don't think I ever want to see another loaf of bread, and believe me, that's close to blasphemy coming out of my mouth." She patted one hip. "I have never met a carbohydrate that didn't make me say, 'Come to Mama.'"

"I know exactly what you mean," I said. I gestured

at the stacks. "You can see that we're not exactly busy tonight. I can tell you that the chairs in the reading area are a lot more comfortable than they look. And there are a couple of big, almost leather chairs in the back corner by the windows that are good for curling up in. You can look out over the water from there."

"That sounds perfect," Kate said. She was wearing ankle-length jeans and a long cream-colored cardigan over a striped long-sleeved T-shirt in shades of brown and orange. A chocolate-colored scarf was wrapped around her neck. Kate always seemed cold. Her shoulders were hunched, her hands jammed in her pockets. Both of her sleeves were pushed back and I noticed the left one was damp, probably from her last cooking session. She looked frazzled, much more than Caroline did. The pressure was on now that there were only six of the original twelve contestants left. I'd seen with Rebecca how finicky sourdough bread could be and I wondered if the stress was getting to Kate now that the semifinals were so close. Patisserie Week had not gone well for her.

I pointed the two of them toward the quiet back corner. "If you need anything, please come find me or you can ask Susan at the desk."

They both thanked me and headed across the floor.

I walked over to join Susan at the front desk. She and Mary had switched some shifts and we hadn't worked together very much in the last couple of weeks. I missed her sense of humor and seeing what she had stuck in her perpetual updo to keep it in place. Tonight it looked like a tiny green plastic trellis.

"They're contestants on the Baking Showdown, aren't they?" she asked.

I nodded. "They are. They're just looking to take a break from everything."

"I don't blame them." She checked the number on the spine of the book on the top of a pile in front of her and then leaned back to place it on the top shelf of a cart. "I used to watch the original version of the show and I know I would never be able to handle baking under those high-pressure conditions. First of all, I would be way, way too slow and, second, the cameras there all the time would freak me out. How could I pick up a cake layer after I'd dropped it on the floor and get way with it?"

I gave her a pointed look.

"Not that I'm saying I've ever done that," she added with a mischievous expression on her face.

"I feel exactly the same way," I said. "Although, if I dropped a cake layer on the floor, it would have two cats all over it before I could even bend down to try to pick it up."

"Trying to make dinner with the twins on either side of me both talking at the same time about two completely different things is hard enough. And I'd only be able to pick up a dropped cake if the boys weren't home."

"Not that you're saying you've ever done that," I added.

Susan grinned. "Of course." She picked up another book and turned it over to check the cover for damage.

"So do you have a favorite baker? I mean other than Rebecca or Ray. I won't tell."

"Honestly, it's hard to choose," I said. I did have a soft spot for Kate. She had such a flair for decorating. I'd loved the ginger cookies she'd made, decorated with kitty faces. "What about you? Are you Team Rebecca or Team Ray?"

"I'll be cheering for both of them, but I think my favorite is Charles. He's been into the café a couple of times."

Charles Bacchus was a former boxer in his midfifties. He had been the episode Hot Shot the previous week. Stocky and balding with a barrel chest and a deep laugh, Charles's massive hands had a deceptively light touch when it came to baking.

"Just talking to him has blown all of my stereotypes out of the water and I love his laugh," Susan said. She nudged her black cat's-eye glasses up her nose. "What are the other contestants like?"

"I've only talked to Stacey once," I said, "and that was when we were introduced. I know Rebecca says Stacey seemed to be the one handling the pressure the best, which makes sense since she's an elementary school teacher."

Susan gave me a knowing grin as she put another book on the cart. "No wonder she's so good at keeping her cool."

"Caroline is very much the mother of the group," I continued. I reached over and pulled a book out of the pile in front of Susan. Its dust jacket was torn. I'd leave it in the workroom for Abigail to repair. "She's always trying to make her bakes healthy, which sometimes doesn't work out so well."

Three preteens came in the front door then. Two of them looked a little lost and the third looked petulant.

"Okay, someone assigned a paper that requires reading an actual physical book," Susan whispered. "Where's Mary when we need her?"

Mary Lowe looked like everyone's idea of a sweet grandmother—and she was. She had soft white hair, she wore a themed sweater for every holiday and she made the best cinnamon rolls I had ever eaten. She was also a champion kickboxer and a big proponent of both reading and getting an education. The kids who came into the library looking for her help were partly in awe of her and partly a bit terrified. According to the middle school rumor mill, Mary had once dropkicked two foulmouthed boys out the front doors of the building. It was supposed to have happened before my time but I knew Mary well enough to know she wouldn't raise a hand or a foot to a child. She would, however, give you a talking-to you wouldn't soon forget.

When I had asked her about the origin of the story she'd just smiled and said, "Sometimes perception is just as important as reality," and left it at that.

Susan held out her arm, hand folded into a fist. She tipped her head in the direction of the three boys. "Rock, paper, scissors?" she asked.

I smiled. "It's okay. I have this."

"You're taking all the fun out of my workplace," she said, wrinkling her nose at me.

"You would have won," I said. "You always win when we do rock, paper, scissors."

She grinned. "I know. That's the fun part."

I shook my head and walked over to the three boys.

Lita came into the library about quarter to eight. Everett's assistant sometimes worked late hours. Kate and Caroline had left by then and I had helped the three boys find the books they needed for their English papers. Now I was dealing with a temperamental computer monitor, muttering to myself under my breath.

Lita frowned at the computer. "Does this happen a lot?" she asked.

"More frequently than I'd like," I said. "That's why I'm looking at starting to replace them all over time, beginning with the next budget. One of these days, banging on the side with the heel of my hand is going to stop working."

"I'll talk to Everett about this," she said.

"I appreciate the offer." I grunted as I leaned over the top of the monitor so I could attach a new cable at the back. "But Everett can't rescue the library every time we need something. We need to make the budget work."

Lita nodded. "I agree, but when Rebecca finds out, I can't guarantee that *she'll* agree."

I sighed. "I know." Rebecca loved the library. It was where she had indulged her love of books as a child and she was happy to spend money for whatever we needed. And if Rebecca was happy then so was Everett. I, on the other hand, felt we needed to run things without Everett always riding to the rescue.

"What I can do is make sure Everett knows what's going on and how you feel about money falling from the sky, so to speak."

"Thank you," I said.

A lot of people in the town and the surrounding area depended on our public-access computers. Even on a quiet Friday night all but the one I was working on were in use. I finished attaching the cable I'd just switched in for what I believed was one with a wonky connection somewhere. I held my breath—at least mentally—and then gave a sigh of relief when the monitor came back to life.

"We're good for another day," I said to Lita. I grabbed the balky old cable and for the first time noticed that she was holding a large white envelope. "You found one." I knew the envelope had to contain a calendar.

She smiled. "Two, actually, in my bottom desk drawer. I set them aside for some reason but I'll be darned if I know why."

I took the envelope from her. "Thank you for finding this and for bringing it over." On the phone I had explained what Eugenie wanted to do. "I don't know if the calendar will generate any interest in Mayville Heights, but it can't hurt."

"You're very welcome," Lita said. There was a teasing gleam in her eye. "Burtis wants to know when you're coming out for a rematch."

We started walking toward the front doors. "That man is a glutton for punishment," I said.

"He's boneheaded stubborn. No argument there."

Lita had been "keeping company" with Burtis Chapman for quite a while now. She was elegant and calm, the kind of person you wanted in your lifeboat. Burtis was larger than life, a self-made man who had worked for the town bootlegger when he was barely a teenager. He and Lita were crazy about each other, and anyone who had dared to comment on their relationship to their faces had been stared into silence.

I considered Burtis a friend and not just because he'd once helped Marcus save me from a burning building. He was loyal and dependable and his word was his bond. That was more than enough for me.

His son, Brady, had bought a pinball machine a while back that he was keeping at his father's house. I had beaten Burtis twice at the game after giving him fair warning that I was a pretty good player. I'd spent a lot of time playing pinball when my parents were doing summer stock when I was a kid. For a while I was making enough money to indulge my comic book habit and then my father found out what I was up to and my days as a pinball shark were over.

"He says the third time is a charm," Lita said. She shook her head.

I smiled. "I love an optimist. Not that optimism is going to help his game. Tell Burtis I'll be out as soon as the show stops taping."

She pulled her keys out of her pocket. "Do you think Rebecca has a chance of winning?"

I nodded. "I really do, but it wouldn't hurt to keep

your fingers crossed, just in case," I said. "And tell that big optimist to keep his crossed as well."

Lita laughed. "I will."

It stayed quiet until closing time. I said good night to Susan and Levi and drove over to the community center. Zach Redmond was at the back door security desk. Zach also worked part-time as a bartender at The Brick. He was taking several of the evening shifts at the desk because he was also taking a couple of online college courses. It was quiet enough most evenings that he had lots of time to study.

Zach had thick brown hair pulled back in a man bun and dark skin. His most striking feature was his deep blue eyes. Most of the time he dressed in black jeans and one of his collection of rock and roll T-shirts.

"How's the chemistry course coming?" I asked as I signed in. I noticed that someone had signed out as just "camera crew." Thorsten was going to get on Zach about that.

"It's a lot of work," Zach said, gesturing at his laptop. "And there's a lot of stuff to remember. But it's not as bad as I expected—at least so far. All those years of keeping drink orders straight have given me a pretty good memory."

I went up the stairs and down the hall to Eugenie's office, hoping that Rebecca would have a loaf of bread still warm from the oven waiting when I got home. I knew I had a bottle of the Jam Lady's marmalade in my refrigerator.

The door to Eugenie's office was open and the lights

were on but she wasn't there. She had said there was a production meeting scheduled, I remembered. It was possible everyone was in the community center kitchen. If no one was working on a recipe in the space, it was where everybody tended to congregate, probably because that's where the coffeemaker was.

I headed for the kitchen hoping maybe there would be a pot of coffee going.

The old brick building had a rabbit's warren of hallways around the main gym/stage area. The double doors to the kitchen were closed. I eased the left one open as quietly as I could in case the meeting was still going on but there was no one inside.

That was odd.

I scanned the room. Only one overhead light was on. I could see a pair of jeans-clad legs in the far right corner of the kitchen. It looked as though someone was bent over the table.

"Hello," I called.

The person, whoever it was, didn't straighten up. Maybe they were wearing ear buds, I thought.

I took several steps into the room. An uncomfortable feeling had settled heavy in my chest. I walked around the large island in the middle of the space. My stomach pitched.

The person I had seen wasn't working at something on the table. She—it was a woman—was facedown in a bowl full of what looked to be whipped cream. She wasn't moving. I made a strangled sound and bolted the rest of the way across the kitchen.

I grabbed the woman by the shoulders. Her body

sagged against mine. Somehow I managed to balance her body weight and lower her to the floor. Whipped cream covered her face and the front of her shirt. It clung to her hair.

I looked around for something to clean her head with. There was a folded tablecloth on the end of the island. I grabbed it and wiped the whipped cream off of her face. It was Kassie, I realized once I could make out the woman's features. At the same time it registered that she wasn't breathing.

Where was everyone?

"Help!" I yelled at the top of my lungs.

No one came.

"Help!" I screamed again, hoping that somehow Zach would hear me down at the back door even as I knew it was a futile effort.

I noticed a scrape on Kassie's lip as I used my fingers to scoop whipped cream out of her mouth so I could start CPR. She didn't respond. She wasn't breathing. I couldn't find a pulse in her neck. It seemed to me that her skin was cool.

I pulled out my phone and called 911.

Where was everyone?

I was still doing CPR when the paramedics arrived I had no idea how many minutes later.

They took over and I stood up and backed out of the way. I wiped my hands on my pants and watched the two medics work on Kassie. She didn't move. She didn't make a sound. I knew she was dead.

4

Zach had come in with the first police officer who was now checking out the kitchen area. He pulled a hand over the back of his neck. "Kathleen, what the hell happened?" he asked, shock etched in the lines around his mouth and eyes.

I couldn't take my eyes off the two paramedics working on Kassie. I wrapped my arms around myself. It was cold in the kitchen. "I don't know," I said. "I came in and found her facedown at the table. She wasn't breathing. I, uh, I called for help but no one heard me." I turned to look at him. "Where is everyone?"

Zach shook his head. Like me, he was finding it hard to look away from the paramedics. "They went down to Eric's to have some kind of meeting. One of the production assistants or somebody was going on and on about the pudding cake that Eric makes and the next thing you know they decide to move the meeting over there. They were supposed to be back about now." His eyes darted from Kassie's body to me. "Is she . . . dead?" he asked.

I let out a breath. "I think so."

"What happened to her?"

"I don't know," I repeated, a lot sharper than I'd meant to. I swiped my hand over my mouth. "I'm sorry, Zach," I said. "I don't know any more than you do."

He nodded. "I'm going back out to the door. There's going to be more police and stuff coming."

"Okay," I said.

One of the two paramedics looked at her partner and shook her head. *I should know her,* I thought. She'd taken care of me once. I couldn't think of the woman's name. I couldn't seem to focus on anything.

The second paramedic reached for the defibrillator. They shocked Kassie once, twice, a third time. I pressed one fisted hand against my mouth, flinching every time her body jerked at the shock. I could see it wasn't working.

Kassie was dead. Kassie had been dead before I found her. They stopped CPR long enough to put her on the stretcher they'd brought in with them.

Marcus walked in then with a uniformed officer. He touched my shoulder with one hand as he passed me. "You okay?" he asked softly.

I nodded without speaking. We'd been in this situation before.

Marcus spoke to the paramedics briefly and they left. He had an even shorter conversation with the two police officers. They both left the room, too, probably to secure the area. Marcus came over to me. He took my hands in his. "What happened?" he asked. His blue eyes were narrowed in concern. He looked down at our hands. "Why are you sticky?"

"It's whipped cream," I said. "I found, uh, I found Kassie facedown in that bowl of it over there." I tipped my head in the direction of the table where I had discovered her hunched over. "I did CPR but . . ." I shook my head.

Marcus frowned. "Kassie?"

"Kassie Tremayne. She's one of the judges on *The Great Northern Baking Showdown*."

"I know. What were you doing here?" he asked. "I thought you were going home after work."

"I was," I said. "I just stopped to drop off one of the cat calendars to Eugenie. She was going to hang it up on the set."

He looked around the empty kitchen. "She wasn't here?"

I shook my head. "She wasn't in her office. I thought she might be here. Sometimes they have meetings in this room." I made a vague gesture in the general direction of the back door. "Zach said they'd moved the meeting down to Eric's. They should be back anytime, maybe even now." My stomach rolled over. "Marcus, all those people worked with Kassie," I said. "They knew her."

"It's okay." He gave my hands a squeeze. "I have an officer at the back door. No one is coming in for now." He studied my face for a moment. "Okay, so you did CPR and you called nine-one-one?"

I took a deep breath and let it out slowly. It seemed

to help settle my stomach a little. "I did. I called for help but no one heard me—there was no one to hear me."

"Think carefully," he said. "Did you see anyone? Did you hear anything?"

I closed my eyes for a moment and pictured myself walking down the hall to Eugenie's office and then coming to the kitchen. All I could remember was how quiet the community center seemed. I opened my eyes again. "I didn't hear anything. I didn't see anyone. I'm sorry."

Marcus gave me a half smile. "It's okay." He let go of my hands and ran one of his through his thick dark hair. "You can go home," he said. "I'll talk to you in the morning."

I nodded. "Okay."

"If anyone asks, please don't say anything more than Ms. Tremayne went to the hospital and that's all you know."

"That *is* all I know," I said. My hands and my jacket were sticky with whipped cream. I just wanted to go home and take a shower.

"I'll walk you out," Marcus said. He was in what I thought of as police officer mode—focused and professional. It was one of the things that made him good at his job. I knew he would figure out what had happened to Kassie.

"There is something I should tell you," I said as we headed toward the back door. I explained about the bit of conversation I had overheard earlier between Kassie and Richard Kent.

"You're sure it was Ms. Tremayne?"

"I'm certain," I said. "I've talked to her several times. It was her voice."

"Okay," Marcus said. "I'll see what Mr. Kent has to say about their conversation. It probably doesn't have anything to do with what happened here."

I raised a hand in good-bye to Zach, who was talking to the officer who had come in with Marcus. "I'll talk to you tomorrow," I said to Marcus.

He ducked his head toward mine. "Love you," he said in a low voice.

I gave him a brief smile. "You too."

A couple of other police officers had cordoned off a large section of the community center's parking lot with sawhorses and two police cars. Eugenie, Russell, Richard and quite a few of the production crew were standing on the other side. I zipped up my jacket and walked over to them. I needed to get to my truck and I couldn't just leave them hanging wondering what was going on.

Eugenie put a hand on my arm. She gave me a long, assessing look. "Kathleen, are you all right?" she asked.

I nodded. "I'm fine."

"What's going on? Who was that in the ambulance?"

I cleared my throat. "It was Kassie. I . . . I found her in the kitchen."

The color drained from Eugenie's face.

"What happened to her?" Richard asked. He looked even paler than Eugenie.

"I don't know," I said. And I didn't, I reminded myself. Not for sure.

Eugenie looked at Richard and Russell. "We should go to the hospital," she said.

I wanted to tell her they didn't need to, but Marcus had asked me not to say anything other than Kassie was being taken to the hospital. I gave Eugenie directions. She gave my arm another squeeze. "I'm glad you were here, Kathleen," she said. She turned to speak to a young man I knew was some sort of production assistant. I didn't see Elias Braeden anywhere in the cluster of people. Marcus would get in touch with him, I knew.

I turned toward the truck and Russell put a hand on my shoulder. "Are you sure you're okay to drive, Kathleen?" he asked. There was genuine concern in his eyes. He might have acted like a goofball a lot of the time but Russell seemed like a good-hearted person. I had noticed how he quietly dispensed encouragement to every one of the contestants.

I gave him a tired smile. "I am, but thank you for asking."

"No worries," he said, smiling back at me.

It wasn't until I was on my way up Mountain Road that I remembered the calendar. I'd left it behind in the kitchen, probably on the floor. It didn't matter now anyway. I didn't think anyone involved in the production would want to keep the show going. I knew that Kassie *was* dead. The skin on her neck and face had been blotchy and her body didn't have the warmth that a living person's did. She hadn't responded to my efforts at CPR or those of the paramedics. I swallowed down the lump in my throat. I wanted to be wrong but I knew that I wasn't.

Owen was sitting on one of the chrome chairs when I stepped into the kitchen. "We've talked about this," I said. "Chairs are for people. You are a cat." I pointed at the floor. Owen jumped down and came over to me. I reached down to stroke his fur. He sniffed my hand and then made a face.

"Whipped cream," I said. "It's a long story."

"Mrrr," he replied, cocking his head to one side as if to say, "Tell me."

"Let me get out of these sticky things." I needed a piece of toast and a cup of hot chocolate with marshmallows. I had a feeling it would be a long time before I wanted whipped cream.

I hung up my bag and took off my jacket. It would have to be washed as well. There was a sticky stain on the left side and up the right sleeve.

Owen trailed me up the stairs. I stuffed my clothes in the laundry basket and put on an old pair of paint-spattered jeans and an equally worn sweatshirt.

"Merow," he said.

I nodded. "Absolutely."

We went back down to the kitchen. I had just put a mug of milk in the microwave to heat when there was a knock on the back door. "That's Rebecca," I said to Owen, running a hand back over my hair. I had forgotten she'd said she would bring some of the bread over for me to try.

It *was* Rebecca. She had her big flashlight in one

hand and in the other she was holding a large plate with one of her beeswax wraps over the top. I could smell honey and something that reminded me of toasted nuts. "I made two loaves so I brought you some of each," she said. "Everett thinks my honey sunflower loaf is best but I'm not one hundred percent sure." She took in my old clothes and my probably pale face. "Kathleen, are you all right?" she asked.

I hesitated.

"The fact that you didn't say yes right away tells me the answer is no," she said. "What happened?"

I sighed softly. "You better come in."

She followed me back into the kitchen, setting the plate on the table.

"I had to make a stop at the community center on the way home," I said. I put a hand on her arm. "I had to drop something off to Eugenie. I . . . I, uh, found Kassie Tremayne in the kitchen. She . . . wasn't breathing. I did CPR and the paramedics took her to the hospital."

Rebecca closed her eyes for a moment. "Oh my word," she said softly. "Do you know how she is?"

I shook my head. I wanted to tell Rebecca that Kassie was dead, but once again my promise to Marcus meant I couldn't.

The microwave beeped.

"Sit," Rebecca said, making a "move along" gesture with one hand.

I sat. I suddenly realized just how tired I was. Owen jumped onto my lap. I wrapped one arm around him and stroked his fur with the other hand.

Rebecca made my hot chocolate and dropped two of the Jam Lady's marshmallows on top before she put the cup in front of me. Then she went to the cupboard where I kept the sardine crackers and offered one to Owen. He dipped his head in thanks and took it, setting it on my leg so he could sniff it suspiciously before he ate it. He had some odd quirks when it came to food.

Meanwhile, Rebecca had taken the wrap off the plate of bread. There were four slices from each of the two loaves she'd made. They smelled delicious. "Spelt or honey-sunny?" she asked.

"You don't have to wait on me, Rebecca," I said. "I'm all right."

She smiled. "I know that. Spelt or honey-sunny?"

I looked at Owen. He looked over at the plate and then back at me. "Merow," he said.

"Honey-sunny," I said to Rebecca. Owen licked his whiskers.

"Toasted?" she asked.

I nodded. "Please."

Once the bread had been toasted and buttered, Rebecca joined me at the table. I told her what had happened, sticking to the details that Marcus and I had agreed on.

"Do you think she could have had a seizure of some sort?"

I shrugged. "I don't know." I gave Owen a tiny bite of toast. He murped his thanks before carefully checking it out. "Do you know if Kassie had any kind of seizure disorder, like epilepsy, or if she was diabetic?"

"She didn't say anything about any health issues and I didn't see her taking any medications." Rebecca's expression changed. "What will happen to the show? What about the people who are working on it?" She gave her head a little shake. "It's horrible of me to even think that, isn't it?"

I shifted Owen on my lap as he stretched a paw toward my plate. "No, it isn't. I don't see how the show can possibly continue. Not if Kassie is . . . incapacitated. I don't know what will happen to the production crew, but the rest of us are probably done."

"I'll hold a good thought for everyone." Rebecca got to her feet. I stood up as well, setting Owen on the floor. I gave Rebecca a hug. "For what it's worth, I'm with Everett. The honey-sunny is excellent."

She smiled. "Well, who am I to argue with such experts? Not that it matters anymore." I walked her out. "Get some rest. And if you hear anything will you let me know?" she asked.

"I will," I promised.

She turned on her flashlight and headed across my backyard to her own house. I watched until she reached her back steps and waved the flashlight at me. Then I locked the door and went back inside.

I made a second cup of hot chocolate and gathered Owen on my lap again. He looked hopefully at the plate of bread. "We'll have some for breakfast," I said. He made a sound a lot like a sigh of resignation.

I looked at my phone. I didn't want to bother Marcus but I couldn't stop thinking about Kassie. Was Rebecca correct? Could Kassie have had some sort of seizure? Was that how she had ended up facedown in that bowl of whipped cream?

I went over the list of things that I knew could cause seizures: epilepsy, diabetes, a head injury. I remembered the abrasion I'd seen on Kassie's lower lip when I started CPR. It looked recent. Could she have had a seizure and banged her mouth when her face hit the bowl? It was possible.

"Or someone could have pushed her head into that bowl," I said slowly. Owen's golden eyes met mine. "I'm jumping to conclusions, aren't I?" I asked him. He continued to look unblinkingly at me.

Maybe I was jumping to conclusions, but based on my past experiences, maybe I wasn't.

5

Marcus called a little after midnight. "Did I wake you up?" he asked.

"No," I said, pulling the quilt up a little higher. "I was reading. I couldn't sleep."

"I just wanted to check in and make sure you were okay."

"It's official, isn't it?" I said. "Kassie's dead."

Marcus hesitated for a moment. "Yes, she is. They pronounced her dead at the hospital."

I set my book aside. "I thought she was, but I wanted to be wrong."

"I know."

"Do you know what the cause of death was?"

"The ER doctor said it wasn't a heart attack or a stroke, at least as far as he could tell from looking at the body, but we won't know anything definitive until the autopsy and that's scheduled for later this afternoon. He thought it was possible she had had a seizure."

So Rebecca's guess could turn out to be right.

"Do you know what will happen to the show now?" Marcus asked.

"I'm assuming that this will be the end of it," I said. "Practically speaking, now they're short a judge, and with Kassie dead I don't see how anyone will want to continue. She died in the kitchen in the community center. Aside from filming the actual show on the set, everything was happening at the center. I don't think anyone is going to feel comfortable working in there again."

I knew I wasn't looking to spend any time in that kitchen. I could still see Kassie slumped over the table with whipped cream spilling down the side of the large bowl. My mind started to head in a dark direction.

"What is it, Kathleen?" Marcus said. I'd been silent a little too long. "Did you remember something?"

"Not exactly."

"It's something from the crime scene, though." I pictured him distractedly running his hand through his hair.

"Maybe I'm overthinking things," I said. "But did you notice the table and the wall behind it?"

"Notice what? There was a little whipped cream on the table but the wall was fine."

"That's what I mean. If Kassie had a seizure, why didn't whipped cream get all over the table and the wall?"

"I remember from my first-aid training that not everyone's body jerks or twitches when they're having a seizure." I had the feeling he'd shrugged as he'd said the words.

I adjusted the pillow behind my head. "That makes sense. But where was the mixer? And why didn't the person who made the whipped cream actually use it for something? Or take it with them? Or at least stick it in the refrigerator."

"So you think someone made a bowl of whipped cream just to, what? Suffocate Kassie Tremayne? That's a big stretch."

"The medical examiner will probably say that Kassie had a seizure," I said. "She was standing by the table and fell forward. With the whipped cream covering her mouth and nose she couldn't breathe."

"But you don't think that's what happened," Marcus said. "You think someone killed her."

"Tell me I'm wrong. Tell me I'm seeing monsters where there aren't any."

He sighed. "I'm sorry. I can't do that. Not yet."

That's what I was afraid of.

The next day didn't get off to a great start because I woke up late. There were no glowing red numbers on the clock next to my bed and no fuzzy face breathing sardine breath onto mine. The clock's plug had been knocked out of the wall. I had no idea where my furry alarms were, either.

I scrambled around and got dressed and ready for work. Downstairs, I discovered Owen sprawled on his back in the wing chair, his head hanging over the edge, his golden eyes slightly out of focus. Someone had been into the Fred the Funky Chicken stash. That explained a lot, including, most likely, how my clock had ended up unplugged. He looked at me upside down and meowed good morning.

"Breakfast in one minute," I said, heading for the kitchen.

I started the coffeemaker, put out food and fresh water for both cats and made myself a messy-looking peanut butter and banana sandwich. I stuffed the sandwich in my bag and filled my travel mug with coffee.

By then Owen had wandered in from the living room. I bent down to give him a scratch on the top of his head. "Have a good day," I said.

"Mrrr," he answered with a loopy smile.

I pulled on my shoes and grabbed my bag and car keys. "Hercules, I'm leaving," I called. About fifteen seconds later I heard an answering meow. It sounded like he was upstairs. I hoped he wasn't doing something he shouldn't be, like spreading my shoes all over the bedroom.

I made it to the library right on time. As I got out of the truck the strap on my messenger bag caught on the seatbelt catch. I yanked at it and when it suddenly let go, I was caught off guard and stumbled back a step. My arm automatically flew up and my hand lost its grip on my mug. The mug arced in the air, landed with a small bounce and rolled along the pavement. The lid hadn't even come off. I sighed with relief. My coffee was safe.

Then Harry Taylor drove into the lot.

The front tire on the driver's side of his truck flattened the metal cup and splattered coffee everywhere.

Harry stopped the vehicle and got out. "Kathleen, I'm so sorry," he said. He bent to look at what was left of the container. The knobby tires on his truck had reduced it to something close to the thickness of a Belgian waffle.

"It's okay," I told him. "I'm the one who dropped the mug. It's not a big deal."

It started to feel like a big deal, though, when I got inside the building and realized there was no coffee there, either. We had run out the day before.

I stood in the staff room and took several deep calming breaths the way Maggie had taught us at tai chi. I decided I'd rather have coffee. I realized then that Susan hadn't arrived yet. I sent her a quick text:

Could you bring me a large coffee, please?
Harry ran over mine. Long story.

A few second later she sent back a thumbs-up emoji and a happy face. All was well.

Except it wasn't.

Susan was coming up the front steps about five minutes later just as Harry was coming out the main doors carrying a stepladder so he could put a new bulb in one of the outdoor lights. As best as I could put together afterward, Susan moved left, Harry moved right and it went downhill from there.

Inside the building all I heard was, "No, no, no! Not

the coffee!" I hurried outside just in time to see the take-out cup tumbling end over end toward the parking lot, where it came to rest, upright, *with the lid still securely on*, between two very startled squirrels.

Apparently squirrels like coffee. And are stronger than they look. They grabbed the cup and started hustling it across the pavement.

Susan threw her head back and looked at the sky. "I shouldn't have added the hazelnut creamer," she said. Then she pulled a knitting needle from her bag and gave chase as the two furry rodents dragged the cup over the asphalt. "Bring that back, you mangy furballs!" she shouted.

"Be careful! They bite!" Harry called to her. He dropped the ladder on the grass and grabbed a broom.

Off to my left I heard someone yell, "Give 'em hell, Harry!"

The Seniors' Book Club had arrived. Based on the cheering, most of them seemed to be Team Squirrels. I could see why. They worked really well as a team.

It was maybe thirty minutes later that Harry appeared in my door with a take-out cup from Eric's, plus a bag of ground coffee and a replacement mug for the one he'd run over.

He set everything in the middle of my desk. "You don't have to talk to me until next week," he said. Then he turned and left.

I reached for the coffee, took a long, very satisfying drink and then leaned back in my chair. All was right with the world. I swung around in my chair so I could look out the window.

What looked to be a large tractor tire sat in the middle of the gazebo.

I swung back around so I was facing the door and had another drink.

Harry changed the burned-out light bulb and dealt with the giant tire. He made a point of staying away from me.

Eugenie called midmorning. "Elias has called a meeting for this afternoon at one thirty. It will take place on the set since the community center is still off-limits. Are you able to be there?"

"I am," I said.

"I'll see you then." She ended the call before I had the chance to say anything else.

It seemed like everyone in Mayville Heights came into the library that morning.

"Karmic punishment for my saying it was too quiet last night," Susan said with a grin as she checked out a towering pile of books for a seven-year-old.

I didn't get a chance to eat, but we did close on time, which meant I made it over to the meeting with a little time to spare. My stomach growled its objections but I decided to wait until after the meeting to eat my sandwich. The streets that ran from one end of Mayville Heights to the other all followed the curve of the shoreline, more or less, so it was a quick and almost straight-line drive across town.

I parked at the community center. Stacey Foster was just coming out the back door of the building. She waited for me. "I take it you're going to the meeting, Kathleen?" she asked.

I nodded. "Yes, I am." We started toward the street.

"That's horrible about Kassie," Stacey said. Her dark hair was cropped in a pixie cut and often stood straight up when she was cooking. She was wearing a green-and-black-striped T-shirt dress with a black sweater over the top. Her hands were jammed into the sweater pockets. "'Poor Silas, so concerned for other folk,'" she quoted in her gentle voice. "'And nothing to look backward to with pride.'"

"'And nothing to look forward to with hope,'" I finished. "The Death of the Hired Man." Robert Frost. It struck me that in some ways the words fit Kassie. I wondered if that was why Stacey had chosen to recite them.

Someone had set up folding chairs on the set. About three-quarters of them were already filled.

"It was good to see you, Kathleen," Stacey said. She started making her way across the room to a couple of people who had waved when she'd walked in. Rebecca spotted me and held up her hand. I made my way over to join her.

"I knew you'd be coming from the library so I saved you a seat," she said, patting the empty chair next to her.

"Thank you," I said.

Caroline was sitting on the other side of Rebecca. She leaned sideways to look at me, a frown of concern knotting her forehead. "Hello, Kathleen. How are you?" she asked.

"I'm fine," I said. I had a feeling that word had gotten around that I had been the one to discover Kassie. Caroline's next words confirmed that.

"I heard you found Kassie and tried to help her."

"I wish I had been able to."

"I wish we'd noticed that she wasn't with us when we left," Caroline said.

"How did you end up going to Eric's Place anyway?" I asked.

"Oh, that was because of Norman." Charles Bacchus had spoken. He was seated in front of Rebecca, half-turned in his chair.

Charles pointed a finger toward the left front corner of the kitchen set. A young man carrying an iPad, his blond hair pulled back in a man bun, was standing there talking to Ray Nightingale. "Norman Prentiss. He's one of the production grunts. Seems he had the chocolate pudding cake at lunch yesterday and he couldn't stop running his mouth about it. And it is pretty damn good by the way. It was going for six o'clock. Everyone was trying to figure out where to eat and there was some talk about a short meeting for the contestants. First thing you know the whole damn bunch of us are headin' down for supper. Wham, bam, thank you, ma'am. And we packed the place."

So many people together in the café like that would make it hard for the police to figure out timelines for everyone.

"Hindsight being what it is, I'm second-guessing that decision now," Eugenie said.

"There's no way you could have known what was going to happen," Rebecca said.

"Damn straight!" Charles nodded. "Kassie was a grown woman. It's not your job to keep track of where everyone is all the time. Not everyone went for supper in the first place and some folks left before the meeting even started."

"So I'm guessing *this* meeting is to tell us the show is over?" I said.

Charles laughed, the sound bouncing around the room. People turned to look. Humor seemed out of place under the circumstances. "Not likely," he said. "You ever hear that old saying, the show must go on?"

"But Kassie is dead," Rebecca said.

"And that's awful, but stopping the show isn't going to make her any less dead. People have a lot of time and money tied up in this production and I don't see something like this keeping the show from going forward."

I looked at Eugenie and she gave a small shrug.

"But what about the fact that the show is now short a judge?" I asked.

Charles gave a snort of derision. "Not a problem." He jabbed a thick finger in the air. "Mark my words. Braeden already has a replacement lined up."

Elias Braeden walked in then, as though our talking about him had somehow conjured him out of thin air. The man was a bit above average height with wide shoulders and a muscular build that even his dark suit couldn't hide. His hair was a mix of brown and gray. He had piercing dark eyes and a lined, lived-in face. His presence alone could be intimidating.

Charles turned in his chair, raising an eyebrow as he did. "You watch," he said, confident in what he had decided was going to happen.

Rebecca leaned toward me. "Do you think he's right?"

I caught sight of the person who had come in with Elias and was now standing off to one side. "Yes," I said. "I think he is."

And Charles Bacchus *was* right. The show was going on, Elias explained. A mention of Kassie's passing would be added to the opening credits of the show that had just been taped and a brief tribute would be part of an upcoming episode.

"Several of you will be asked to share your remembrances of Kassie," Elias said.

Charles gave another snort of contempt and from the corner of my eye I saw Eugenie and Russell exchange a look.

Then Elias looked to his left. "Obviously the show can't continue without two judges. I'm happy to report that local business owner Marguerite LeClerc is stepping in to help us. If you've been out to eat at Fern's Diner, you've already met Marguerite, better known as Peggy Sue."

From the sidelines Peggy Sue walked over to join him. Instead of her fifties carhop outfit, she was dressed in slim black trousers with black heels and a crisp white shirt with the cuffs turned back. She looked competent and professional and it struck me that this might just work. Peggy was knowledgeable about food. For several years she had written a column for *Food & Wine* magazine. She had a bachelor's degree from the New England Culinary Institute and had worked in several restaurants in Chicago and

Minneapolis before coming home to Mayville Heights. She was savvy about business and people. She had a great sense of humor. And most importantly, she was available.

Charles looked over his shoulder. "You heard it here first," he said, a huge grin on his face.

Elias turned the microphone over to one of the associate producers, who quickly explained the changes to the schedule for the next two weeks. Then the meeting was over.

Eugenie and Russell already had their heads together. Charles was making his way toward Ray. I turned to Rebecca. "What do you think?" I asked.

"I can't say I wasn't surprised at Peggy being chosen as the new judge," she said, "but the more I think about it, the more it strikes me as being an excellent choice. Did you know she has a degree in culinary arts?"

I picked up my messenger bag that I had set at my feet. "I did. And I agree with you. I think Peggy is the perfect choice. She'll be very easy to work with."

Rebecca wrapped a long, multicolored scarf around her neck. "That will make the transition easier," she said. "Not to speak ill of the dead, but Kassie could sometimes be . . . challenging." She tucked the ends of the scarf inside her jacket. "I'm guessing the autopsy is today?"

"It is," I said. "By the end of the day we might know exactly what happened."

"It would be good to have some answers. I wonder if Kassie has . . . had a family."

Kate Westin was standing behind Rebecca. "She has . . . had a son who is about twelve or thirteen."

I hadn't pictured Kassie as someone's mother.

Rebecca frowned. "I didn't know Kassie had a child. I never heard her talk about him."

Kate folded her arms over her midsection, her shoulders once again hunched up around her ears. "She . . . she mentioned it once."

"It's sad, nonetheless," Rebecca said. She turned her attention to Kate. "Do you know if anyone has collected her things, her clothes, her makeup?"

Kate shook her head. "I don't, but I can ask around."

Rebecca smiled at her. "I know Kassie had some things over at the community center. Her son might want them."

"I'll see what I can find out," Kate said.

"You might want to wait until the police have finished their investigation," I said.

"Kathleen's right," Rebecca said. "I didn't think about the police."

Kate nodded. "Okay. I'll wait." She glanced across the room. "Excuse me. I see someone I need to talk to."

"Do you need a ride home?" I asked Rebecca.

"Thank you, but I have a meeting with Lita and then Everett is taking me out to dinner."

"Lucky Everett," I said, smiling back at her.

Rebecca winked. "That's what I keep telling him!" She headed toward the back of the set.

I fished my keys out of my pocket and turned toward Eugenie and Russell. When I'd taken over the research position, Eugenie had given me a filming schedule for the show so I knew in advance what the theme for each week was. She had added notes for each week letting me know what information she needed. If there was a mystery ingredient for a particular week, I'd find that out just a couple of days before filming and Eugenie was happy with two or three details she could use.

During Pie Week the mystery ingredient had been bison meat and Eugenie had explained to the show's future audience that what we think of as buffalo roaming the plains out west are really bison.

I touched her shoulder now to get her attention. "I'm sorry to interrupt," I said. "I'm going to get started on next week's research this weekend. If you think of anything else that you need, please let me know." Cake Week was coming up next. Eugenie had already asked me to find out if Marie Antoinette really had said, "Let them eat cake," or the equivalent in French. (There was no record of it.)

"I will," she said. "And thank you for the calendar. Now that I know we're going to be continuing I'll make sure it gets hung on the set as soon as possible."

I stared at her, feeling a little confused. "You got the calendar?"

"Yes. It was on my desk this morning. I just assumed you left it."

I shook my head. "It wasn't me. But I'm very happy you have it."

"It must have been elves," Eugenie said with a smile.

I had a feeling it had been one tall, blue-eyed, dark-haired elf in particular.

We said good-bye and I walked out to the truck.

I was just setting the table for supper when Marcus came in the back door.

"Something smells incredible," he said, leaning over to kiss me.

"Merow," Owen commented loudly from his place by my chair.

"In case you don't speak cat, that meant spaghetti and meatballs," I said.

Marcus took a step toward the stove where the tiny meatballs were still sizzling in a pan. He didn't take a second step because Owen had jumped down and was blocking his way.

"You're wasting your time if you think you're going to be able to swipe one of those meatballs," I said. "If Owen isn't getting one, nobody is."

The cat meowed again loudly as if to emphasize the point.

Marcus looked down at him. "I would have shared," he stage-whispered.

Owen wrinkled his nose as though he might be rethinking his actions.

"So how was your day?" Marcus asked.

"When I got to work there was a tire from a road grader in the gazebo." I gave the sauce a stir. "And that wasn't the worst part of my day."

"Should I ask what *was* the worst part of your day?" he said, trying and failing to stifle a smile.

"I got out of the truck in the parking lot and dropped my travel mug. And it was holding my first cup of coffee because some furball managed to unplug my clock." I shot a look at Owen over my shoulder. He decided to play innocent and look over his own shoulder.

"Did you dent it?"

I shook my head. "No. The top didn't even come off. Of course, it did when Harry drove over the mug with his truck." I held up my thumb and forefinger about an inch part. "It's that thick now."

Marcus leaned over and kissed the top of my head. "I'm sorry," he said.

"Oh, the story's not over yet."

He raised one eyebrow. "Okay."

"Harry apologized, of course, but I still didn't have my coffee."

"Why didn't you just make coffee?"

"Because there wasn't any to make." I lowered the heat on the meatballs just a little. "Abigail had taken money from petty cash to get a bag. I sent a text to Susan and because she is a kind and good person she got me the largest take-out cup of coffee Eric has. She was just coming up the steps with it when Harry came out the front door carrying the stepladder."

"I'm sensing a theme here." His lips twitched.

"Apparently the cup hit every one of the steps on the way down and then went top over bottom all the way to the parking lot." I held my hand up once more. "*But*, the lid stayed on."

"So the coffee was okay?"

"You'd have to ask the two squirrels that dragged the cup away."

"Hold on a second," he said, holding up a hand. "Squirrels?"

"Uh-huh. To be fair, it was hazelnut flavored. And for the record, Harry and Susan did try to stop them. There was a broom and one, possibly two, knitting needles involved. It did provide a fair amount of entertainment for the Seniors' Book Club when they arrived. It seemed the smart money was on the squirrels."

Marcus was shaking with laughter. "So did you ever actually get a cup of coffee this morning?" he asked when he got himself under control again.

"About half an hour after all that Harry arrived back at the library with another take-out cup from Eric's, a new travel mug *and* a pound of ground coffee from that micro-roaster in Red Wing."

"Poor Harry," Marcus said, still grinning.

"There's a small postscript to the story," I said.

"I love postscripts."

"When I went out to the truck at lunchtime I found the empty take-out cup sitting on the hood."

Marcus held up both hands. "So to sum up your morning, Harry destroyed your coffee not once but twice and you were flipped off by two squirrels."

"Don't forget there was a road grader tire in the gazebo."

"And there was a road grader tire in the gazebo." He started to laugh again. "And to think some people believe the library is boring!"

I pointed my spoon at him. "Go wash your hands

because we're almost ready to eat." I shifted my attention to Owen. "And you move out of the way or you're going to end up with a heap of spaghetti on your head."

They shared a look and then Marcus went to wash his hands and Owen moved back to where he'd been sitting before he felt the need to defend the meatballs. No arguing, no adorable cute faces from either of them.

How did I do that? I asked myself.

I was setting our plates on the table when Marcus returned. Both cats were enjoying one meatball each. I rationalized that one wasn't going to cause them any harm, and given their other "attributes" it was quite likely they didn't have ordinary digestive systems, either.

"So are you mine for the evening?" I asked.

Marcus smiled across the table. "I am. There's a group playing in the bar down at the hotel—just a couple of guys with guitars—but they're supposed to be pretty good. Do you want to go down later for a listen?"

"I'd like that," I said. "It's been a crazy week. I'd like to just put my brain on idle."

"I'll second that." He picked up his fork and speared a meatball, rolling it through the sauce before he popped it in his mouth. "Oh, that is good," he said after a moment.

He leaned sideways and held up his hand to Owen as though they were going to high-five. The cat, who had finally finished checking out his own meatball and now was starting to eat it, lifted his head and gave Marcus a blank look. Marcus straightened up again, a grin on his face.

"One of these days you're going to do something like that and Owen is going to actually high-five you with one paw."

Marcus shrugged. "Hey, it's not impossible. He can just become invisible anytime he wants to. How hard could a high five be?"

I had kept the cats' abilities secret for such a long time that it felt weird now that Marcus knew. He had taken the news a lot better than I had expected. I'd requested several physics textbooks for him via inter-library loan. He was trying to find an explanation for both Owen's ability to disappear and Hercules's trick of walking through walls that depended on science, not woo-woo magic.

"Have you seen my black pen?" he asked. "You know, the skinny one I bought at the bookstore?"

I shook my head. "I haven't seen it. Where did you last have it?"

He made a face as he twirled spaghetti around his fork. "That's the problem. I don't remember."

"It'll turn up," I said. It was probably buried on his desk at work.

I told him about the meeting while we ate.

"I think Peggy will be a great judge," Marcus said.

"That seems to be the general consensus."

"From what I've heard so far, Kassie Tremayne wasn't that popular." He leaned back in his chair. All that was left on his plate was a smear of sauce.

"You know that expression that Burtis uses about someone being like the cow that gives a bucket of milk and then kicks it over?"

"You're saying Kassie was like that?"

There was a lone strand of pasta in the middle of my plate. I picked it up with my fingers and popped it into my mouth. "I don't like to speak ill of someone who isn't here to defend herself, but yes, from what I saw she was."

"Some people are hard to warm up to."

I shook my head. "I think it was more than that. To me it was like she was . . . mean-spirited. She seemed to be happy when things went wrong for other people."

Marcus laced his fingers and rested his hands on top of his head. "That sounds like a pretty crappy way to go through life."

"Did you get the autopsy report?" I asked. It didn't seem like dinner conversation but it wasn't the first time we had talked about a case at that table. The day we'd met we'd sat across from each other in the library's staff room and talked about the death of Gregor Easton over mugs of coffee. Of course, Marcus had thought I had been having a torrid affair with the temperamental composer and conductor. And I had thought Marcus was, well, a jerk.

We'd both been wrong.

"Just some preliminary results," he said. "There are some tests that will take a few days."

"She died from asphyxiation, didn't she?" I said. It seemed to be the most logical cause of death given what I had seen.

He nodded slowly.

"I take it you don't know exactly how it happened."

One hand rearranged the knife and fork on his plate. "No. We don't. Not yet. You know I can't get into a lot of details with you."

"I know that," I said. "But hypothetically speaking, you—or anyone for that matter—would have to ask how Kassie ended up facedown in a bowl of food. Did she pass out? And if she did, what caused that to happen? The only injury I saw was that scrape on her lower lip."

Marcus nodded but didn't say anything.

I leaned back in my chair and pulled one leg up underneath me. "Continuing in this hypothetical world for a minute, you—"

"—or anyone for that matter," he interjected with a smile pulling at the corner of his mouth.

"Or anyone," I continued, smiling back at him, "would be looking for some indication that she passed out. Did she have a stroke or a seizure? Did she fall and hit her head? Did she choke on something? The answer to all of those questions has to be no."

"Because?"

"Because you"—I held up my hand before he could interrupt me again—"hypothetical you, would have had both the cause of death and the manner of it if the answer to any of those questions was yes. So the manner of death isn't obvious. That's why you're waiting for those test results."

"The hypothetical me," he said.

I nodded.

Hercules launched himself onto my lap then. He had been so quiet up to now, eating his meatball, washing every inch of his fur. "Hello," I said.

He murped a hello back at me and then moved around until he was settled. He leaned his head against my hand and I scratched behind his ear. His eyes closed and he started to purr.

I looked across the table at Marcus. "The hypothetical you is probably looking at a window of about two and a half hours for time of death."

"How did you come up with that number?" he asked.

"I found Kassie at approximately eight thirty, give or take a few minutes. I know from talking to the people at the meeting they probably left around six o'clock."

"More or less." He hesitated. "Kassie made a phone call at about twenty after six."

"So more like a two-hour time frame in which her death had to have occurred."

Marcus smiled. "Hypothetical me would not argue with that."

"Someone killed her," I said. I felt better saying out loud what I had been thinking for the last twenty-four hours.

His expression grew serious. "We're not talking in hypotheticals anymore, are we, Kathleen?" he said.

"No." I shifted on my chair again. Hercules opened one eye and shot me a look of annoyance. "I did CPR on Kassie and I didn't get any response. Her face was purple and blotchy and she wasn't really warm. She was dead well before the paramedics got there. She was dead before I got there. There was no one else in that building other than Zach, and I'm pretty sure he couldn't kill a spider. The whole thing doesn't make any sense. What was she doing at the community center when everyone else was at Eric's having supper?"

Marcus raked a hand back through his hair. "Maybe she was hungry and was looking for a snack. Maybe she forgot something and went back to get it."

I was shaking my head before he finished talking. "She would have been at that meeting. It was a chance to needle everyone and stir up trouble. That's the kind of person Kassie Tremayne was. I saw her in action at the meetings I went to." I put one arm around Hercules as I leaned forward to make my point. "Someone killed her, Marcus. You know that just as well as I do. She wasn't a nice person but she didn't deserve that."

For a long moment silence hung between us.

"I know," he said finally. "That's why I'm going to catch whoever it was."

6

It was Wednesday before the medical examiner declared that Kassie Tremayne's death was a homicide. He had ruled out a stroke, a heart attack, any kind of a seizure and an accidental fall. He'd also discovered lorazepam in her system, which would explain why there weren't any injuries on her body other than the cut lip. She hadn't struggled before her death because she had been drugged. I knew lorazepam was prescribed for anxiety among other things, and one of the drug's side effects was drowsiness.

Marcus had found no prescriptions for lorazepam in Kassie's name and no pills on her body or in her things. It suggested that whoever had killed her had planned to do it.

Elias had made putting together a tribute to Kassie a priority. I knew Richard and Eugenie were both participating, as well as Russell, Caroline and one of the associate producers.

Filming was done outside along the Riverwalk and inside at one of the baking stations on set. "Kassie would love it, you know," Eugenie said as we sat in her office Thursday morning, each of us with a cup of tea and a butterscotch oatmeal cookie. "She did so like to be the center of attention."

I had traded shifts with Abigail so I could spend all day Thursday at the show. Along with working at the library, Abigail was also a children's book author. In June she was going on a short book tour and I'd be able to (happily) repay the favor then.

The show schedule had been adjusted once again and the latest episode was going to be filmed on Saturday and Sunday. It meant the crew would be paid overtime. They all seemed happy about that.

Eugenie had been tasked by Elias with bringing Peggy up to speed. "I need your help, Kathleen," she'd said when she had called me Wednesday night. "Peggy doesn't need to understand all the nuances of the show to film the next episode but she does need to understand a little about the remaining contestants and how we do things."

"What would you like me to do?" I asked.

"Could you put together a basic biography for the six contestants that are still in the competition, please? As well as a bit of background on Richard? We wouldn't want his nose out of joint because Peggy didn't know how many celebrities he's cooked for." I could picture her smiling on the other end of the phone.

"I can do that," I'd said.

"Here comes the difficult part," Eugenie had said.

"Can you put it all together for tomorrow morning? Elias will pay you double what you usually receive for your research."

I didn't have anything planned after work other than watching Netflix with Hercules. "I can do it," I said.

Putting together the biographies turned out to be easier than I expected. I already knew enough about Rebecca and Ray. The newspaper had published an article on the show and talked to Kate and Charles. I discovered Stacey had been profiled by her hometown paper. And Caroline was happy to answer a few questions when I got in touch with her.

There was plenty of information about Richard online. The problem I had was deciding what to leave out.

I handed Eugenie what I had come up with now. "Stacey reads poetry to her kindergarten class? How marvelous!" she said as she scanned the pages. "Charles can tap dance?" Her eyes widened in surprise.

I nodded. When Maggie had invited Charles to our tai chi class he had asked if being a good tap dancer would help. Maggie had thought for a moment and then said, "It couldn't hurt."

I spent more than an hour going over every bit of information with Peggy. She knew Rebecca well, and Ray well enough to get by, which meant she only had to learn the backgrounds of the other four contestants. Eugenie had given us a brief rundown of everyone's strengths and weakness as bakers: who handled the pressure well—Stacey, Rebecca and Ray—who got overwhelmed—Kate—and who had to be reminded to watch their language when something went wrong—Charles and, surprisingly, Caroline.

"How do all the contestants practice?" Peggy asked. "Ray and Rebecca live here so they're okay but what about the others?"

"All the contestants are living in town while the show is filming," I explained. "They all have places with fully stocked kitchens and anyone can work in the kitchen here if they want to."

Peggy finally slumped against the back of her chair and smoothed both hands over her hair. "There's a lot to remember," she said, pushing aside the pages I'd printed.

I straightened the pile of notes into a neat stack. "Be yourself. That's what they hired you for."

Peggy smiled. "Harrison said the same thing."

"Harrison Taylor is a very smart man," I said.

She let out a soft sigh. "I keep having the sensation that I'm about to walk out on a stage stark naked."

I shrugged. "If you do that, you won't have to worry about what to say because no one will be paying attention to what's coming out of your mouth."

Peggy laughed and I knew she was going to do just fine.

I had brought my lunch with me and since the sun was shining and the temperature had gone up, I sat on a bench by the water to eat it. That morning was the longest amount of time I had spent working with everyone from the show. I'd spent a few minutes here and there with the bakers, Eugenie and Russell and even Richard and Kassie, but I hadn't spent much time with the crew. It turned out everyone—from Norman, the PA with the obsession for Eric's chocolate pudding cake, to the set designer who had happily hung the cat calendar for Eugenie—was so nice, so quick with a smile and an offer of a cup of coffee. I took a drink of the coffee I'd brought out with me. It was the good stuff, from the camera guys' stash.

Maybe whoever killed Kassie wasn't part of the show. I couldn't think of a single person I seriously suspected. True, no one had really liked her all that much. And no one was really that broken up about her death. Elias had improved security, keeping more lights on in the building at night and installing temporary alarms on the other main-floor doors that would sound if they were opened.

Harry had replaced Zach in the evening since the latter had been letting people come and go with nothing more than "camera crew" or "backstage crew" for sign-ins. Once those changes were in place people had seemed to settle back in the routine.

No one seemed to miss Kassie, which left me feeling a little sad. Had her killer just been someone who had managed to get in the building, maybe through one of those other doors, looking for something to steal? Had Kassie just been in the wrong place at the wrong time? No, that didn't make sense, either. How had she ended up with lorazepam in her system? I realized I liked the idea of the killer being a stranger because it was better than thinking I was working with a murderer.

I had just finished the applesauce I had brought with me and was wishing that I'd made and frozen more back in the fall, when I saw Russell coming toward me across the grass. He was wearing a yellow T-shirt with his black skinnies and a pair of Mickey Mouse Vans with a pink toe and yellow tongue.

"Hey, Kathleen, do you have a minute?" he asked as he came level with the bench.

"Sure," I said, sliding sideways. "Have a seat."

Russell sat beside me, resting his elbows on his thighs and linking his fingers. "Your boyfriend is the police detective."

He didn't phrase the words as a question but I nodded anyway.

"Ruby Blackthorne says you could probably figure out what happened to Kassie. She says you've done it before. She says you figured out who killed her old teacher."

I had helped catch Agatha Shepherd's murderer. I had also almost gotten myself—and Owen—blown to bits in the process.

"I didn't know you knew Ruby," I said, mostly because I wasn't sure what else to say.

"Elias introduced us." Russell was wearing a gold signet ring on the middle finger of his left hand. He played with it, twisting it in slow circles. The ring looked old. I wondered what its significance was.

I cleared my throat. "I did figure out who killed Agatha, yes," I said. "But so did the police."

"Ruby said people tell you things that they don't always tell the police."

I nodded. "Sometimes they do."

"Kathleen, I did something I shouldn't have done," Russell said, his eyes fixed on his brightly colored shoes.

My chest tightened and my mouth was suddenly dry. "What did you do?" I hoped he wasn't going to say he killed Kassie.

"That bowl of whipped cream? I'm the one who made it."

I looked at him, incredulous. "Why?" I said.

He finally looked at me. "I was going to use it in a magic trick that sadly would go terribly wrong with Kassie being the beneficiary."

"You mean the old pie-in-the-face trick."

Russell nodded. "And you don't have to tell me how juvenile the idea was. I do know."

"Eugenie couldn't have been in on that."

"She wasn't."

The breeze lifted a stray strand of my hair and I tucked it back behind my ear. "So you made the whipped cream. Then what did you do?"

"The dishes. I don't like messes." He made a face.

"Why did you leave the bowl of whipped cream on the table?"

"Because I heard Eugenie calling my name and I didn't want her to come into the kitchen. I knew if she saw the whipped cream she'd guess what I was planning. I figured I'd just come back later and get it. Nobody was going to be in the kitchen. Then we all ended up down at the café and I started to think maybe my plan wasn't such a good idea after all." He blew out a breath. "You know the rest."

"Why did you want to pull Kassie into one of your . . . stunts?" I said. "She didn't strike me as the kind of person who . . ." I hesitated.

"Who had a sense of humor?" Russell asked.

"Who would have wanted to do anything that would have left her looking silly."

He put his hands together back to back and interlaced his fingers. "That was kind of the point. To make her look silly." He looked at me again. "I got tired of the way she took little digs at the bakers. For someone like Charles or Rebecca, well, they're pretty confident people. They can handle it. But for Kate and Stacey—she made them doubt themselves."

Russell wasn't wrong, but I didn't think a face full of whipped cream would have changed Kassie's behavior.

"Kassie was like a crow," he said. "She liked to collect shiny things, but in her case the shiny things were bits of information about people. Then she would use what she knew like a little sword to jab the person."

His words left me with an unsettled feeling. I remembered what I had heard Kassie say to Richard.

"What shiny thing did Kassie have on you?" I asked.

Russell laughed. "See? That's the thing. She didn't have anything on me. That's why I was the person to even the score." He raised an eyebrow and gave me a cheeky grin. "Lucky for me all of my shiny bits have already been shown to the world, so to speak."

7

I pulled out my phone and called Marcus. I explained what Russell had just told me.

"Can he come down to the station now?" Marcus asked. I pictured him sitting at his desk, papers piled everywhere.

I relayed the question to Russell, who nodded. I said good-bye to Marcus, gave Russell directions to the police station and then walked back to the community center with him so he could get his rental car. I spent the next couple of hours looking ahead at the show's schedule with Eugenie and making notes on topics she wanted me to research. Dairy and dessert weeks were still ahead.

Maggie poked her head in Eugenie's office about two thirty. She was carrying a plate with a green flowered napkin on top. "Caroline sent me with these," she said, setting the plate in the middle of Eugenie's desk.

"Wonderful," Eugenie exclaimed. She peeked under

the napkin and then lifted her gaze to Maggie. "Sour-dough biscuits?"

She nodded. "With lemon curd."

"I'm going to put the water on," Eugenie said. "You'll join us?" she asked Maggie over her shoulder as she went to fill her kettle.

"I would love to," Maggie said. She smiled at me. There was a smudge of rust-colored paint on her left cheek. "I saw Peggy. She told me how much help you were to her."

"All I did was give her some basic information," I said. "She's going to do a good job because of the kind of person she is. Adding her to the show was a good decision on Elias's part."

"Do you think Ruby had anything to do with Peggy getting the job?" Maggie asked.

"Ruby had everything to do with her getting it," Eugenie said, coming back in with the kettle. "We needed another judge if the show was going to continue. Ruby suggested Marguerite—I mean Peggy." She plugged in the kettle and set it on top of the bookcase. "That piece of information came right from the horse's mouth, Elias being the horse, so to speak."

"It was a good idea no matter whose suggestion it was," I said. I gathered my notes into a pile and set them to one side.

"There isn't any problem with the show continuing, is there?" Maggie asked.

"I don't think so," Eugenie said, reaching for a metal canister on the middle shelf of the bookcase. "Why do you ask?"

"Because I saw Elias leave about half an hour ago. He looked preoccupied. He didn't speak to anyone. His energy felt off. Usually he comes in to say hello and to see what we're all working on but this time he didn't."

"As my mother used to say, Elias has a lot of irons in the fire." Eugenie dropped four teabags into her squat teapot. "I'm sure there's no problem with the show."

There was no problem with the show but there was a problem for Elias. Late in the day, Marcus arrested him for the murder of Kassie Tremayne.

Ruby arrived just as we were finishing the form at the end of tai chi. Her orchid-colored hair was disheveled, she was pale and she kept picking at the front of her sweater as she stood just inside the door waiting for us to finish. As soon as we were done she came across the floor.

"Kathleen, did you know Marcus arrested Elias?"

"What?" Maggie said, her green eyes narrowing.

Ruby nodded. "Just a little while ago."

I put a hand on her shoulder. "I didn't know, but my phone is in my bag so he probably left me a message."

"This is some kind of stupid mistake. Elias couldn't kill anyone. I know people think he's some kind of thug because he worked for my grandfather a million years ago, but he's not that kind of person. He's filming the Baking Showdown here and he didn't have to do that, but he did because he cares about this town."

Maggie put an arm around Ruby's shoulders. "Take a breath," she said.

Ruby pressed the heel of her hand hard against her breastbone and took a couple of deep breaths.

Ruby and Marcus had clashed during the investigation into Agatha Shepherd's death. It had taken her a long time to rebuild a friendship with him. Now it looked like all that work had been destroyed.

"First of all, Elias is a very smart man," I said, "with an accomplished team of lawyers. They will have him out on bail in no time. Second, you know Marcus is a good detective and more importantly a good man." I kept my eyes locked on hers until I saw an almost imperceptible nod. "Just because Elias—or anyone for that matter—has been arrested doesn't mean he's going to stop digging until he has incontrovertible proof of who killed Kassie." What I didn't say was that Marcus wouldn't have arrested Elias in the first place if he didn't have evidence that implicated the man.

"Find out who did it," Ruby said.

"Elias's lawyers have investigators who are probably already looking into the case."

"I trust you."

I pulled a hand over my neck. It was clammy with sweat. "I can't do anything they won't be doing, that the police won't be doing," I said.

Ruby's eyes stayed locked on mine. "Please, Kathleen," she said.

I thought about what a good friend she'd always been. I thought about how when it came to families I had won the life lottery no matter how crazy mine made me sometimes, and how Ruby hadn't. Elias was Ruby's family. Ruby was my friend. If the enemy of my enemy is my friend, what did that make the friend of my friend?

I took a breath and let it out slowly. "All right," I said.

Ruby pressed her lips together and nodded. It was the closest I had ever seen her come to crying. She took a couple more deep breaths. "I have to go," she said. "Thank you."

Maggie gave her a quick hug and she was gone. We walked over to the tea table together.

"What did I just do?" I said.

She smiled. "You said you'd help a friend."

I hoped it wasn't a bad idea.

"He knew, didn't he?" Maggie said as she leaned over to plug in the kettle for tea. "That's why Elias seemed so off this afternoon."

"Probably," I said. I pulled the elastic off my ponytail and shook out my hair.

"Do you think he killed Kassie?" she asked.

I shook my head. "No, I don't. Elias Braeden is too shrewd a businessman to have killed Kassie by suffocating her in a bowl of whipped cream. That makes no sense to me." On the other hand, why had Marcus arrested him? "I need to check my phone and I need to go home and have a shower," I said.

Maggie gave me a hug. "Call me if I can help. I'll hold a good thought that the universe will work things out."

I changed my shoes, grabbed my hoodie and

headed down the stairs. I waited until I was in the truck before I checked my voice mail. As I'd expected, there was a message from Marcus.

"Hi, it's me," he said. "I wanted to be the first to tell you that we arrested Elias Braeden. I know Ruby is going to be upset but there's evidence that he's our killer and the prosecutor doesn't want to wait." I heard him turn away from the phone and speak to someone. Then he was back. "I have to go. I'll try to call you when you're done with class."

I put the phone back in my bag and drove home. There was a welcoming party of two in the kitchen. I put my phone on the table, hung up my tai chi bag and went to the refrigerator for the milk. I filled a mug and put it in the microwave. Then I stuck a slice of Rebecca's bread in the toaster and got the peanut butter, hot chocolate mix and marshmallows from the cupboard. Hot chocolate and peanut butter toast were my versions of comfort food.

Out of the corner of my eye I saw Owen and Hercules exchange a look. "Marcus arrested Elias Braeden," I said. "Ruby is upset."

"Merow," Hercules said. His right ear twitched. He liked Ruby. So did Owen.

The microwave beeped. I made my hot chocolate, added three marshmallows and took a drink. I set the cup on the table and got two stinky crackers for Hercules and two for Owen—their version of comfort food.

Once the toast was made I sat at the table. Hercules lifted his head and eyed my messenger bag, which was hanging from the back of one of the chairs. Then he looked at me. "Yes, we're going to help her," I said, pulling my toast into two pieces. "But first I have to talk to Marcus." Would he even tell me what evidence he had?

My cell phone warbled. Owen raised his head then, looked at me and meowed loudly. "Yes, I know it's the phone," I said, reaching across the table to grab it.

Owen dropped his head again, muttering almost under his breath as though he was saying, "I was only trying to help."

It was Marcus. "I'm sorry I missed you earlier. I wanted to talk to you before you left for tai chi but the time got away from me."

"It's okay," I said.

"I'm guessing you saw Ruby at class." It wasn't really a question.

I pulled one foot up onto my chair so I could prop my chin on my knee. "I did. She's very upset."

I heard him exhale. "Believe me, I get that," he said. "I didn't want to arrest Braeden. But I have to go where the evidence points. The prosecutor was ready to charge him."

"It's your job," I said. "And I know you wouldn't have done it if there wasn't some kind of proof."

Marcus lowered his voice. "His fingerprints were on the table."

"Everyone's fingerprints are probably on that table," I said. "Including mine."

"His were the only fingerprints on it other than Kassie Tremayne's."

I pushed my bangs off my forehead. "That doesn't

make sense. Everyone has been in that kitchen touching things."

"It makes sense when you know that your friend Russell is a bit of a clean freak. After he made his little bowl of whipped cream he cleaned up after himself. I'm serious, Kathleen. The guy has some sort of obsession with clean kitchens. I think he scrubbed down every flat surface in there."

"Okay, just because Elias's fingerprints were on the table doesn't mean he killed Kassie. He could have just gone into the kitchen looking for someone or to get a cup of coffee." I felt compelled to be the counterpoint to Marcus's evidence.

"His were the *only* other fingerprints. And it's not like we had a long list of suspects. We eliminated the crew pretty quickly aside from one guy who couldn't tell us where he was because he was so drunk he has no idea. Rebecca has an alibi as well, not that she was ever really a suspect."

"Oh," I said. I wasn't sure what counterargument to make against all of that. "But you didn't arrest him just because of those fingerprints."

I guessed that he was rubbing the space between his eyebrows or swiping a hand over his stubbled chin right about now. "Elias was in the building."

"But I don't remember seeing his name in the book when I signed in. And why didn't he come when I was yelling for help?" Both Hercules and Owen seemed to be listening to my side of the conversation.

"That's because Braeden let himself into the building via another door, which was supposed to be locked."

"Okay, that's not good," I said.

"No, it isn't, and then add in the fact that Braeden told more than one person how much he regretted hiring Kassie Tremayne but that he was stuck with her now . . ." He let the end of the sentence trail off.

I could see why the prosecutor had pushed for an arrest. There was more than enough evidence to take to court.

"Look, I'm still asking questions. The investigation isn't over yet. There are things we've discovered that I don't even know whether they're important."

"Like," I said. I wasn't sure he'd tell me.

"Like she changed her name," Marcus said. "Kassie Tremayne was Kelly-Anne Sullivan, daughter of Sean Sullivan, a politician and businessman with some dubious connections. He's a boxing promoter and he owns a gym in Chicago among other things. His nickname for his daughter was Kassie from her initials, K, A, S. She wanted to distance herself from her father, but not too far, it seems."

Marcus had said he had to go where the evidence points. And that the investigation was continuing. He hadn't said he thought Elias Braeden was guilty.

"Do you think the name change is important?" I asked.

"I don't know," he said. "Probably not. I do know that Sean Sullivan and Elias Braeden are acquainted with each other."

"So maybe Elias was doing Kassie's father a favor by hiring her."

"Maybe."

I heard a squeak, which told me Marcus was sitting at his desk. No matter what he'd tried he couldn't seem to get his desk chair to stop squeaking.

"I am sorry Ruby is caught up in all of this."

He couldn't see me, but I nodded just the same. "Me too."

"Before I forget, have you seen that key-chain knife I have?" Marcus asked. "I kept it in the car and now I can't find it anywhere."

He'd found the key-chain knife at a flea market in Red Wing. The tiny folding knife, shaped like a house key, had a very sharp blade and had been useful on occasion.

"I haven't seen it," I said, "but I'll look around here."

"I probably stuck it in a drawer somewhere at home. I'm getting forgetful in my old age." Again, he turned away from the phone to speak to someone. "I have to go," he said when he came back. "Be careful, and if you find out anything, promise you'll let me know."

Marcus knew I was going to try to figure out whether Elias was guilty or if someone else had killed Kassie, I realized. "Promise," I said. "I love you."

"You too," he said and I could hear the smile in his voice.

I ended the call and set the phone back on the table.

I looked down at my two furry cohorts. It was time to get started.

8

Friday morning Elias called a meeting in the community center's gym for everyone involved with the show. A judge had granted bail and he had only spent a few hours in custody. He stood in the middle of the room and we all gathered around him, most people with a travel mug or a take-out cup of coffee.

Elias looked around. "Is everyone here?" he asked. We all looked at one another. I was standing with Eugenie and Russell. Maggie and Peggy were across the circle from us. Rebecca and Harry were next to them, talking earnestly about something. I saw the rest of the bakers standing around—Caroline, Kate, Ray, Charles and Stacey. If some of the crew was missing, I couldn't tell.

Thorsten was on the far side of the room by the main doors to the gym, which had been propped open when we arrived. Elias nodded. Thorsten flipped up the metal kickstands at the bottom of each door. They swung closed and he stood in front of them.

Elias raised a hand but the buzz of conversation continued around us. Suddenly a piercing whistle cut through the chatter. Everyone stopped what they were doing; stopped talking, stopped drinking coffee, stopped swiping through their phones. Eugenie dropped her thumb and forefinger from her mouth and smiled at Elias.

"Thank you, Eugenie," Elias said with a smile. He looked around the ragged circle of people. "Thank you for coming in so early. I'll get right to the point. Yesterday I was arrested for killing Kassie Tremayne." He didn't need a microphone. His voice carried throughout the space.

I didn't think there was anyone who hadn't heard about his arrest but hearing Elias say the words so plainly out loud obviously made us all feel a little uncomfortable. Around me people shuffled their feet, ducked their heads, studied their shoes.

"I didn't kill Kassie. And I don't know who did. But it is my intention to find out, not just to clear my name, which yes, is my priority, but also to bring the real killer to justice. Since I did nothing wrong, and I have nothing to hide, I will be continuing in my role as executive producer of *The Great Northern Baking Showdown*." The words had probably been written by his lawyer.

I realized that Elias was looking directly at me now. I met his steady gaze with my own, wondering if Ruby had told him about her conversation with me last night. I wasn't surprised that he was continuing to work on the show. The man had a level of confidence that bordered on arrogance.

"If you remember *anything*," Elias said. "If you saw anything the night Kassie was killed, if you overheard a conversation, if you saw her arguing with someone, please talk to the police. Don't let some misguided loyalty to the show or to me keep you from speaking up. If the police want to talk to you, please cooperate and answer all of their questions." His eyes finally flicked away from mine. "As far as *The Great Northern Baking Showdown* is concerned, it's business as usual. Thank you for your time, everyone. Let's get back to work."

After a moment's hesitation, people began to move toward the doors, which Thorsten was propping open once again. Elias closed the distance between us. "Kathleen, do you have a minute?" he asked. Since it was Friday and I didn't go into the library until lunchtime, Eugenie and I were planning to work a little more with Peggy since they would be filming her first episode on Saturday.

Eugenie touched my arm. "We'll be in my office," she said.

I nodded.

Russell winked at me and the two of them left together. Elias waited until the room was empty before he spoke. "I know what Ruby asked of you last night."

I didn't say anything. It wasn't as though he'd asked me a question. I waited for him to tell me that he didn't need my help.

"I'll pay you whatever fee you want to set," was what he said instead.

I looked at him, dumbfounded. "I'm not an investigator, Elias," I said. "And I know you probably don't think so right now, but the police are very good at what they do. They will find out who really killed Kassie."

He smiled but there was no real warmth in it. "So you don't think I killed her?"

I shook my head. "I don't know. Shoving someone's head in a bowl of whipped cream doesn't strike me as your . . . style."

Elias laughed. "Don't believe everything you hear about me, Kathleen." He adjusted the cuff of his suit jacket. "I saw what you did in the case of Simon Janes's father. And I know you were also involved in catching the person who murdered Agatha Shepherd. I'm serious. I'll pay whatever dollar amount you name to find the person who killed Kassie."

I wondered what it was like to go through life having your influence and your money get you so many of the things you wanted.

I smiled back at him. "I told Ruby I would do what I could because she's my friend. I'm not a private detective and if you need one, you should hire one."

"You don't like me," he said.

I raised an eyebrow. "I don't know you well enough yet to decide."

That made him laugh again. He pulled his cell phone out of his pocket, glanced at the screen and then put it away again. "What would you like to know?" he asked. "Ask me anything. I'm an open book."

Somehow I doubted that was true. "Did you know who Kassie really was?" I asked. "That she was Sean Sullivan's daughter?"

He nodded. "Yes."

"You hired her as a favor to her father." It was a guess, but a pretty easy one to make. I slipped the strap of my messenger bag off my shoulder and set the bag between my feet.

"I did."

"Were you in the kitchen the night Kassie was killed?"

"You know that I was. I'm guessing you know they found my fingerprints on an otherwise clean table. I went to get a cup of coffee." He adjusted his cuff again.

I wondered if Elias had already practiced the answers to these kinds of questions with his attorney.

"Kassie was there." Another guess, but from the way his mouth tightened for a moment, a good one.

"Yes, she was," he said. "She was upset over an argument she'd had with someone. She wouldn't say who it was."

It was probably the conversation I had overheard between Kassie and Richard earlier in the day. I shifted the strap of my bag from one hand to the other.

"There's something I don't understand," I said. "Why didn't you sign in at the back door?"

Elias waved a hand dismissively. "It's a pain in the ass. This is my project. I got a master key from Thorsten—we go way back—so I could come and go as I please."

I studied the way he was standing, the expression

on his face. There were no little tics to suggest he was being evasive.

"I've been using a space up on the second floor as an office so I can get away from the chaos down here—another perk of knowing Thorsten."

I'd guessed that, since the second floor was supposed to be off-limits to the show.

"So you didn't hear me when I was yelling for help."

"I have a desk in the production office but it's a busy spot. I didn't see or hear anything that night because I was a floor away. I'm sorry. And I didn't say anything to the police about being in the building because I knew it looked bad."

The expression on his face told me he knew how ill advised that had been.

I picked up my bag. "I don't have any more questions and Eugenie is waiting for me," I said. "Like I said, I'll help Ruby any way that I can."

He smiled. "Helping her will probably help me," he said.

I nodded. "I know that."

"Which means I'll be in your debt."

This time I was the one smiling. "I know that, too."

Eugenie and I ran Peggy through the details of what would happen on Saturday on the set. Peggy was ready. She was familiar with all the bakers and their backstories, and there was already an easy camaraderie between her and Richard. Russell put a hand on her shoulder and pulled a tiny foil-wrapped bee from behind Peggy's ear. "It's a new bee," he said solemnly as he handed it to her.

Eugenie groaned and shook her head at the bad pun, but Peggy and I laughed, and in the end we all decided Russell should try the same bit during filming.

I didn't have to be at the library until one thirty. Susan was covering the extra hour for me, and Levi was working because the kids had the day off for teacher development.

About twelve thirty I went outside to eat on the same bench where I'd had lunch the day before. I needed to figure out what I was going to do next. How did I start trying to figure out who had killed Kassie Tremayne?

I could hear my mother's voice in my head saying, *"Start at the beginning; proceed through the middle; and when you get to the end, stop."*

But where was the beginning?

I took a bite of my grilled chicken and pepper sandwich. Caroline had given me some of her bread to try and I had used two slices for my lunch. It was made with whole-wheat flour, flaxseed and molasses, she'd explained. It was delicious. Rebecca's honey-sunny bread was going to have some serious competition from Caroline.

Maybe what I needed to do was talk to everyone who had been a possible suspect before the police and the prosecutor decided Elias was the culprit. Marcus had said that he had pretty much eliminated all of the crew. That left Richard, Eugenie and Russell and the rest of the bakers, minus Rebecca because I remembered Marcus saying she had an alibi.

I looked at my watch. I had enough time to head back over to the community center. Richard had been trying on shirts. He might still be around and I could find out why Kassie had threatened him.

I drank the last of my coffee, folded my sandwich wrap and put it in my bag and stood up. When I turned around I saw Charles coming across the grass toward me. He raised a hand in acknowledgment. I smiled in return.

"You got a second?" he asked as he reached me.

"Sure," I said. "What's up?"

He gestured at the bench. "Mind if we sit for a minute? I've been on my feet all morning making bread."

"It's fine with me," I said, sitting back down. Charles joined me, leaning back against the wooden slats and stretching his muscled arms along the top of the bench.

"How many loaves of bread have you made in the last week?" I asked. I knew Rebecca had made four, maybe five.

"Six," Charles said. "Seven if you count the loaf that didn't rise right. That one didn't make it into the oven."

"How do you keep making the same thing over and over again? Don't you ever want to throw something out the window in frustration?"

Charles laughed. "What do you think happened to that loaf that didn't rise right?"

I grinned.

His expression grew serious. "You're a librarian, right?"

I nodded. "I am."

"How do you go to work and put the same books back on the shelf day after day?"

I propped my arm on the back of the bench and thought about his question for a moment. "First of all, there are thousands of books in the library so I'm not putting the same ones away all the time. And even more importantly, I love books." I leaned toward him. "Don't tell anyone, but I like some books more than I like some people."

Charles smiled. "It's the same for me. There are thousands of recipes to try and tinker with and I love cooking probably the same way you love books."

"I've tried your cooking," I said. "You should try my library."

"You don't have to sell me on the library," he said. "How do you think I learned to cook?"

"Seriously?"

"Absolutely. I grew up with a single mother who hated to cook. The only way I was going to get anything other than canned spaghetti and Ding Dongs was if I learned to make it myself. So I did."

I smiled. "I'm impressed." I meant the words. Charles was a very creative cook. When the judges had surprised the bakers with bison as their mystery ingredient he had created a spicy orange bison filling for his meat pie.

Charles swiped a hand across his mouth. "Well, I guess I've stalled enough. I wanted to ask you something."

"Go ahead," I said. I had a few more minutes before I needed to be at the library.

"I heard Rebecca say that you and the police detective that arrested Elias are a couple."

"We are."

Charles nodded as though that was the answer he'd been looking for. "There's something I need to tell the police."

"Okay." Russell had made the whipped cream and, it appeared, sanitized the kitchen. Elias had a master key so he could come and go as he pleased. What was Charles about to confess to?

He looked out across the water and then he looked at me. "I was sleeping with Kassie."

9

I hadn't seen that coming.

"I don't exactly seem like Kassie's type, do I?" he said.

"More like she didn't seem like your type."

A small smile flashed across his face. "She liked slumming."

I didn't like the word and I didn't like Charles using it to refer to himself. "I don't think Kassie was slumming by being with you and I think anyone who knows you would feel the same way." I had noticed how quick Charles was to encourage the other bakers or to offer a hand if things were going downhill.

"I spent almost six years in prison for manslaughter, Kathleen."

I folded one arm up over my head and looked at Charles sitting there beside me. Manslaughter. He had killed someone. Not planned and not with malice but Charles had taken someone's life. "I don't know what to say." After telling me he was sleeping with Kassie

I hadn't expected to hear anything else that would surprise me.

"I get that a lot," he said. "At least you didn't ask me if I like *The Shawshank Redemption*." He blew out a breath. "I shoved a guy outside a bar. I wasn't looking to kill him. He'd just hit the woman he was with. Turns out he'd broken her nose." He held up one hand. "I'm not telling you this to excuse what I did because my reasons for going after the guy don't make it okay. I pushed him. I was bigger. I was stronger. He lost his balance. He hit his head on the curb and he died. I spent more than five years in jail. I want you to understand that I'm not ever going back. I learned my lesson."

"So you wouldn't have killed Kassie."

Charles shook his head. "No, I would not. She could be a piece of work, don't get me wrong, but I wouldn't get locked up again for her."

I went out on a limb. "She was blackmailing you, wasn't she?"

"Wouldn't have slept with her otherwise," he said. "Like you said, she wasn't my type." He gave me a wry smile. "And it turned out to be a pretty stupid thing to do. All I did was give her more ammunition to use against me."

"What do you mean?" I asked.

"She threatened to say I was sexually harassing her unless I did her a favor. Like I said, she was a piece of work."

I slid my hand down over the back of my head and rubbed my neck. "What kind of a favor?"

"She wanted me to throw the show."

I frowned. "She wanted you to lose?"

"More like she wanted someone else to win."

"Do you know who?"

"Yeah. Your friend Rebecca."

"Rebecca?" I was pretty sure my mouth gaped for a moment.

Charles seemed to find my reaction amusing. "Oh yeah. Kassie was betting on who was going to win the competition."

"You can bet on something like that?"

"You can bet on anything."

"Why?" I said. "And why Rebecca?"

He shrugged. "The girl liked to gamble. She owed money. It was a way to get even or even come out a little ahead. As for why Rebecca, when we started filming she was the long shot. Little old lady from the middle of nowhere. No offense."

I shook my head. I wasn't offended but I was surprised that anyone would bet on the outcome of a TV show. On the other hand, as Charles had just pointed out, people bet on just about everything else. But there was something else that was bothering me. "I thought the show did background checks on all the contestants," I said. "How did they miss the fact that you've been in prison?"

"When no one said anything, I just assumed somehow they didn't know," he said. "And yeah, I know how lame that was. When my charm in the bedroom didn't win Kassie over, I decided the best thing to do was to out myself. So last Wednesday I went to Elias and told him the truth. I told him I would quit and go home. They could explain it any way they wanted."

"You told him about Kassie?"

Charles nodded. "I told him everything. Turns out he'd known all along. He was planning on spinning the whole thing as an inspiring tragedy-to-triumph story that would have the added bonus that Kassie would have nothing to hold over me."

I could see Elias coming up with that idea.

"Problem was, a couple of days later Kassie was dead." He dropped both his arms and looked at me. "I didn't kill her, Kathleen. I didn't have a reason to after I talked to Elias and I wouldn't have done it anyway. But I get that it looks bad."

"It looks like you have a motive," I said.

"I get that," he said with a shrug. "That's why Elias told me to keep my mouth shut."

I could see Elias coming up with that idea, too. I closed my eyes for a moment and shook my head to clear it. Then I opened them again and looked at Charles. "You need to tell the police the truth."

"I know," he said. "If nothing else, it shows there's some reasonable doubt at least as far as Elias being guilty."

It could also put Charles into the middle of a murder investigation. But the truth was what mattered. As my mother liked to say, *"Tell the truth. It's easier to remember."*

So once again I pulled out my cell phone and called Marcus at the station.

"I'm standing in the parking lot right now," he said. "Stay put and I'll come to you. I won't be long."

I would just be able to make it to the library on time. I explained where we were and Marcus said he'd see us in a few minutes. Charles and I sat on the bench and talked about the show. It seemed the general consensus was that everyone already liked Peggy. At least something was working out.

When Marcus arrived I walked over to meet him. "Charles is a good guy," I said.

"Is that your way of telling me to be nice?" he asked.

I stood on tiptoe and kissed his cheek. "No," I said. "*That's* my way of telling you to be nice."

"For the record, I like that second way."

I smiled at him and swung the strap of my messenger bag over my shoulder.

Marcus caught my arm. "Do you remember the other night when we came down to the hotel to listen to those two guys?"

I nodded.

"Did you take the half a pack of gum that was in the cup holder?"

I shook my head. "I don't even remember seeing anything in the cup holder."

He made a sound of exasperation. "This case has me distracted."

"I'll get you more gum," I said. "Right now I have to get to the library."

"I'll talk to you later," he said.

I got to the library with maybe a minute to spare. Susan was at the circulation desk. "How was your morning?" she asked. "Tell me some backstage gossip. Is Rebecca secretly a terrible baker? Does Ray make cookies that look like little ducks? Does Eugenie Bowles-Hamilton expect you to curtsey when you go into her office?" She cocked her head to one side. "C'mon, Kathleen. You have to share something. You're my inside source."

I smiled and held up my left index finger. "Okay. Let me see. Rebecca is *not* secretly a terrible baker. In fact, I've probably eaten about five pounds of her sourdough bread in the last week." I held up a second finger. "Ray actually did make little duck cookies. They were chocolate hazelnut. And they were delicious." I added a third finger. "And no, Eugenie definitely doesn't make anyone curtsey, although she does do a perfect one herself."

In fact, Eugenie had shown her curtsey to Peggy and me just that morning. "My mother insisted that all we girls knew how to do a proper curtsey," she'd said. "Just in case the queen happened to come for tea."

"I have to meet her," Susan said, gushing like the fangirl she obviously was. "She looks so cool and elegant. Please, Kathleen."

"I'll see what I can do," I said, heading for the stairs. Susan gave a little squeal of excitement.

I loved her zest for life in general. Her boys had the same enthusiasm. And since they were scary smart, life was never dull at Susan and Eric's house.

During my supper break I started looking into the

backgrounds of everyone I figured had been on Marcus's suspect list before Elias Braeden moved to the top, doing a deeper dive than I had when I was putting together the information for Peggy. I couldn't just sit on a bench by the water and wait for the answers to come to me, although that had worked twice so far.

Just as he'd told me, Charles had spent close to six years in prison for manslaughter in the death of the man he had shoved outside a bar. I'd missed that when I'd been putting together that basic profile on him for Peggy. The sentence had been reduced due to extenuating circumstances—the fact that the man had just hit his girlfriend hard enough to break her nose.

Charles had learned to box in prison and had had a short-lived professional career when he got out. He'd trained at Rival Boxing in Chicago. I leaned back in my chair, laced my fingers together and rested my hands on the top of my head.

Charles had boxed in Chicago. Sean Sullivan owned a gym in Chicago. Could there be a connection? Had Charles known who Kassie really was? Did he know why Elias had hired Kassie? I had questions for the next time I saw Charles.

I had a few minutes left to see what else I could learn about Caroline Peters. She didn't have much of a social media presence and what she did have showed that she was very much the earth mother I saw her as. I knew she liked to keep her baking as healthy as possible. She favored natural products like the beeswax wraps she'd taught Rebecca how to make and she was an active protester over climate change. While Caroline may have been a gentle earth mother most of the time, I discovered she did have a temper when she was provoked. She had tangled with a counterprotester at a global warming panel discussion in her hometown and had hit him over the head repeatedly with her protest sign. She'd only stopped because other people pulled her off the man. He had needed stitches to close the gash on the back of his head.

No charges were brought against Caroline. Maybe because the police found bomb-making supplies in the guy's car.

I studied the photo that accompanied the story I had found in the *Milwaukee Journal Sentinel*. The photographer had caught the protester curled in a ball, cowering on the ground. Caroline had her sign raised above her head ready to swing it again. Her hands clenched the wooden post so tightly that even in the small photo on the paper's website I could see the skin of her hands pulled tight over her knuckles. As I studied the image all I could think was that she looked angry enough to kill.

Had she?

10

After I finished work at the library I headed over to Maggie's. Roma was joining us and we were going to look at photos from her and Eddie's wedding. The ceremony had been held out at the house with just family and close friends. Maggie and I had been bridesmaids along with Roma's Olivia and Eddie's Sydney. They hadn't had a formal photographer, but Ruby had brought her camera and taken lots and lots of shots.

"The girls are nagging me," Roma had said on the phone. "They want me to make a wedding album. Ruby put all the photos on a flash drive and said I can use whatever I want. But I don't have a clue how to get started."

"We need Maggie for this," I had immediately replied.

With her artist's eye I knew Maggie would select the best of Ruby's photographs, not that I thought there would be very many that weren't great.

Ruby's photos often looked like little works of art to me, probably because she was an artist. She had a knack for finding an unusual angle or a unique perspective. That's why the calendar had been so successful. I was looking forward to seeing the pictures from the wedding. When I took photos I was happy if I managed not to chop anyone's head off.

"We're up here," Maggie called when I knocked on her door. I headed up the stairs and found Roma on the sofa in the living room with her computer on her lap. Maggie was in the kitchen making tea.

"Do you want a cup?" she asked.

"I think I do," I said over my shoulder as I hung up my jacket in her little coat closet. I looped the strap of my bag over the hanger. "I think I had too much coffee today. I realized tonight when I was helping someone with an Internet search that I was talking really fast."

"I didn't know that there was such a thing as too much coffee as far as you're concerned," Roma said as I dropped onto the sofa next to her.

I stuck my tongue out at her and she laughed.

"This is vanilla rooibos tea," Maggie said, holding up the pot. "Naturally caffeine-free."

"As your sometimes doctor, I approve," Roma teased. Although she was a veterinarian, Roma had taken care of me more than once since she was also trained in first aid—for people.

I bumped her with my shoulder and leaned sideways to look at the computer. "Let me see the pictures," I said.

"We have to wait for Maggie," Roma stage-whispered, moving her laptop to the left, out of my range of view.

"It's okay. I'm ready," Maggie said as she came from the kitchen carrying a large tray with three cups of tea, milk and sugar and three plates with what looked to be slices of Swiss roll.

"Oh, that looks good," Roma said, setting the computer next to her on the sofa.

Maggie put the tray on the small coffee table. She had found the rickety piece at a flea market and bought it for five dollars. Marcus had glued and repaired all the joints and she and I had sanded and painted it black. I liked Maggie's apartment. It was warm and welcoming just like her.

"Rebecca or Charles?" I asked, gesturing at the cake. I knew next week was Cake Week and I knew both of them liked to work ahead.

Maggie smiled and handed me a cup of tea. "Ray actually. It's red velvet cake with cream cheese filling." She held up a small jug I hadn't noticed. "And raspberry coulis."

"Thank you, Ray," I said.

I took one corner of the couch, Roma took the other and Maggie curled up in the big chair. We had tea and cake and talked about our week, which meant Maggie and I mostly talked about what we'd eaten.

"Does the show need a veterinarian?" Roma asked. She was wearing her sleek dark hair in a slightly longer bob and it suited her.

Maggie laughed. "I went up to Barry's Hat with a

bunch of the crew. They had beer and wings. I've seen farm animals with better table manners." She nodded slowly. "So possibly, yes."

I ate the last bite of my cake. "I had no idea Ray could make something like this," I said, pointing my fork in Maggie's direction.

"If he'd made one of these Swiss rolls for the co-op board, everyone would have forgiven him pretty quickly," Maggie said.

Roma licked raspberry coulis off the back of her fork. "Do you think he has a chance of winning?" she asked.

"Yes," I said.

Maggie nodded in agreement.

I set my plate on the tray. "Ray is very steady. He doesn't get rattled when things go wrong. Neither does Rebecca."

"I could definitely see Rebecca coming in first," Maggie said. She reached for her tea. "I know you've been working with Peggy. Is she ready for tomorrow?"

"I think so," I said. "She has good chemistry with Richard from what I've seen, and all the bakers like her."

"Everyone likes Peggy," Roma said. Her head was bent over her plate as she tried to scrape the last of the cream cheese filling off.

Maggie grinned. "Roma, would you like another slice of cake?"

Roma looked up. "I shouldn't."

"I didn't ask if you should have another piece. I asked if you wanted to have another piece."

Roma nodded and held up one hand with her

thumb and forefinger about half an inch apart. "Just a little bit, please."

Maggie got to her feet and looked over at me. I shook my head. She took Roma's plate and went into the kitchen. "Hey, Kath, do you know who Russell is seeing?" she asked as she sliced the cake.

"I don't think he's seeing anyone," I said.

"Yeah, he is," she said, "and I'm pretty sure it's someone on the show."

I looked up at her, frowning, as she came back with Roma's cake. "What makes you say that?"

She sat down again, curling one leg underneath her. "You know how the bakers and the camerapeople were doing a walk-through yesterday?"

I nodded. Watching Roma eat her cake was making me rethink my decision not to have a second slice.

"Well, it seems Garry is interested in one of the camera guys."

Roma held up a hand. "Wait a minute. Who's Garry? I thought we were talking about Russell."

"Garry is the illustrator Maggie is working with," I said.

"Okay," she said.

Maggie continued, "So Garry is interested in one of the camera guys, which meant he kept coming up with excuses for us to be out there, and every time we were on the set Russell was on set, too."

"That doesn't mean he's involved with anyone. We're all trying to help Peggy. In fact, Russell has a magic trick they're going to do. They were probably just working on that."

Maggie made a face. "No, I don't think that's it. Yesterday and Thursday he shaved twice, both days."

Roma jabbed a finger in the air. "You're right. This guy's definitely interested in somebody. A man does not shave twice a day unless there's someone he's trying to impress." She smiled. "Ask me how I know."

Maggie stretched out a foot and gave Roma's leg a playful nudge. "We all know you're married to the perfect man," she said with a teasing smile.

Roma's cheeks turned pink. "Eddie is pretty terrific."

I was still trying to wrap my head around the idea that Russell was involved with someone. I had just found out that Charles had slept with Kassie. Eugenie seemed to flirt with Harry Taylor every chance she got and now it seemed that Russell had his eye on someone from the production. TV people weren't a lot different from theater people, it seemed.

I realized both Roma and Maggie were looking at me. "Sorry," I said. "Did I miss something?"

They exchanged a look. "I just asked how your Mr. Perfect is," Roma said.

I smiled. "He's good. This case is keeping him busy."

Roma's expression turned thoughtful. "I saw Ruby getting coffee at Eric's this morning. Do you think Elias Braeden could be guilty?"

I shook my head. "I want to say no. I know he has a reputation for being pretty hard-nosed when it comes to business, but that doesn't mean he's capable of killing someone."

"Wasn't he a suspect in the murder of Simon Janes's father?" she asked.

"He was a person of interest, very briefly. That's all."

"It would break Ruby's heart if he's convicted."

"That's not going to happen," I said.

Roma looked at me for a long moment without speaking. "Okay," she said finally.

Maggie pointed at the computer. "Pictures," she said.

Roma reached for the laptop again and I moved over to sit next to her. Maggie sat down on the other side where the computer had been.

"Both Olivia and Syd want a good photo of Eddie and me. Whatever that means," Roma said. She made air quotes around the word "good." "I'd like one of the four of us if Ruby took any, and one with Mom and Dad." She looked at me, a smile pulling at her mouth. "Ruby said there are a couple of nice photos of you and Marcus that you're welcome to have. You never know when you might want a nice picture of the two of you."

"Say, for an announcement of some kind," Maggie finished. She batted her eyes at me.

I moved my index finger back and forth between the two of them. "Don't start!" I warned.

Maggie leaned her cheek against Roma's and they both gave me their most innocent looks. "We're not starting anything," Roma said.

"Nothing at all," Maggie added.

They had both conspired to get Marcus and me together and now they were being about as subtle as dumping a Gatorade cooler of water and ice over my head, trying to keep us together for life.

I gestured at the computer. "Let's see some photos," I said.

Roma clicked on the flash drive icon on the laptop screen. Of course the photo that appeared on the screen was one of Marcus and me. Roma struggled not to laugh. Maggie held out her hands. "Don't look at us," she said. "It's just the universe trying to send you a message."

I rolled my eyes at her. I had a feeling "the universe" had blond hair and green eyes.

It took more than an hour, but we managed to cull the photos down to a manageable number. "Thank you both," Roma said, wrapping her arms around her knees. She'd set the laptop on Maggie's coffee table. "I'll get these printed on Monday. Both Olivia and Syd stressed that they want 'real' photos."

We'd found two wonderful photos of Roma and Eddie with Sydney and Olivia. All four of them had looked so happy. I remembered the day and I knew they hadn't just looked happy, they'd felt that way, too.

Roma and I hugged Maggie good-bye and neither of us argued when she gave us each a slice of the Swiss roll to take home. We went downstairs together. When we reached the sidewalk Roma stopped. "I need . . . I need your opinion on something," she said.

Her expression was serious, her mouth pulled into two thin lines.

"What's wrong?" I asked.

"Friday night I was late leaving the clinic. I knew

Eddie wouldn't be home and I didn't feel like cooking, so I drove over to Eric's for some takeout. I was walking down the street from where I'd parked just beyond the café, and I heard raised voices. There were a couple of men standing by the bookstore. It looked to me like they were arguing but it didn't seem like a big deal." She sighed.

"Did you know them?"

Roma shook her head. "One of them had his back to me and the other I didn't recognize, at least not at the time. I watched them out of the corner of my eye and it didn't seem to be anything more than a disagreement. I figured there was a pretty good chance that Nic Sutton was working and I thought I would get him to just step out and make sure everything was okay."

Nic Sutton was built like a hockey goalie, strong and solid. He tended to get people's attention.

Roma twisted her wedding ring around her finger. "Just as I got to the door the man with his back to me shoved the other guy and stalked away."

"Was the second man hurt?" I asked. I wasn't sure where the story was going.

"No, he was fine. The problem is what the first man said before he pushed the other guy."

I put a hand on her arm. "Roma, what did he say?"

"He said, 'I'll take care of it. Keep your mouth shut, Charles, or I will bury you so deep you'll never come up for air.' And I really didn't think about the conversation again, but you and Maggie were talking about the contestants on the show and the more I think about it, the more I'm certain that the man whose face I could see was Charles Bacchus and the other man was Elias Braeden."

I rubbed the back of my head with one hand. This didn't look good for Charles or Elias.

"I should tell Marcus, shouldn't I," Roma said. She knew the answer so she didn't frame the words as a question.

I nodded just the same. "People say stupid things when they're arguing. It doesn't mean the conversation had anything to do with Kassie Tremayne's death. It's more likely they were talking about something to do with the competition. I've seen things get pretty heated on the set but people cool off pretty quickly after they've vented a little." I gave her a hug. "Yes, tell Marcus, but I don't think what you heard is a big deal."

She smiled. "Thank you. I'll call him in the morning." She reminded me that we were moving the cats from the old carriage house into their new home on Sunday, and I promised I would be there.

Roma got into her car and I got into the truck. I resisted the urge to pound the steering wheel with one hand. Both Charles and Elias had left a few things out when we'd talked. I needed to get those blanks filled in.

Rebecca had offered to check in on Owen and Hercules before she left to come down for filming so I wouldn't have to go home after work, and Abigail had offered to close the library for me, so I made it over to the community center by five after one on Saturday.

Basically it was my job just to be available in case Eugenie had any questions or drew a blank on something.

"If you don't mind," Eugenie had said when she had asked me to be there. "I think we'll all be off our game a trifle."

Since it was Peggy's first episode I was filling the same role for her.

The crew was almost ready to start filming when I arrived. All the ovens had been tested and were working properly. I'd learned that they were checked before every show so there could be no complaints later that someone's bake hadn't turned out because of a wonky oven.

I had also been fascinated to find out that the show had a recipe researcher whose job was to make sure the Back to Basics segments of each show were something the bakers could complete in the allotted time.

Because of the change to the schedule we were also filming the episode out of order. Usually the show was shot in sequence: Favorites, where each baker showed off their personal recipes; Back to Basics, which tested how much they knew about baking and which was blind judged; and Outside the Box, which was each contestant's chance to showcase their creativity. Today the Outside the Box segment was going to be filmed and tomorrow they'd go back and do the Favorites and the Back to Basics sections.

It was a long afternoon. Eugenie wanted another fact about sourdough starter to use when she talked to Ray. Russell wanted to know if the sourdough museum was a legit thing. (It was.) And every time Peggy came out she had a question. I could see she was nervous. She kept rubbing the side of her right thumb against her little finger.

"You've got this," I said as we stood by the Riverwalk.

"I didn't think I would be this nervous," she said.

"Well, it doesn't show. If you do get stuck, just turn to Richard and smile. He's got your back."

I had decided not to talk to Charles until everything was finished on Sunday. It didn't seem fair to do anything that might throw him off. However, there was no reason not to talk to Elias.

Right after filming finished for the day I saw him standing with Richard and I made my way toward them. I got waylaid by Eugenie.

"I should have guessed you'd know about the museum," she said, smiling at me.

"It's nice to have a use for all the random facts that just seem to stick in my head."

Eugenie held out a brown paper envelope. "Kathleen, I know you're busy, but would you have time to go through this?"

"What is it?" I asked, taking the envelope from her. It felt about an inch thick, filled with papers I guessed, since it wasn't very heavy.

"It's the contents of Kassie's show file. I flipped through it very quickly and it just seems to be notes and some things she printed out on Richard, on me and on some of the contestants. The police didn't want it and one of the producers gave it to me thinking there might be something Peggy or someone else would find useful. I was going to toss the whole thing in the recycling bin but perhaps someone should go through the papers, just to be certain, before I do."

Somehow the job of fact-checker/researcher had turned into me being a jack-of-all-trades. I didn't really mind. Paperwork was easy to handle. Popcorn in the book drop? That was a real problem.

"I can do that," I said. "I'll pull out anything I think Peggy would find helpful and I'll give you back the rest. You can recycle it or file it or let Russell make little paper animals with it."

I'd discovered that along with magic tricks Russell also did origami. I had gone to get coffee during filming and when I came back there was a tiny origami mouse sitting on my notes.

"That's a splendid idea," Eugenie said, "especially that last part."

"Is there anything else you need?" I asked.

She shook her head. "There isn't." She looked around. Richard's conversation with Elias seemed to have ended. It looked as though he was headed back to the community center. "I need to catch Richard. I'll see you tomorrow."

I took a couple of steps so I was directly in Elias's path. "Do you have a minute?" I asked.

"I do, but not much more than that," he said. "What is it?"

There wasn't any point in beating around the bush. "You didn't tell me that Charles was sleeping with Kassie."

A tiny pulse flickered just below the corner of his

right eye. It was the only indication he was surprised that I knew. "He told you."

I nodded. "He did. He also said that you told him not to tell anyone, including the police."

"I knew it made him look bad," Elias said. "And I know Charles—he couldn't have killed Kassie."

I raised an eyebrow. "But he has killed someone else."

"That was a long time ago and it was an accident." He looked at his watch. "Is that it?"

"No," I said. "This is where you tell me that you and Charles had an argument on the street outside Eric's Place a couple of hours before I found Kassie's body."

He pressed his lips together for a moment. It was the only sign I could see of the annoyance I was guessing he was feeling. "Is there anything you don't know about?" he asked.

I held up both hands. "I don't know what the two of you were arguing about."

Elias waved away my words. "It was nothing. Charles was having an attack of conscience. He thought he should tell people about his relationship—such as it was—with Kassie. I disagreed."

"I told Ruby I would help you and you're making it difficult when you keep secrets like this." It was hard to keep the exasperation out of my voice.

"Oh, please, Kathleen. You don't really believe Charles killed Kassie. It's just unthinkable."

"Why not?" I said. "After all, the police think you killed her."

He looked at me for a long moment. "Touché," he said softly.

"What did you mean when you told Charles you'd bury him so deep he wouldn't be able to come up for air?"

Elias tugged on his cuff the way he had the last time we'd talked. Nervous habit, maybe?

"Not what you think," he said. "I know Charles is trying to turn being on the show into bigger opportunities. Hell, he's not the only one. All of the contestants have an agenda. What I meant was if he was foolhardy enough to make what should be kept private public, I would have no choice but to make sure not one single opportunity would come his way. Nothing more. Now are we done?"

"For now."

"I'd like to say it's been a pleasure, Kathleen," he said.

"So would I," I said with the slightest of smiles. I had caught his meaning and I was certain he'd caught mine.

I stuffed the envelope Eugenie had given me in my messenger bag. My feet hurt from being on them so long all day. All I wanted to do was climb into the bathtub with one of Maggie's herbal soaks and stay there until I looked like a prune. I didn't want to make supper. Marcus was out of town for the weekend at a coaching seminar in Minneapolis. He'd been helping with the high school girls' hockey team and it was something he was good at—no surprise, because he was pretty athletic. I was happy the case hadn't derailed his plans.

I unlocked the truck, dropped my bag on the seat and decided to head to Eric's to get some supper to take home. I found a parking spot on the street just a couple of spaces down from the café, a sign, I decided, that the universe did not mean for me to cook tonight.

The restaurant was fairly quiet with about half the tables occupied, typical for a Saturday evening this time of year. I took a stool at the counter just as Nic Sutton was coming from the kitchen with a tray of food.

"Hey, Kathleen," he said. "Give me two minutes and I'll be right there."

I nodded. "Take your time."

Nic expertly delivered the orders, smiled and gave what from my vantage point looked like directions to the Stratton Theatre all quickly and efficiently. He scanned the room to make sure no one was trying to get his attention and then came back and slipped behind the counter.

"What can I get you?" he asked. "I'm assuming since you didn't grab a table that you want takeout." Nic was about medium height and stocky, with light brown skin and deep brown eyes. He had grown a goatee a few weeks ago and I thought the closely cropped facial hair suited him.

"I do," I said. "How about a noodle bowl?"

"Good choice," he said. "How about chicken and shrimp?"

There was a better than average chance that I would end up with a paw in my bowl if I said yes to the shrimp but I did it anyway. "Are there any cheese biscuits?" I asked.

Nic shook his head. "But we do have some fresh naan bread. It's made with caramelized onions." He raised his eyebrows in a question.

I smiled. "That sounds good, too."

"I'll go put your order in," he said. He grabbed his tray and headed for the kitchen. When he came back he gave me an appraising look. "Leaded, unleaded or no coffee at all?"

"Better make it decaf," I said. He poured me a cup in a take-out container and I gave myself a mental kick for leaving my new stainless-steel mug at home.

"Were they taping the Baking Showdown today?" Nic asked as he set the cup and a lid in front of me.

"I just came from there," I said, reaching for the cream and sugar.

"Any hints on who's in and who's out?" he asked, a teasing smile lighting up his face. "I would not breathe a word to a soul. I swear. And on a totally unrelated subject we have chocolate cheesecake."

I laughed. "Nice try but my lips are sealed."

Nic made a face. "Overplayed my hand a little with the cheesecake, didn't I?"

I nodded. "Little bit, maybe."

"Can you at least tell me how Charles is doing?" he asked.

I took a sip of the coffee. It was hot and strong, just the way I liked it. "You know each other?"

"Kind of," he said. "I was working last week when

it seemed like pretty much everyone from the show showed up for dinner. We were swamped. Claire's shift ended at six and she hadn't been out of the door five minutes."

"So Charles was here?"

Nic scanned the room again to see if anyone needed anything. "Good thing he was. Like I said, we were swamped. First thing I know, Charles is getting coffee for people. Next thing he's helping me wait tables. I wouldn't have gotten through the night without his help."

"So you're saying he waited tables here for two hours?"

He nodded. "Yeah. Eric wouldn't let him pay for his own food. I never could have handled so many people all by myself." He reached for the coffeepot. "I'll just go top up some cups and your food should be ready."

"That's fine," I said. I took another sip of my coffee. Charles had been here helping Nic with customers the night Kassie Tremayne was killed. There was no way he could have killed her, and I was happy about that because I did like the big baker. On the other hand, Charles had had an alibi all along. Why hadn't he said so?

11

I drove out to Wisteria Hill early Sunday morning. I'd had to drag myself out of bed. It had been a long week.

Roma had decided early in the morning was the best time to move the cat colony. For the past several weeks she had been slowly moving their feeding station, which was at the back of the carriage house, over to the door, literally a few inches at a time. I had helped her as often as I could. The first couple of times Lucy had looked perplexed, but I noticed after carefully checking out the food and the water she'd eaten, the others had followed her lead.

Today, for the first time, the feeding station was in the doorway of the cats' new home. Eddie had done an excellent job on the twelve-foot-by-twelve-foot shed. It was insulated, with a roof that didn't leak and new shelters for each cat made from plastic storage bins by Rebecca, Ella King and Harry's daughter, Mariah.

I was surprised by the knot of anxiety that lay in my stomach like I'd swallowed a large rock. This was such a big change for the cats. What if they didn't like their new home? What if they all just disappeared? We'd never be able to find them again. And I wasn't sure it was a good idea to rehome Smokey at the clinic, at least not now. The colony was his family. Just because he was old didn't mean there wasn't a place for him.

Roma had asked me if I would put out the cats' food and water for the first time.

"Of course I will," I'd said at once. Lucy trusted me as much as she trusted anyone, and Roma hoped the cat would accept the change more easily if she saw me.

Roma and Eddie stayed across the driveway as I headed for the carriage house with the food, the dishes and two jugs of water. Her arms were folded tightly across her chest and I knew she was probably as apprehensive as I was.

I propped the side door of the carriage house open and then went over to the new building. That door was wedged open as well and the feeding station was set up in the doorway. Eventually it would be moved farther inside. Eddie had built a small flap in the larger door so the cats could come and go as they pleased. There was a partial wall dividing the shelter area from the rest of the space so the cats would feel secure. The shelters themselves were up on a long shelf about waist height. There was a small step about halfway between the floor and the top of the platform so the cats could easily get up and down. I knew even Smokey could navigate the distance if I could just come up with a way to convince Roma that he needed to stay.

The building was sheltered by a clump of evergreen trees and some other bushes, which Eddie felt would mitigate the extremes of both the summer and the winter temperatures.

I set out all the dishes and filled them with food and water. Then I backed away, crouched down and waited. I had probably stayed like that for maybe five minutes, although it felt a lot longer. The lump in my stomach felt heavier and harder. I had cramps in both my legs but I was scared to move, afraid that if I did it would be just the moment the cats would appear and I'd frighten them away.

Then, finally, I saw movement at the door of the carriage house. Lucy poked her head out. She looked at me and it seemed to me she looked confused. I didn't blame her. After the loft had fallen down in the carriage house we didn't see her or any of the cats for two long days. They didn't touch any food. Roma kept putting out water and insisted they would come back. Later she'd admitted she was trying to convince herself as much as she was me.

"They did come back, Kath," she had reminded me earlier. "This will work, too." I wondered if, like before, the reassurance was for herself as much as for me.

I watched Lucy. Lucy watched me. Neither of us moved. I was holding my breath, I realized. I let it out and then called softly to the little cat. "Hi, puss. Breakfast is ready."

She took a step outside and her whiskers twitched

as she sniffed the air. Could she smell the food at that distance?

"C'mon, Luce," I said. "This is your new home. It's safe. I promise." I thought about the little cat finding Marcus and making such a fuss he'd realized something had to be wrong and headed for the carriage house in time to help save Syd and Olivia.

Lucy cocked her head to one side. She seemed to be weighing my words. Or maybe she was just deciding whether to go back inside the carriage house or bolt for the trees.

Maybe this was a bad idea. Maybe I was just going to have to convince Roma and Eddie to let the cat colony have the carriage house to themselves until they were all gone after very long and happy lives.

And then Lucy took a step forward. And then another. She meowed loudly and Smokey stuck his gray head around the carriage house door. He stepped outside and started for the feeding station. After a moment the other three cats followed. They all seemed a little apprehensive and skittish, even Lucy, but they all came and ate and then Smokey went inside. He had always been the most curious of the group and the most fearless. I leaned sideways and watched him sniff everything and then disappear back where the shelters were. Roma had put a couple of the sardine crackers I made for Owen and Hercules in front of each shelter as what she called a "welcome home" gift.

After Lucy had eaten she sat and washed her face while the others finished and then followed Smokey inside. Finally she turned, looked at me and meowed again.

"I'm glad you like it," I said. I had to blink away a sudden, unexpected prickle of tears. Everything was going to be all right. Lucy turned back around and went to explore her new home.

I stood up, shaking my left leg, which had fallen asleep because I had been crouched down so long. I walked back over to Roma and Eddie, hobbling a little as the feeling came back to my leg.

"It worked!" Roma exclaimed, bright-eyed. She'd come close to tears herself, it seemed.

We hugged and then I leaned back. "Don't make Smokey go live at the clinic," I said. "Please."

Roma shook her head. "I'm not."

I stared at her for a long moment. "You're not?"

"I'm not. This is his home and his family. Eddie convinced me I was wrong. And that's why he built that extra step between the ground and the platform. So Smokey could make it up and down easily."

I looked up at Eddie, who was smiling at me. The former hockey player really was a softie. "I love you, Crazy Eddie Sweeney," I said.

The smile turned into a grin and he wrapped me in a bear hug. "Love you, too," he said.

I told Roma I would call her later that afternoon to see how the cats were and then I got in the truck and headed home.

I'd had fruit and yogurt before I had driven out to Wisteria Hill. Now I was hungry again. I found Hercules sitting on the back steps, green eyes cast skyward. He had some weird rivalry going on with a grackle—or maybe it was several grackles, I wasn't sure.

I leaned down and picked him up. "How do you feel about a breakfast sandwich?" I asked.

He murped with enthusiasm and nuzzled my neck.

"Where's your brother?" I asked.

Hercules suddenly wriggled to get down. That was *not* a good sign. As soon as I stepped inside the kitchen I knew why Hercules had suddenly gotten squirmy. Owen was under the kitchen table and based on the bits of dried leaves surrounding him, he had been playing air hockey with a Fred the Funky Chicken. For once he hadn't bitten the head off and spread catnip everywhere. This would be easy to sweep up. There was just a tiny split in the side of the cat toy.

Owen gave an indignant meow when I picked up the chicken.

"Yes, I know it's yours, but you made a mess on my clean floor."

The cat looked around the room and then fixed his narrowed golden eyes on me. I remembered that I hadn't actually washed the floor on Friday. I had gone to Maggie's with Roma instead.

"Okay, my almost clean floor," I said. "That's not the point. I don't see your little paws working the broom when there's catnip everywhere."

He lifted one paw and stared at it. I couldn't help laughing. I leaned down to scratch the top of his head. "Okay, Fuzzy Face," I said. "First I'm going to clean up your mess. Then I'm going to make a breakfast sandwich."

Owen murped his enthusiasm for both ideas and tried to grab the yellow chicken I was holding. I snatched it out of his reach. "Say good-bye to Fred," I told him, straightening up and taking the catnip toy to the garbage can. It was one good swat away from splitting open and spewing a whole lot of dried catnip all over my semiclean floor.

I grabbed the broom from the porch and swept up the mess Owen had made. He muttered and grumbled a little but he knew when he'd lost. I kicked off my shoes, hung up my hoodie and went to wash my hands. I knew there were eggs, tomatoes and cheese in my refrigerator and one last slice of Rebecca's spelt bread in the breadbox. I scrambled the eggs, toasted the bread and added a couple of slices of tomato and two slices of cheese. The boys got a tiny bit of egg with two sardine crackers.

I set my sandwich on the table and got my laptop. I didn't have to be down at the show for a while. I wanted to see if I could learn a little more about Kassie.

I was reading an article on an entertainment site about the revival of *The Great Northern Baking Showdown*, when Owen launched himself onto my lap and leaned in front of me as though he wanted to read what was on the screen, too. After we finished the article—Owen, if he was indeed reading, was pretty quick at it—we scrolled down to the comment section. The first episode hadn't even aired and already people were critical about Kassie's casting and her lack of experience and training when it came to cooking in general and baking in particular. They picked on everything from her hair to her penchant for heels to the way she pronounced the word "recognize" in her online videos. A lot of the comments were spiteful. I wondered if Kassie had seen any of them, and if she had, how they had made her feel. I felt uncomfortable and sad reading them and they weren't directed at me.

I got up to get another cup of coffee, setting Owen on the chair. When I came back to the table he was on his hind legs, one paw on the edge of the laptop, looking at the screen with what seemed to me to be a very self-satisfied expression on his face. Somehow in the short amount of time I had been up he'd managed to find Kassie's Instagram feed. I scooped him up and set him on my lap.

"Not even going to ask how you did this," I said. "But I'll give you a pass for the catnip." He licked my chin.

Kassie's Instagram feed was a carefully curated collection of images. There was no way my kitchen ever looked that good.

"Where are the clumps of cat hair on the floor?" I said to Owen. "Where are the funky chickens and stinky cracker crumbs?"

He leaned forward for a better look at the screen and then seemed to shake his head. Clearly he was baffled, too.

We spent a little time sifting through the photos Kassie had posted before her death. She had been showing more of what was happening on set than

Elias had wanted posted online and while she didn't mention any of the contestants by name, she did manage to work in little comments on their baking. Very quickly I picked up a pattern in what she was saying and showing. She favored Ray. Although she didn't use his name it wasn't hard to figure out to whom she was referring. Anyone who had checked out the show's social media would realize it was Ray.

There was already a lot online about *The Great Northern Baking Showdown* and the contestants. Elias's promo people seemed to be trying to generate as much buzz as possible, probably because they felt it would help find a buyer for the final product. It was hard to believe that people actually cared about the outcome of a program no one had seen yet.

I remembered Charles telling me that Kassie had bet on the winner of the show being Rebecca. "This doesn't make sense," I said to Owen. "Why was Kassie piling on the not-so-subtle praise for Ray when her money was on Rebecca?" If anything, she had seemed to pick on Rebecca's efforts a little.

"Mrrr," he said.

"Unless . . ."

Owen looked at me, cocking his head to one side.

"We know people bet on the show. They bet on who will make it to the top three. They bet on who will win. If someone is perceived to be a long shot, then the payout will be greater if they win."

"Mrrr," Owen said again. So far he seemed to be following me.

I took a drink of my coffee. "So if Kassie gave people the impression that Ray is becoming the front-runner and Rebecca doesn't have much of a chance of winning, they're more likely to bet on him, which moves the odds with respect to Rebecca winning more in Kassie's favor." Could that have actually happened?

It took a little searching and a couple of lucky pokes of the keyboard by Owen but eventually we managed to find an online gambling site that gave the odds of each one of the bakers taking first place on the show. People would bet on anything, it seemed.

"Look at that," I said. Owen followed my finger. Ray was favored to win, although as I tracked the odds back over the previous ten days his advantage had slipped a little. On the other hand, the chances of Rebecca winning had increased a little over the same period of time.

I didn't think Rebecca knew what Kassie had been doing. Had Ray? "Very interesting," I said to Owen.

He murped his agreement.

I got down to the set about half an hour before filming started, which gave me plenty of time to check in with Eugenie and deal with any last-minute questions from Peggy. They were shooting Back to Basics and then Favorites. The Basics section would take the least amount of time. After that had been filmed we'd break for lunch—catered by Eric—and then finish with Favorites.

Everyone was wearing the same clothes they had worn on Saturday and I watched a member of the production crew check shoes, hair and jewelry for continuity's sake since we were filming the first part of the show last.

Everything went just as well as it had the day before. Peggy and Richard already had an easy, relaxed chemistry—not flirtatious, more like siblings without the sibling rivalry. I could see that Ruby had been right to suggest Peggy as the replacement judge.

Russell came to stand next to me while we were waiting for the set to be cleaned up before the Basics judging. He was wearing a long-sleeved orange T-shirt that still managed to show off his muscled arms and his ubiquitous Vans—this pair was orange and red. When I used to watch the original version of the show I'd always wondered why everywhere was so clean during the judging. Did the bakers scurry around after they were finished to make each station presentable? It turned out a bunch of production assistants and a couple of producers were the ones scurrying around to make everything look good again, while the bakers got to step outside for a few minutes' break.

"Thank you for the mouse," I said to Russell. "It's so small and perfect."

He held out his closed hand and when he opened his fingers another tiny mouse sat on his palm. "One for Hercules and one for Owen," he said with a smile. "I have their names right, don't I?"

"Yes, you do," I said, taking the little paper creation from his hand. "Thank you for mouse number two. You know, I think they need names."

Russell wrinkled his nose and pulled his mouth to

one side as though he were deep in thought. "Russell is a very nice name," he said, "or so I've heard."

I nodded and held up the paper mouse. "Russell, meet Russell."

The human Russell bowed his head. "It's a pleasure."

"If this is Russell, then the other mouse has to be Eugenie, don't you think?" I said.

"Eugenie and Russell," he said thoughtfully. "Russell and Eugenie. In either combination the names do work well together."

"Then it's settled," I said with a smile.

He gestured at his paper creation. "Be careful. You know what they say: When the cat's away, the mice will play."

He gave me a cheeky smile and walked off.

Everything ran so smoothly that filming actually finished a bit early. To my delight Rebecca was chosen Hot Shot—the week's best baker, in other words. For the Favorites segment she'd made her honey-sunny bread. Richard had complimented the flavor and Peggy had noted both the texture and the crispness of her crust.

Caroline had made a spicy tomato sourdough loaf, which had coaxed a smile from the usually serious Richard. And Ray's sourdough focaccia with rosemary, sea salt and garlic had filled the set with its delicious aroma as it baked.

Sadly, Stacey was eliminated. Her basic sourdough loaf hadn't held its shape and was overbaked. And both Richard and Peggy had felt her sourdough biscuits were too heavy and too bland.

Maggie and I had been standing together, watching the final judging segment. We hurried over to Rebecca.

"I knew you were going to win Hot Shot," Maggie said, folding Rebecca into a hug.

"The credit has to go to my mother's recipe," Rebecca said, bright-eyed with excitement.

"The credit has to go to you," I said, stepping up to hug her as well.

Stacey came up behind Rebecca and tapped her on the shoulder. "Congratulations, Rebecca!" she said with a smile. "You deserve being the Hot Shot baker this time."

"I'm sorry you're leaving," Rebecca said. "It's been such a pleasure to get to know you."

Stacey nodded. "You as well."

Maggie leaned toward me. "I have to get going. I have some more illustrations for next week that I have to work on."

"I had fun Friday night," I said. "We have to do it again."

"Pizza?" she said, raising an eyebrow.

I loved Maggie's pizza. "Absolutely."

Maggie raised a hand in good-bye to Rebecca and headed for the community center.

Caroline, Ray and Eugenie joined us then. Ray and Caroline were still wearing their aprons and Caroline had a dusting of flour in her hair.

"I need to try that bread," Ray said to Rebecca.

"So do I," Caroline said. "What made you think of adding walnuts?"

They dragged Rebecca away, all of them talking at once.

Beside me, Stacey still had a smile on her face.

"That was nice of you," I said.

"You're wondering why I'm not sulking and going off somewhere to lick my wounds," she said.

I shook my head. "No. I'm just impressed by the way you're handling the fact that you have to leave the show. It isn't easy to be gracious about someone else's win when you lost something."

"Actually it is easy," Stacey said, brushing a bit of what looked like orange zest from the sleeve of her sweater. "I never expected to make it on the show, let alone get this far. I've gotten way more out of this experience than I ever expected, so I'm happy."

"I'm sorry to see you leave," I said.

"I'm not going yet," she replied. "I've already taken the time off so I've decided to stay here a bit longer, maybe explore the town a little."

I smiled. "Come see the library if you have time."

She smiled back at me. "I'd like that."

Richard was heading in our direction.

"Excuse me, Kathleen," Stacey said. "I have to let Richard tell me he thinks I'm a great baker even though we both know by the face he made when he tried my biscuits that he's a little iffy on that."

She was still holding her apron and she leaned over now and set it on the end of Rebecca's workstation. As she did, the fine silver chain she was wearing around her neck slid out of her dress. I caught sight of what looked like a tiny red heart-shaped paper pendant hanging from the chain. I hoped that meant Stacey had someone special to commiserate with. Even though she hadn't expected to make it this far, being ousted had to sting a little.

I started for the truck when I realized that Charles was ahead of me, headed in the same direction. I caught up with him at the curb.

"We need to talk," I said.

He shrugged. "Yeah, I figured this was coming." He gestured at the grass. "You wanna walk?"

I nodded and we started walking away from the building that housed the set.

"I saw you talking to Elias yesterday," Charles said.

"When you told me that Elias warned you not to tell anyone that you slept with Kassie, why didn't you tell me the two of you stood on the street and argued where anyone could have heard you?"

"Duh! Because it doesn't make him look good."

"Him shoving you doesn't make *him* look good?" I said. "That's what you were worried about?"

Charles held up a hand. "First of all, I may have been a crappy boxer but I still could have laid the dude out right there if I'd wanted to. But I didn't and I wouldn't. Like I told you before, I learned my lesson about getting physical with people. I let him shove me like that to let off a little steam. And second, like I said, it doesn't look good for Elias to be putting his hands on me and saying he'll take care of things and then a couple of hours later, Kassie is dead. I know how the police think."

I exhaled loudly. "Well, it looks worse when the information comes from a witness who heard the two of you instead of from Elias or you."

"Look," he said. "I just don't think he killed her. I really don't. And the guy's been good to me. I wasn't going to hang him out to dry."

Charles just didn't seem to see he hadn't made things better.

"You also didn't tell me that you used to box in Chicago."

At least this time he had the good grace to blush. "Where Kassie's father had a gym. Yeah, I probably should have said something about that. I only knew the guy by reputation, which was enough, believe me. I swear, though, I didn't know Kassie was his kid at first. Do you think I would have slept with her if I had? Jeez, I don't have a death wish."

I kicked a rock and sent it bouncing along the ground in front of me. "When did you find out who she was?"

"Elias told me when I told him about the two of us hooking up."

I had no reason to disbelieve him but I wasn't sure I *should* believe him, either. Not that it really mattered. "How did you get down to Eric's the night of the murder?" I asked.

"I drove down with some of the crew, Norman and a couple of the camera guys."

The last piece slid into place. "Well, unless you happen to be some sort of sprinter, you have an alibi for Kassie's murder."

Charles grinned and patted his ample midsection. "The only time I run is for free donuts."

"So why didn't you say where you were from the beginning?"

"What does it matter?" he said. "You know, and I assume you'll tell your boyfriend so the police will know. And anyway, I'm not even a suspect."

I was pretty sure Fred the Funky Chicken would have been able to tell he was hiding something. "Oh, humor me," I said.

His mouth moved but no words came out.

There was a bit of a breeze and the wind lifted my hair. I pushed it away from my face. "Charles, I hope you don't play cards," I said.

"Why do you say that?" he asked.

"Because you can't bluff to save your life. Tell me why you didn't mention you had an alibi or I'm going to think there's a reason you don't want everyone to know you were helping wait tables at the café."

His gaze slipped away from mine.

I stopped walking. "Wait a minute. That's it, isn't it?"

"No," he said. He really wasn't a very good liar. A lot of people weren't.

I just stood there looking at him.

Charles swiped a hand over his face. "Okay, okay. I didn't tell you because I was trying to downplay the whole thing."

"Because?" I prompted.

"Because I've been watching you. Sometimes you're too smart for your own good."

I wasn't sure if that was supposed to be a compliment or a criticism.

"I was afraid you'd figure out what I was really trying to do that night," he said.

"Which was?"

He shook his head. "I was trying to get into the kitchen, okay? I wanted to find out what Eric's secret ingredient is in that chocolate pudding cake. Dessert Week is coming up."

I stared at him, dumbfounded. "You were going to steal Eric's recipe? You've got to be kidding. You couldn't have fooled anyone. Every single person in Mayville Heights has eaten that pudding cake. More than once."

"I wasn't trying to steal anything," Charles said, his jaw clenched. "I just wanted to know what his secret was so I could make a couple of adjustments to *my* lava cake recipe. No harm, no foul."

I sighed. "There is no secret ingredient, unless it's the fact that Eric puts his heart into every recipe he creates." I had liked Charles up to now, but suddenly I wasn't so sure how I felt about him.

He was shaking his head again before I finished speaking. "I'm an ex-con, Kathleen. I'm not like Caroline, making healthy versions of comfort food for her five kids. Or like Rebecca, using recipes that go back three or four generations. I was raised by a single mother who was also raised by a single mother. Neither one of them knew how to cook."

"No one is asking you to be Rebecca or Caroline or anyone else," I said. "Be who you are. For all you know there will be someone watching who will get inspired by you." I looked at him for a long moment and then I turned and walked away.

I drove home and had a late supper with Owen and Hercules. I had left chicken soup in the slow cooker and the delicious smell filled the kitchen. After I'd eaten and the boys had given me their most mournful looks, Hercules decided to go out into the porch and stare out the window—maybe looking for his grackle nemesis. Owen decided to stay in the kitchen and do everything possible to get in my way.

The phone rang as I was finishing the dishes. It was Marcus. "Hi," he said. "I just wanted you to know that I'm having dinner with a couple of the guys from the workshop and then we're heading back."

"I miss you," I said. "Drive safely."

"I will," he promised. "Did Lucy and the other cats like their new place?"

I explained how well things had gone that morning. Then I told Marcus how I had discovered that Charles had an alibi. I realized from his response that he already knew.

We said good-bye and I set my phone on the counter. I finished the dishes and tidied the kitchen. Then I got out the envelope that Eugenie had given me on Saturday.

I spread the papers across the table, deciding that I would sort things into three piles: one for Peggy, one for Eugenie and one for anything I was unsure about.

Everything else could be recycled. I was just getting started when my phone rang again. It was Roma. I had called her during the afternoon to check on the cats—who seemed to be adjusting well. She had said she'd call me after supper.

"Smokey went back to the carriage house maybe an hour ago," she said. "Which made me a little anxious, but Eddie saw him return to the cat house about five minutes ago. I think that's a good sign."

"Number one, you have to come up with a better name than 'cat house' for their new home. And number two, has Eddie been out in the yard watching the cats all day?" I asked.

"No," she said, somewhat indignantly. There was a brief hesitation. "He's been watching from the porch. With binoculars."

I couldn't help laughing. "Roma, that man loves you to the moon and back."

I pictured the goofy smile she got on her face whenever the conversation turned to Eddie. "I know," she said.

I told Roma if she needed me in the morning to call. "I'll be up. Owen thinks if he's up, everyone should be up."

She laughed and said she would.

I said good-bye and turned back to the table. My furry early-riser had jumped onto a chair and seemed to have started sorting the papers without me.

"Owen," I said sharply.

He jumped at the sound of his name and one paw knocked a pile of pages on the floor. I groaned and I might have muttered a word under my breath that librarians generally did not use.

Owen immediately jumped down and started nudging papers toward the table.

I crouched down next to him and began to gather the rest.

"Merow?" he asked, a little tentatively it seemed to me.

"No, I'm not mad," I said. "Just next time wait for me, please." I realized if anyone had heard the conversation they would think I was talking to a person and not a cat.

Owen suddenly peered in the direction of the refrigerator. He stretched out a paw and snagged a piece of paper that had slid partway underneath.

"Thank you for your help," I said as I took it from him. It looked to be a photo of a couple of teenagers, maybe fifteen or sixteen years old.

Owen just sat there staring at me.

Okay, it seemed that I was missing something. I took a closer look at the picture. The two teenagers, a boy and a girl, were on a tire swing. She was wearing a bikini top and a tiny pair of white shorts. He was wearing denim cutoffs and a tank top. I recognized the boy. "That's Ray Nightingale," I said, tapping the page with a finger.

Owen murped his agreement and began to wash his face.

I studied the girl. "Hang on a minute. That's Kassie."

The cat's golden eyes flicked to me for a moment without missing a pass of his paw over his face.

I straightened up, still holding on to the picture.

"Ray and Kassie knew each other when they were kids?" I had recognized who they were pretty quickly. They had to have recognized each other.

"Why didn't Ray say something?"

Owen seemed as puzzled as I was.

Could he have been involved in Kassie's death? No. That didn't make sense.

I probably should have just called Marcus with the information, but I didn't. I reached for my cell and called Maggie instead. She was probably still in her studio at Riverarts.

Maggie confirmed that Ray was there or at least he had been about ten minutes earlier when she'd gone down to her Bug to get the new paintbrush she had left in the car.

I told her I needed to talk to Ray and she didn't even ask me why. She just said she would be at the back door to let me in.

I stuffed all the papers back in their envelope except for the photo. That I took with me. Owen disappeared into his basement lair. Figuratively for a change, not literally. Hercules had gone out onto the back step and was staring at the sky again. I stopped to give him a head scratch.

"Please don't start a war with the grackles," I said. "I don't want to come home and find out I'm living in *The Birds*."

As promised, Maggie was at the back door to let me into Riverarts. Ray was one of the newer members of the artists' co-op. He'd had to wait a while for studio space in the converted school, and he was there a lot.

"Come on up when you're done with Ray," Maggie said. "I'll show you next week's illustrations."

I said I would and she headed back to her studio, her long legs taking the stairs two at a time.

Ray's space was on the second floor of the building on the right-hand side of the hall at the end. I knocked on his half-open door and after a moment he called, "Come in."

The space was incredibly tidy. A huge commercial shelving unit, painted black, filled one end wall. The opposite wall held several glass display cases with Ray's collection of vintage ink bottles.

There was a big drafting table next to the window and a long workstation in the center of the room.

Ray was working by the window. He looked up, surprised to see me. "Hey, Kathleen," he said. "Are you looking for Maggie?"

"No," I said, "I'm looking for you."

"What do you need?" he asked. "No offense, but I have a tight deadline on a project and the show has put me behind."

I put the printed photo of him and Kassie on the drafting table.

"So Kassie and I knew each other when we were kids," he said with a shrug. "We went to the same school in Chicago for a while. We hung out sometimes. What's the big deal?"

"The big deal is she's dead and you didn't tell anyone you knew her."

"I hadn't been around her in I don't know how long. We didn't know each other anymore. Kassie was as surprised to see me as I was to see her."

"Did either of you tell Elias you knew each other?"

"No. Neither one of us wanted it to look as though there had been some kind of collusion between us. She didn't want to leave the show and why should I? I worked hard to get to be a contestant. Probably harder than she had to be a judge. So we agreed to act like we didn't know each other. It wasn't a big deal. So we hung out when we were teenagers. It wasn't like that gave me an advantage or anything now."

He seemed indifferent to the fact that someone he had been friends with had been murdered.

Ray glanced at the photo again. "Look. It has to have been at least fifteen years since I saw Kassie. We might as well have been strangers. I can't tell you or the police anything about her. I don't know anything."

"Do you know where this picture came from?" I asked. I reached over and took it before Ray did something to it.

"I don't have a clue," he said. "Maybe she found it somewhere and was going to show it to me and then she didn't get the chance."

I remembered when I'd first met Ray. It was after the murder of artist Jaeger Merrill. Jaeger Merrill had been a mask-maker who could take what other people saw as garbage and turn it into art. He was also a liar and a forger, in essence a *con* artist. He reproduced religious icons—top-quality fakes. He had fooled some of the best art experts in the world. And he used everyone he met. He and Ray had been friends, as much as someone like Jaeger Merrill had friends.

Ray had tried to further his career by fudging an

endorsement from another artist. Not only had he not thought about the damage it could do to the co-op's reputation, it had been clear he didn't care. All he'd seemed to think about were his own self-interests.

"My work will stand on its own merits. All I'm doing is getting someone to pay attention for a minute," he had insisted when he was caught.

There wasn't anything else to say in respect to his friendship with Kassie. I thanked him and headed for the stairs up to Maggie's studio.

One thing I was sure of, Ray had lied to me the first time we'd met and I was certain he was lying now.

12

I found Maggie standing in front of her easel frowning at the drawing that was propped on it. "Hi," I said.

She turned and gave me a distracted smile. "Hi," she said. "How did it go with Ray?"

I held out my hand and waggled it from side to side.

"Does this have something to do with Kassie?" she asked. I noticed her eyes flick back to the drawing.

I ignored the question for the moment and went to stand beside her. I studied the pen and ink drawing and the color swatches Maggie had propped beside it.

She leaned her forearm on my shoulder. "I can't get the green right for the kiwi." She made a gesture over her shoulder toward her computer. "I've been looking them up online for the last half hour but the color still feels wrong." She'd also been running her hands through her hair and her curls stuck up all over her head. Once again I thought she looked like a green-eyed lamb.

"Mags, just go down to Eric's," I said. I tipped my head gently to the side so it bumped the top of hers.

"I already had supper."

"Not for supper," I said. "You need to look at a real kiwi. Not a photograph of one." Maggie would have realized that herself if being overworked hadn't given her tunnel vision. "The grocery store is closed or you could just go buy one, but Eric will have kiwi in his kitchen. Once you see the real thing you'll be able to get the color right."

A smile spread across her face and she straightened up. "Super Librarian to the rescue!" she said.

I tossed my hair back and pressed a hand to my chest. "I live to serve, one good idea at a time."

Maggie threw her arms around my shoulders to give me a hug. "We really need to get you a cape and tights."

"I think I would look very good in a cape," I said.

She laughed. "I'll get right on that," she said. She let me go and studied my face, her green eyes narrowing. "Tell me what happened with Ray. This does have something to do with Kassie's death, doesn't it?"

I handed her the picture of teenage Kassie and Ray.

She studied the image for a moment then her eyes met mine. "That's Kassie with Ray. They're just kids but they're both recognizable."

I nodded.

Maggie turned the sheet of paper over. "How did you get this?"

I explained about Eugenie's request and how Owen had knocked the papers off my kitchen table.

"It looks like she—or someone—scanned the original photo and then printed the scan." She handed the page back to me. "What did Ray say? I'm assuming that you asked him if he knew where the image came from."

I looked at the picture again. "He said he didn't know, that maybe Kassie found it and was going to show it to him but didn't get a chance."

"So why did they act like they didn't know each other?"

"According to Ray neither one of them was willing to give up their place on the show. They knew it would look bad if anyone found out they had been friends years ago, so they decided to just keep quiet."

"You think he's telling the truth?"

I made a face. "I think what he told me was true, as far as it goes, but I think there are some things he left out."

"That sounds familiar," Maggie said. I knew she was referring to the forged letter.

"I need a favor. If it makes you uncomfortable, please just say no."

"Okay, now I'm intrigued. What is it?"

"Could you get me a copy of Ray's CV?"

I knew from Maggie and Ruby that an artist's CV—curriculum vitae—was necessary when submitting work to galleries and exhibitions. Unlike a résumé, which focused on education and experience, a CV highlighted professional accomplishments; awards, exhibitions, publications in which the artist had been featured, collections that held his or her artwork, teachers the artist had studied with.

Maggie picked up a paintbrush that had been lying on her worktable and turned it over in her fingers. "Do you actually think Ray could have had something to do with Kassie's death?"

I shrugged. "I don't know. I do think he's lying about how close they were. He was very offhand about any connection between them, almost as if he was trying to convince me it was no big deal—which makes me wonder if maybe it was. Maybe it's that picture of the two of them, or maybe it's just a gut feeling, but I think Ray and Kassie were more than just a couple of kids who knew each other and then lost touch. I want to see if they could have connected anywhere else in their lives."

"There's a copy of everyone's CV available at the store," Maggie said. "Sometimes a collector comes in with a question about an artist's background or who they've studied with. As far as I'm concerned, that makes that information more or less public." She set the paintbrush down again and moved over to her laptop. "I can print you a copy."

"Thanks," I said. I watched her connect the computer to the printer. "You don't trust Ray, do you? You haven't trusted him since you found out his connection to Jaeger Merrill."

Jaeger Merrill had been killed in the basement of the co-op's store. Maggie and I had found his body floating in several feet of water that had filled the space after some serious flooding to downtown.

Maggie hit several keys on the laptop and the printer began to do its thing. She turned around to look at me then. "Ray has worked hard to regain everyone's trust."

"But," I prompted.

She shook her head. "But sometimes I think he's making the effort just to win us all over, not to make up for his mistakes because he understands what he did was wrong. Does that make any sense?"

"Yes, it does." It was exactly how I felt. I had never gotten the sense that Ray felt much, if any, remorse for his actions. I thought what he felt bad about was being caught.

Maggie handed me Ray's CV.

"Thank you," I said. "I need to get going. I still have those papers to sort through."

"Let me shut my laptop off and I'll walk down with you," she said. "I'm going kiwi hunting."

Maggie came over to the truck with me. Her Bug was parked several spaces away. "Don't work half the night," I said, giving her a hug.

She smiled. "Back at you." We said good night and Maggie headed for her car.

I laid the photo and Ray's CV on the front seat of the truck. A large crow flew overhead, cawing at something. I remembered what Russell had said about Kassie, that she was like a crow, but instead of collecting shiny things she collected information on people. I wondered what shiny thing she'd had on Ray.

13

The *Mayville Heights Chronicle* had been around for more than a hundred years. It was one of a shrinking number of small-town newspapers that was still turning a profit. Much of the credit belonged to publisher Bridget Lowe. Under her watch the Chronicle had won a number of awards for reporting. Not only did everyone in the area read the paper, it also had a significant number of online subscribers from out of town. Including my mother, which was why it didn't really surprise me when she called about half an hour after I'd gotten home.

I had almost finished sorting through the envelope of papers. Owen had been content to sit on my lap and keep his paws off the papers, though he occasionally meowed his disagreement over which pile a page ended up in. Most of them were printouts of baking terms, recipe ideas and details about the original version of *The Great Northern Baking Showdown*. I realized that Kassie hadn't known anywhere near as much about baking as any of the contestants had.

I was happy to get up and stretch when my home phone rang. I carried Owen with me into the living room, dropped into the big wing chair and set him on my lap as I reached for the phone. He would have followed me and hopped onto my lap anyway. I was just removing a step from the process.

"Hello, sweetie. How are you?" Mom said.

As always, when I heard my mother's voice, I felt a sudden pinch of homesickness. My mother made me crazy sometimes, but she loved me with the fierceness and protectiveness of a grizzly bear. She loved all three of us that way.

"I'm fine," I said, stretching my legs out onto the footstool while Owen stretched himself out on me the way we'd done too many times before to count.

"How's Marcus?" she asked, a teasing note in her voice.

"He's perfect, as always."

"He has a new case, I see."

I was right about why she'd called. "He does," I said.

"So what have you unearthed so far?"

I knew there was no point in trying to pretend or outright lie that I wasn't involved. Mom had some kind of mother's instinct that told her when Ethan, Sara or I were lying. She also seemed to know when we were about to come down with a cold.

"Not a lot. Kassie was sleeping with someone on

the show. Don't ask me who because I'm not telling you."

"Well, from what I've seen online, that young woman liked the male gender, so that doesn't leave a lot of choices. It certainly wasn't Richard, I know that."

Owen shifted on my lap and I had to put a hand on him so he didn't roll off onto the floor. He gave me a slightly embarrassed look. "Hang on, Mom," I said. "How do you know it wasn't Richard? You said yourself, women love him."

"Well, of course they do, sweetie." I pictured her making a dismissive wave with one hand. "He's very attractive with those dark eyes and that smile, but Richard has almost always dated the tall, athletic type, with an occasional attraction to a slightly older woman."

"No, no, no. We are not going there," I said.

On the other end of the phone she was laughing. "Just because Richard was very much attracted to me doesn't mean anything happened. Your father is the only man for me."

I knew she meant that. She wouldn't have married Dad twice if she hadn't. They wouldn't have had so many dramatic fights and so many equally dramatic makeups if they weren't absolutely wild for each other.

Owen shifted again so his head was on my stomach. "What's Richard like, I mean as a person?" I asked. "I've barely spent any time with him. I know Eugenie and Russell a lot better."

"I don't think he could have killed Kassie Tremayne,

if that's what you're asking," Mom said. "He doesn't have it in him. And from a purely practical standpoint he would never do anything that might make a mess on his clothes. Have you noticed how particular he is about them?"

I *had* noticed. Eugenie had told me that after Saturday's filming, the body-hugging shirt Richard had been wearing had been sent out to be laundered and ironed so it was fresh for him to wear on Sunday. In his favor, it was the only diva-like behavior I had noticed about him.

"I did notice," I said.

"Richard can be nitpicky, but he never crosses the line into being cruel. And I'm willing to bet, if the online rumors are true, that Ms. Tremayne *was* coming down hard on some of the contestants, which means Richard would have gone to bat for them. I've seen him do something similar in the past. He's going to be a big star, you know."

"He did go out of his way to make sure the change in judges went well."

"Sweetie, Richard is a complicated man. He can be harsh one moment and incredibly kind the next. He makes fantastic food and he also has a secret passion for McDonald's apple pies."

"I'll keep that in mind," I said. "Thanks, Mom. Now tell me how Dad is."

"Incredibly handsome and incredibly annoying. Luckily, your father has gorgeous legs in a pair of tights."

Mom and Dad were working on *As You Like It*. He

was starring and she was directing. I knew from past experience the play would be fantastic, but sparks—and words—would fly until opening night.

We talked for a few more minutes. "I love you," I said. "Give Dad a hug and a kiss from me."

"I will," she said. "I love you, too, Katydid."

I finished sorting the papers, put them into labeled envelopes and put all three of those in my bag. Owen sat on my lap, got down for a drink, got back up for a snuggle and generally made the process go more slowly.

I kissed the top of his head. "I love you even when you get in the way."

He nuzzled my chin. I was pretty sure that was cat for, "Back at you."

There was a tap then on the kitchen door and I turned around to see Marcus standing there smiling at me. "Hi," he said.

I set Owen on the closest chair, got up and threw my arms around Marcus. "I didn't expect to see you tonight," I said after I had hugged him and kissed him twice.

"I couldn't wait until tomorrow to see you," he said. He kissed my ear, my cheek and then the side of my mouth. I had been going to say something but the words seem to float right out of my head.

Then I realized he was hugging me with only one arm. I pulled back and looked up into his gorgeous blue eyes and had another brief moment of amnesia. Finally I got ahold of myself. "Why do you have one hand behind your back?" I asked.

One eyebrow went up. "Do I?" he said.

I pulled on his arm. "Yes, you do. What are you hiding back there?" He wasn't really trying to resist so it wasn't difficult to get his arm out where I could see it.

He was holding a small box wrapped in bright green paper and tied with green and silver ribbons.

"Is that for me?" I asked.

"It is."

Owen gave what seemed to be a perturbed meow.

"I didn't forget you," Marcus said, pulling a small paper bag from his pocket.

I recognized from the size of the bag what the contents likely were. "No, no, no," I said, shaking my head. "Please tell me you didn't bring him a catnip chicken."

Marcus put a hand over his heart. "I swear to you that I did not buy Owen a Fred the Funky Chicken."

I continued to eye the bag with suspicion. "And no one gave you a Fred the Funky Chicken?"

"And no one gave me a Funky Chicken," he said solemnly. There was a glint in his blue eyes. He was up to something.

"Merow," Owen exclaimed. He was not very patient.

Marcus set the paper bag on the chair seat. Owen eyed it with as much suspicion as I had. Then he stuck a paw inside and pulled out something small and green that smelled unmistakably like catnip. "Mrr," he said happily. He picked up the small green critter and disappeared toward the living room. Disappeared as in vanished. All I could see was the catnip toy bobbing along, seemingly floating in midair.

"I don't think I'm ever going to get used to seeing him do that," Marcus said.

I slugged him on the arm. "You said you didn't bring him a catnip chicken."

"First of all, oww! And second, that's not a catnip chicken. Didn't you notice that it was green?"

"What is it, then?" I asked.

He grinned. "It's a catnip frog. To be specific, it's Ferdinand the Funky Frog, cousin to Fred."

I leaned against him laughing. "You're making that up."

He folded his arms around me. "I swear I'm not. That's how they're being marketed. How could I not buy it for Owen?"

"Wait a second," I said. "How can Fred have a cousin that's a frog? Chickens and frogs are very different species."

"What? You've never heard of adoption?"

That started me laughing all over again. The idea of Fred the Funky Chicken having an adopted frog cousin was, to use one of Eugenie's favorite words, marvelous.

I was still holding the gift-wrapped box in one hand.

"Are you going to open your present?" Marcus asked.

"It's not a catnip frog, is it?" I said.

He shook his head. "It's not a catnip frog—or a catnip chicken."

I took Owen's seat, undid the pretty ribbons and carefully took off the wrapping paper before opening the box. It held a white ceramic mug with the words, *Cats, Books & Coffee, Yes Please!* in black script.

"It's perfect!" I exclaimed. I reached up, grabbed the neck of his shirt and pulled him down for a kiss. "Thank you."

"I got something for Hercules, too." He held up one hand. "Not treats because I know how Roma feels." He pulled another bag out of his pocket. "It's a mechanical mouse. You shake it and when you set it down it just runs randomly across the floor. I have to say it was a big hit at dinner tonight."

"Hercules will love that," I said. "He used to have a little purple mouse just like that. It came to an unfortunate end in Owen's water dish."

Marcus dropped into the chair across from me. "So did you miss me?" he asked with a teasing smile.

I set my mug on the table. "I missed you a lot. All I did was work while you were gone."

He groaned. "I have lots of that waiting for me tomorrow morning. I don't suppose you happened to hear anything that will prove Elias is guilty or that someone else is? All I have at the moment is people giving me the runaround or, in the case of Mr. Kent, avoiding my questions altogether."

"Sorry," I said. "Aside from learning that Charles has an alibi—which you already knew—the only other thing I discovered is that Ray and Kassie knew each other when they were kids." His expression didn't change. "And you knew that, too."

He nodded. "What I don't know is where the lorazepam Kassie had in her system came from."

"You're positive she didn't have a prescription and she didn't have any pills with her things or in her apartment?"

"I'm positive. And before you ask, Elias doesn't have a prescription for that or any other similar drug. I might as well tell you. I figure either he or Ruby will."

He looked tired all of a sudden. "I'm guessing no one else in the cast or crew does, either."

"That wouldn't be a bad guess," Marcus said. He stood up, grabbed my hands and pulled me to my feet. "I'm sorry. I need to get going. I have to see how Micah is and I need to check in at the station for a minute." Eddie had kept an eye on Marcus's cat. She'd probably come away from the weekend more than a little spoiled.

Marcus glanced around the kitchen. "Any chance I left a memory stick behind the last time I was here?"

I shook my head. "I haven't seen one."

He exhaled loudly. "That means I must have lost it at the rink."

"What was on it?" I asked.

"The tentative summer workout schedule for the girls' hockey team. At least Brady has a copy. I can get it from him."

"I'm sorry I couldn't help." I stood on tiptoe and kissed him.

"That helps," he said with a smile. He left with three more kisses and a promise we'd have lunch or supper or something in the next couple of days.

Owen wandered in from the living room. He didn't have his Funky Frog, but he did have the blissful expression that told me he'd been chewing it. He made his way a little unsteadily to his water dish and noisily had a drink.

My phone rang and Owen started. A little water splashed on his paw. He made a cranky face.

It was Keith King calling. He was one of the newest additions to the library board and he ran a storage business up on the highway. "Hey, Kathleen," he said. "I'm sorry to bother you at home."

"That's not a problem," I said. "What can I do for you?" Owen had started to gingerly lick the water off his paw.

"I'm cleaning out a unit for nonpayment and I came across a box of what are clearly library books. Some are from our library but some of them aren't. What do I do with them?"

One of my pet peeves—no surprise—was people not returning their books. I would happily waive the fine just to get a book back on our shelves. To me, keeping a book was almost as bad as defacing one, and no, not all of the culprits were children using a piece of gum as a bookmark.

"Are you going to be there for a while?" I asked.

"Based on the contents of this storage space at least a couple of hours."

"I'll come get them. I can track down where the other books belong."

"That would be great," Keith said.

"I'll see you soon," I said.

I looked over at Owen, who looked back at me, although his golden eyes seemed a little unfocused. "I have to drive out to Keith's to get a box of books. Why don't we skip the whole you-sneak-into-the-truck-and-I-catch-you thing and you just come along for the ride?"

He seemed to consider my offer for a moment and then he headed for the door walking more or less in a straight line. I stepped into my shoes, grabbed my purse and my keys and followed.

There was no sign of Hercules in the porch or the backyard. "Do you know where your brother is?" I asked Owen. I didn't get an answer. Then I remembered that Everett should be home from his latest business trip and I had a pretty good idea where Hercules was.

There was more traffic than I had expected on the way out to Keith's business. The box of books that was waiting for me when I got there was a lot bigger than I expected as well. "We should be able to figure out where the other libraries are and get their books back to them," I said to Keith.

"Thanks," he said. "I would hate to see them end up at the recycling center or worse."

I smiled. "Not on my watch." I lifted a flap and peeked inside the carton. There had to be at least a dozen hardcover books inside.

"I was talking to Lita a couple of days ago and she mentioned the library is going to need some new computers," Keith said as he carried the box out to my truck.

I nodded. "She came in when I was trying to fix one of the monitors."

"You know how to repair a computer? I'm impressed."

"Only if you consider whacking the side with my hand to be repairing."

Keith laughed. "I think we took the same repair class." His expression became serious again. "Look, Kathleen, I know there are some manufacturers that provide public access computers at cost to places like libraries and schools. I'll see what I can find out before the next library board meeting."

"That could help a lot," I said. "Thank you."

He put the box in the truck, setting it on the floor of the passenger side, and we said good night. Owen leaned down and tried to poke his head inside the cardboard carton, sneezing twice in succession.

"Get out of there," I said, lifting him away from the box. "That box has been in a storage unit for who knows how long. It's full of dust and probably a spider or two."

Owen shook his head and moved a little closer to me.

I fastened my seatbelt and started the truck. Traffic was backed up and stopped in front of the business's driveway. I craned my neck to look down the street. I caught sight of a huge RV, as big as a bus, waiting to make a left turn. Owen meowed impatiently.

I reached over and put my hand on his head. "Relax," I said. "It's just a little backed-up traffic. Things will get moving again in a minute."

That didn't seem to satisfy him. He stood on his hind feet and put his paws on the dashboard, eyeing the vehicles that were blocking the street in front of us.

"Glaring at the other drivers isn't going to make things move any faster," I said.

Owen ignored me. He seemed fixated on a small red car that was three vehicles past the entrance to Keith's storage business. He looked at me and then looked back at the road again. "Merow," he said. When I didn't immediately lean forward to see what had caught his attention he meowed again, louder and more insistently.

I hooked my thumb around my seatbelt and pulled it a little looser so I could shift sideways just a bit and get a better view of the red car. There was only one person inside, a man. All I could see was part of the back of his head, but something about him was familiar. As I continued to stare, the driver turned and glanced at something on the seat beside him.

It was Richard Kent. No, it couldn't be, I told myself. It was someone who looked like Richard. I just thought I was seeing him because I had just been talking about the man. Then I noticed the driver's right arm, propped on top of the steering wheel. He was wearing a black watch. A distinctive black watch. I was willing to bet it had a black rubber strap and a sapphire crystal.

"That *is* Richard," I said to Owen.

He gave me a look that could best be described as, "Well, duh!" and then he sat down again and began to wash his face.

I leaned back against the seat. The traffic was starting to move. "What's he doing up here?" I asked. The cat didn't seem to know.

I had my turn signal on to make a left turn, down the hill toward home. I looked at the red car moving away down the street. "This is crazy," I said, more to myself than to Owen.

The final car in the line passed by in front of me. There were no vehicles coming in the opposite direction. I started to pull out and at the last second went right instead of left. We were far enough back that I didn't think Richard would notice us, but even if he did, I figured the last thing he would be expecting was for someone to be following him.

Owen finished washing his face and moved along the seat so he could look out of the passenger window. Even when the traffic thinned out a little it wasn't hard to stay back and still keep the red car in sight.

It wasn't until Richard flipped on his left turn signal that I realized where he was going. I kept two cars between us and crossed my fingers that he wouldn't use the drive-thru.

Luck was with me. He didn't. Richard pulled into a parking spot, and I found one that was out of his direct line of sight but still gave me a pretty good view of the inside of the McDonald's we were at. I watched Richard go inside. I watched him order. I watched him take a seat and devour not one but two hot apple pies. He wasn't famous enough yet that anyone recognized him.

What had my mother said? *"He makes fantastic food*

and he also has a secret passion for McDonald's apple pies."
I used my phone to take a couple of photos.

Owen moved across the seat and leaned against me. I looked down at him. "There's no point in doing your cute face. We're not getting anything."

He made an annoyed sound and his tail flicked against the seat. Then he disappeared. It was his version of the silent treatment.

I backed out of the parking spot, pulled onto the street and started for home. There was nothing else I needed to see. I hadn't taken Mom seriously when she'd mentioned Richard's penchant for fast food. I could see how from his perspective it wouldn't look good for a celebrity baker to have a secret love for that kind of food even though millions of people did. It probably wouldn't be the kind of thing that he would want to get around.

Marcus had said that Richard was avoiding his questions. "Maybe that's because he was here," I said.

Owen still wasn't talking or showing himself, so I didn't get a response. "Maybe that's why he keeps avoiding Marcus's questions." Still no furry response.

It wasn't the strangest idea I had ever come up with.

As soon as I pulled into the driveway I got my phone out and called Marcus. "You said Richard has been avoiding your questions."

"And I shouldn't have," he said.

Owen winked into sight. He walked across the seat and climbed onto my lap. Apparently all was forgiven, plus he probably wanted to be carried to the back door.

"This is going to sound, well, crazy, but I think I might know where he was the night that Kassie was killed."

"I'm listening," Marcus said.

I explained what Mom had told me on the phone and how I hadn't taken it seriously. I told him how Owen had spotted Richard's car and how we'd followed him. "There he was, sitting in the dining area wearing sunglasses and his five-thousand-dollar watch eating two hot apple pies. I have a couple of photos if you want them."

"Send them to me. I think I'll have another conversation with Mr. Kent. Maybe even tonight."

"That's it?" I said. I knew my theory was a little far-fetched.

He laughed. "Yeah, that's it. The whole case is just weird enough for this to be true." He told me he'd call me in the morning and let me know what he found out.

If I was right, we had just eliminated a suspect.

14

Marcus called while I was eating breakfast the next morning. My guess had been a good one. Richard had an alibi. He had been indulging in his love for fast-food pie at the time of the murder. Marcus had the time-stamped security video from the restaurant to confirm it.

"And I found my pen," he said.

"Where was it?" I asked as I added just a tiny bit more brown sugar to my oatmeal.

"At the back of one of my desk drawers. But I still can't find that missing thumb drive and I think Brady swiped the lighter I keep in the car." Marcus was tidy in every aspect of his life except for his desk at the police station. I had a feeling the missing lighter and the missing thumb drive were either on the desk or in one of the drawers.

Mary Lowe was waiting for me at the bottom of the library steps. She was carrying a quilted bag that I fervently hoped held a container of her cinnamon rolls. She wore a bright yellow sweater with red tulips on the pockets and a giant bouquet of tulips on the back. Mary had a cardigan for every season and for every holiday. She had one for National Chocolate Chip Cookie Day. Turns out it's a real thing. Happens every August. And who was I to quibble about a day that celebrated one of my favorite cookies?

"There are fifteen bales of hay in the gazebo," she said as I came up the walkway.

"Please tell me that's the title of Abigail's new book," I said.

Mary shook her head. "No such luck, kiddo."

I blew out a breath and shook my head. "First the grader tire, now this. Do you think it's the same people who are vandalizing the book drop?"

"I don't," she said. "The stuff with the book drop smacks of a group of kids egging each other on. Gum, slime, popcorn, it's all been childish stuff. The gazebo on the other hand, that's taken planning. You'll see when you go take a look. Those hay bales are stacked precisely on top of each other: five, four, three, two, one."

I let Mary into the building and then walked around to the back to see the gazebo for myself. Just as she'd described, the bales of hay were stacked neatly with five on the bottom all the way to one on the top. She was right. This had taken planning. And it was going to take planning to catch the culprit. I headed back inside to call Harry.

Harry came and collected the hay and we talked about what to do next. He suggested a security camera for the back of the building. "We are probably going to have to go that route," I said. "But I hate to spend money on cameras that could be spent on books."

"Let me check prices," Harry said. "Maybe a little more information will help you make a decision."

"Where would someone get all those hay bales this time of year?" I asked.

"Whoever it was probably swiped the hay from different places a bale at a time. It's what I'd do." He gave a slight shrug. "Not that I'm saying I've ever done something like that."

The rest of the day passed uneventfully. Marcus brought wonton soup and egg rolls for supper. He was determined to master chopsticks and refused to use a fork. Owen and Hercules happily sat on either side of him and dealt with the fallout.

After Marcus left for a hockey training session I washed the kitchen floor and swept the porch while it dried. I was at the table going over the latest notes for Eugenie, when there was a knock at my door. I was surprised to discover Russell, of all people, standing on my back step.

"Hey, Kathleen," he said. "I hope it's okay that I stopped by without calling. I wanted to see your cats." He held out a foil pan. "I brought food to make up for my gaucheness."

"It's okay," I said. "C'mon in. I was just working on some stuff for Eugenie."

Owen and Hercules, who had disappeared to who knew where when Marcus left, were now sitting side by side in front of the refrigerator.

Russell smiled at them. "Hercules is the black-and-white cat and Owen is the tabby, right?"

I nodded.

"And they don't like to be touched."

"Only by me," I said.

"I don't like to be rubbed the wrong way either, guys," Russell stage-whispered.

He took a seat at the table and the boys moved to sit beside his chair. It seemed they recognized a kindred soul.

I took the top off the foil pan.

"Ham and cheese rolls," Russell said. Two furry heads swiveled in unison toward me. "Don't worry, I didn't make them. Caroline did."

"Will you have one with me?" I asked.

Russell smiled. "That's kind of why I brought four."

"Coffee or tea?"

"Tea, if it's not too much trouble," he said. "I've been spending a lot of time with Eugenie."

I opened the cupboard door. "Well, you can tell her I have a teapot *and* a tea cozy."

He grasped the lapels of his gray sweater and sat upright in the chair. "This is my suitably impressed face."

I made the tea and poured us each a cup. Caroline's ham and cheese rolls were delicious. We each had one and I pretended not to see Russell sneak a bite to the boys.

Once there was nothing left but crumbs on my plate I pulled both feet up so I was sitting cross-legged and smiled at Russell. "I know a bribe when I see it—

and eat it. You didn't just come by to meet Hercules and Owen. What's going on?"

"I lied to the police."

I sighed. Apparently the first time hadn't been enough. "What about?"

He studied the top of the table for a moment. "I let Eugenie use me as an alibi."

"So the two of you weren't together all evening when Kassie was killed?"

He shook his head. His spiky hair looked like little porcupine quills.

"Russell, you're not just Eugenie's alibi. She's yours."

He traced along the metal edge of the table with his index finger. "I have a real one." He looked up at me. "The police have been back asking more questions. I suck at lying."

"Start at the beginning," I said. "And by the way, being a terrible liar isn't a bad thing. So why did you cover for Eugenie in the first place?"

He looked at me like the answer was obvious. "Because it was Eugenie, Kathleen. She's my friend." He took a breath and let it out. "I overheard her and Kassie fighting, the day before Kassie . . . died. I've never seen Eugenie so angry. She doesn't get angry. I was afraid . . ." He didn't finish the sentence.

I raked a hand back through my hair. I didn't believe Eugenie had killed Kassie. "What did the two of them argue about?"

"Eugenie didn't like how Kassie had been bullying Kate and Caroline. It wasn't just the little cracks on camera. She took digs at both of them every time she was around them." He hesitated. "Eugenie threatened to have Kassie replaced."

"But we both know she couldn't do that."

Russell shrugged. At his feet Owen and Hercules seemed to be taking in everything he said. "I'm not so sure, Kathleen," he said. "I heard her say if it came down to her or Kassie that Elias would pick her. I don't know what she meant by that."

"How did Kassie react?"

"She didn't act like she felt threatened at all. She said, 'You're not getting rid of me that easily.' Then Eugenie came back and said, 'Child, if you knew more about me, you wouldn't be nearly so smug.'" He leaned forward with his elbows on his knees. "I have to talk to Eugenie about all of this first. Will you come with me?"

I nodded. "I will, but there's something I need to know first. What's your real alibi?"

A tiny smile tugged at his lips. "I was doing hot yoga with Stacey."

I dropped my feet to the floor and stood up. "Did you know Maggie teaches yoga classes? I'm sure she'd love to let the two of you try one."

Russell started to laugh. "*Hot* yoga, Kathleen."

"I know what that is," I said. "The temperature and humidity of the room are raised so everyone sweats a lot."

He was still grinning. "In this case it wasn't the room that was hot," he said. He licked the end of his index finger, touched it briefly to his shoulder and made a sizzling sound.

I got what he meant then. I remembered the tiny paper heart I'd noticed Stacey wearing on a chain around her neck. I should have made the connection the moment I had seen it.

"So if you were Eugenie's alibi, who was Stacey's?" I asked. This was all so convoluted. I thought about what my mother always said about telling the truth: *"Tell the truth. It's easier to remember."*

Russell smiled down at the cats. "The thing is, Stacey's the kind of person who's always kind of in the background helping out—probably because she's a kindergarten teacher and she does that all day. Anyway, people tend not to pay a lot of attention to where she is or isn't. But if you ask they'll say, 'Sure, Stacey was there.' She got to Eric's ahead of Eugenie and me and when the two of us left no one really paid attention. A couple of people said she was there all night and so we just left it at that."

Marcus had said that eyewitness testimony wasn't always infallible. I could see why he felt that way.

"I know it seems like Stacey has it all together, but lying like this just makes her anxiety worse. I don't want to hang Eugenie out to dry, but I think I have to tell the truth."

We needed to talk to Eugenie now and clear things up. "Do you know where Eugenie is?" I asked.

Russell frowned. "As far as I know a bunch of them were going out to Fern's to try the pie. They might still be there. I can text Norman and find out."

"I think that would be a good idea."

I leaned against the counter while Russell texted

the PA and waited for his reply. "They're still there," he said, looking up from the phone.

"Let's go," I said. I slid my feet into shoes, pulled on a sweater and grabbed my wallet and keys. "I'll follow you," I said to Russell.

He leaned forward and smiled at Owen and Hercules. "It's been a pleasure to meet you, fur dudes," he said.

Hercules bobbed his head and Owen meowed. They seemed to feel the same way.

Peggy was behind the counter when we got to Fern's. She smiled when we walked in. "Sit anywhere, Kathleen," she said.

We took a booth beside the table of people from the show. Caroline smiled and gave a little wave, which I returned. Charles was deep in conversation with one of the camera operators.

Peggy came over to us.

"Just coffee for me," I said, "And it probably should be decaf."

"What kind of pie has everyone been having?" Russell asked, peering over at the table next to us.

"Banana cream and apple," Peggy said.

Russell rubbed his hands together. "Umm, I think I'll try the banana cream. And I'll have tea." He looked at me. "Are you sure you don't want any pie?"

I shook my head. "No thanks." I wondered what he did for a workout given that he seemed to have more of a sweet tooth than I did.

As if he could read my mind, he raised an eyebrow and said, "Hot yoga burns a lot of calories."

I was wondering how to get Eugenie to join us, when she solved the problem by picking up her tea and coming over to the booth. She slid in next to Russell. "This is a delightful surprise," she said. She looked at him. "I thought you had something to do."

"I did," he said. "And now it's done."

"Marvelous," Eugenie said. She smiled across the table at me. "And it's good to see you, too, Kathleen."

"Actually, we need to talk to you about something," I said.

Eugenie looked a little puzzled. "Of course. What is it?"

Peggy came back then with Russell's pie and our coffee and tea. "Let me know if you need more hot water," she said to Eugenie.

Russell took a bite of pie and made a little groan of happiness. I had had the banana cream pie and it was that good.

I looked at Eugenie. "Where were you the night Kassie was killed?"

Her eyes shifted uncertainly from side to side. "I already told you that. Russell and I were at Eric Cullen's lovely café." She looked sideways at Russell and smiled. He suddenly looked like he was eating sawdust instead of pie. "What's going on?" she asked.

"Were you with Russell the entire time?" I said.

She continued to keep her gaze on Russell. "What did you tell Kathleen?" she said.

I repeated the question. "Were you with Russell the entire time?"

Finally, she shifted her attention to me. "The fact

that you're asking me that question tells me that you know that I wasn't."

Russell put his fork down. He put a hand on Eugenie's arm. "I'm sorry," he said. "I overheard you and Kassie arguing and I didn't want the police to think you could have killed her and when you didn't have an alibi I said we were together all night but I'm just not very good at lying." The words all came out in a rush.

Eugenie looked . . . surprised. "My dear boy, you told the police we were together to give *me* an alibi?"

He nodded.

"I thought you did it to give *yourself* one."

"Okay, hang on a minute," I said. I pointed at Russell. "You gave Eugenie an alibi because you'd heard her fighting with Kassie."

He nodded. "I'm sorry," he said. "I know you didn't kill her."

"Heavens no," she said. "I didn't have to resort to murder to get rid of her."

"We're coming back to that," I said. I gestured at Eugenie. "You thought Russell had said he was with you to give himself an alibi."

"Yes. I have one."

"You have one?" Russell exclaimed.

I rubbed the space between my eyes. I had a headache.

Eugenie took a sip of her tea. "It's not one I'd like to share with many people but I do have it." She reached over and patted Russell's shoulder. "Honestly, all you had to do was ask me. I would have told *you*."

"Tell us now," I said. "Start with explaining what you meant when you said you didn't have to resort to murder to get rid of Kassie."

"This isn't something I want spread around," she said.

"I'm not planning on doing that," I said.

She exhaled slowly. "You know that I've lived in Canada for quite a while but I grew up in London."

Both Russell and I nodded. I wasn't sure where Eugenie was going.

"One of the reasons I left London—left England altogether—was so that I could live my life on my terms." Her long fingers played with her cup.

Russell frowned at me. He seemed as confused as I was.

"Eugenie, I'm not really sure where you're going with this," I said.

"Have you heard of Hamilton House?" she asked.

"If you mean the plumbing supply company, then yes. I have a big, deep Hamilton House bathtub in my bathroom." It seemed as though I actually heard a tiny *click* as my brain made the connection. "You're one of those Hamiltons."

"Yes," she said.

I glanced at Russell, who hadn't made the connection. "Thomas Hamilton invented the little flapper piece that lifted up and let water into a toilet when you flushed it." All the odd and obscure things I'd been asked to research over the years meant I was really good at trivia night.

"Okay," he said slowly, clearly still lost.

I shifted my gaze to Eugenie. "Your great-grandfather?"

She nodded.

I turned back to Russell again. "That invention was the beginning of one of the largest plumbing supply companies in the world."

Eugenie cleared her throat. "The biggest, actually."

"So what you're saying is you're rich," Russell said. "Are we talking Tony Stark rich?" He was referring to the billionaire character in the Iron Man movies.

"Nothing like that," she said. "But I do have more than enough money to relieve Elias of any financial obligation he might have to Sean Sullivan, Kassie's father. So as you can see, I had no reason to hurt anyone."

"And what about your alibi?" I said.

She looked around the restaurant and then leaned forward. "Again, Kathleen, this is something I'd prefer to keep as private as I can."

"I understand that," I said. "And I don't plan on sharing what you tell me with anyone, although I think you need to share it with the police."

"I should have done that from the beginning," she said. She hesitated for a moment. "I was in a smoking club in Red Wing."

Russell's eyes grew wide. "You smoke?" he exclaimed.

Eugenie looked around to see if anyone had heard him but no one was paying attention to us. "Cigars," she said. "No cigarettes and none of that silly vaping. It's just that it doesn't go with my image."

Smoking didn't go with Eugenie's image and fast-food pies didn't go with Richard's. At least the "hot" yoga made sense given what I knew about Russell. I had no doubt everyone's new alibis would check out.

I picked up my coffee and took a long drink. I knew Ruby would be devastated, but it was looking more and more like Elias had killed Kassie.

15

Marcus showed up the next morning with a mint chocolate chip cupcake for me from Sweet Thing. All of the alibis had checked out. Eugenie, Russell and Stacey were in the clear.

"Thank you," I said. I would have kissed him but we were standing just inside the library door.

"Did you bring enough of those to share with the class?" Mary asked from the circulation desk.

"As a matter of fact, I did," Marcus said, bringing a cardboard box with the Sweet Thing logo on it out from behind his back. He set it in front of Mary with a flourish.

She smiled approvingly. "Nice work, Detective Gordon."

He smiled back at her. "You'll notice two of them are mocha fudge, which are your favorite." He caught my hand and gave it a squeeze. "I have to go. I'll talk to you later."

Mary watched him leave. "If I were you I'd get some rope and tie—"

Still holding the little bag with my cupcake, I put my hands over my ears. "I'm not listening," I said, heading for the stairs. Even with my ears covered I could still hear her laughing.

It was a busy morning at the library. I gave a class of fourth graders and their teacher a tour and was pleased by how many of the kids were readers. Keith King dropped off some information about a program he thought the library might qualify for that would give us a thirty-percent discount on the new computers we needed.

"I'm still looking for other options," he said. "I'll keep you in the loop."

Harry stopped by before lunch with a couple of prices for security cameras. I looked at the numbers and shook my head.

"I know," he said. "That has to be out of the library's budget. How do you feel about a jerry-rigged temporary solution, just until we catch whoever keeps putting stuff in the gazebo?"

"Jerry-rigged suggests it's not going to cost a lot of money," I said. "I like the sound of that."

Harry squeezed the brim of his Twins baseball cap. "Probably just the price of a few rolls of duct tape, I'm thinking."

I smiled. "I like that a lot. What do you have in mind?"

"You remember when Mariah was doing that project for school and she put together that drone?"

I nodded.

Harry's daughter had done more than just put together a drone. She'd figured out how to attach a camera and fly the drone. She'd also recorded footage that gave a potential murder suspect an alibi. What she hadn't done was tell her father or anyone else what she was up to.

"Well, it turns out Uncle Larry was giving her a little help."

Harry's younger brother, Larry, was an electrician who liked to tinker with anything electronic. It struck me that maybe he'd be able to come up with a way to keep our computer monitors working.

"I hope you don't mind that I talked to him about what's been happening down here," Harry said. "He thinks he might be able to rig some kind of camera along the roofline at the back of the building. It won't cost you a cent. Larry has a workshop full of junk and after what happened with Mariah, he figures he kinda owes me." He grinned. "Might as well take advantage of it."

"Yes," I said. "If Larry can come up with some way we can catch the culprit, why not?"

"I'll give him a call," Harry said.

It was about quarter after twelve when Levi Ericson came in. Mary had taken the early lunch break. I was putting books on our holds shelves.

"Could I talk to you about something?" he asked. His expression was serious and I hoped he wasn't going to tell me he was quitting.

"Of course," I said. "We can go up to my office. I just need to get Abigail."

"Here is fine," he said. He cleared his throat. "Did you know World Mental Health Day is in October?"

I shook my head. "No, I didn't."

"I was wondering, could we do something here at the library? Maybe on the day or during the week? Some kind of display, or maybe a talk or . . . something?"

"Yes," I said. "We could do all of it."

A smile lit up his face. "Really?"

"Really." I was happy not to be losing Levi and his suggestion was a good one.

"I, um, I kind of have some ideas for what we could do," he said, swiping his hair back out of his eyes with his long fingers. "I have this friend who has anxiety. She looks like she has her life together but it's not how she feels inside. I think a lot of people feel that way and they're scared to let anyone know."

"Put your ideas on paper," I said. "You don't have to do anything fancy. I'm not asking you to write an essay. Just organize your thoughts. Then you and I will sit down and come up with a plan."

"I can do that this weekend," he said. He couldn't seem to stop smiling.

I smiled back at him. "I can't wait to see what you come up with."

He started for the door and then turned around. "Thank you, Kathleen. Really, thank you."

"You're welcome," I said.

Levi all but bounced out of the door. I loved his enthusiasm and how much he obviously cared about his friend. *"She looks like she has her life together but it's not how she feels inside.*" I realized that the way he had described his friend sounded a lot like the way Russell had talked about Stacey just last night: "*I know it seems like Stacey has it all together, but lying like this just makes her anxiety worse.*"

Stacey had anxiety? How was she managing it? I knew that not everyone with anxiety used medication. I also knew people were sometimes desperate enough for help that they bought drugs illegally. Marcus had said that no one involved with the show had a prescription for the drug found in Kassie's system. Was I jumping to conclusions thinking Stacey could be the source of the lorazepam?

At one o'clock I took my lunch break and headed to the community center to give Eugenie my research into making butter. It would have been easier to e-mail everything, but she liked to check the information while I was with her and it really wasn't that big of a hassle.

I stopped to say hi to Maggie and let her know I might be late for tai chi. Roma wanted to check Hercules's leg one more time. She was squeezing us in at the end of the day and I was going to pick him up as soon as I left the community center. I was lucky Mayville Heights was the kind of place where my cat could spend the afternoon at the library and no one would think that was strange.

Stacey was just crossing the parking lot when I came out the back door. She waved and changed course to intercept me. "I'm glad I saw you," she said.

"I wanted to thank you for encouraging Russell to talk to the police."

"You're welcome," I said. "I was just a little moral support. Russell already knew what he needed to do."

Stacey fingered the strap of her brown leather cross-body bag. "I don't like lying, especially to the police. I was getting so anxious I started having panic attacks."

"I'm claustrophobic," I said. "I know a little about how panic feels."

"Usually I can manage my anxiety with meditation and exercise but, being on the show, it's been a lot harder." I noticed that her nails were very short and the cuticles on both hands looked ragged.

I smiled. "I think you may be doing better than you realize. I didn't notice anything."

Stacey ducked her head for a moment. Her fingers were still fidgeting with the strap of her bag. "That's because I'm pretty good at fooling people, and, to be honest, I've been taking something—not all the time. Just when I need it."

"Is there anything I can do?" I asked. "I know we're not friends but I sometimes think librarians are like bartenders—you'd be surprised the things people tell us."

That made her smile. "I appreciate the offer but now that I'm not on the show most of the pressure is gone. I'm glad I did it, but I don't think I'd do something like that again." She shook her head. "I got so anxious I swiped a few pills from a friend who has a prescription for antianxiety medication. Dumb, right?"

"Not dumb," I said, choosing my words with care, "but maybe not the best way to handle things."

"Russell said the same thing, and I am going to see my doctor when I get home." Her gaze slipped away from my face for a moment. "Last night I gave him the ones I had left and he got rid of them. I wasn't really keeping track of how many I took and I know that isn't good."

"I'm glad you're not self-medicating anymore and I'm glad you have Russell." I touched her arm for a moment. "Russell has my number. Please use it if you want to talk or just get a cup of coffee. Or tea."

Stacey nodded. "I will."

We said good-bye. She headed for the door and I made my way across the lot.

I got in the truck and dropped my bag on the seat. I propped my elbow on the armrest and leaned my head on my hand. There was a good chance Stacey was the source of the medication in Kassie's system. By her own admission she hadn't kept track of those pills she'd taken from her friend. It would have been easy for someone to borrow one or two. But if I told Marcus what I had just figured out, Stacey would know I'd betrayed her confidence. I couldn't do that. There had to be some other way for him to get the information. I just needed to figure it out.

I drove home and found Hercules upstairs, seemingly rearranging the shoes in my closet. "I'm not even going to ask," I said, bending down to scoop him up.

"Want to come and spend the afternoon at the library?"

He squirmed in my arms. His green eyes narrowed and one ear turned sideways. He was rightly suspicious. "You can sit in my chair. You can shed cat hair all over my desk."

He seemed to think about it for a moment. Then he stopped squirming. I wondered if it was the chair or the shedding that had won him over.

Hercules climbed in the cat carrier bag without complaint. I felt a little guilty because I knew he would feel I'd tricked him when we ended up at Roma's clinic after work. I also knew I was attributing a lot of human emotions to a small black-and-white cat.

When we got to my office I set the carrier bag on my desk and unzipped the top. Hercules climbed out, stretched and then jumped down onto my chair, which sent it slowly spinning in a circle.

"You're going to make yourself dizzy," I warned.

He gave me a slightly loopy look as the chair swung past me. Hercules may not have cared for catnip the way his brother did, but he did like going around in circles in my chair.

The next time an arm of the chair passed me I grabbed it. I leaned my face close to his and he licked my chin. "I love you, too," I said. "Please stay in here. The last thing I need is to have to explain what you're doing here. I don't think anyone is going to believe you came to borrow a book."

He gave an indignant murp as though the idea that he couldn't read was insulting. For all I knew maybe

he could. Both Hercules and Owen were far from ordinary.

I gave him one last scratch under his chin and
headed downstairs.

"Would you give Lita a call when you have a
chance, please?" Abigail asked. "She called about half
an hour ago." She reached over and plucked a clump
of black cat hair from my shirt.

"Hercules is in my office," I blurted.

"Oh, I know," she said. "He waved a paw at me as
you skulked past the desk."

"I did not skulk." I wasn't going to argue about the
waving.

"Please," Abigail said with an eye roll. "If Hercules
was a Great Dane instead of a cat, it would have been
an episode of *Scooby-Doo*." She glanced in the direction of the stairs. "Does he have to go see R-O-M-A?"

I laughed. "I don't think he can hear you all the way
in my office. And yes, he does. She just wants to check
his leg one more time."

"You know, Kathleen, Hercules is a pretty smart cat.
Pretty soon he's going to figure out that every time he
gets to come to the library he ends up you-know-where."

"That's what I'm afraid of," I said.

Hercules stayed in my office—or at least, if he went
roaming around, he didn't get caught. When I went
up for my break he was sitting in the middle of my
desk. It looked like he was reading something.

"What are you doing?" I asked.

"Mrrr," he said, putting a paw on the page in front
of him. It was Ray Nightingale's CV.

I hadn't had much time to look for more information on the connection between Ray and Kassie.

"I need that," I said to Hercules. I tried to pull the sheet of paper away from him but he kept his paw in place and there was a stubborn jut to his chin.

"Mrrr," he said again.

I looked down at the page. The cat's paw was resting just below the listing of the artists Ray had studied under. *Tim Dougall*.

"Why does that name seem familiar?"

Hercules didn't seem to know.

I reached for my computer. I wasn't sure why that name mattered, but it did. A quick search told me that Timothy Dougall was an artist who had done the illustrations for more than two dozen children's books.

"Maybe Abigail mentioned his name to me," I said.

Hercules wasn't interested anymore. Now he was sitting in the middle of the paper, carefully washing his tail.

I went back downstairs. Abigail was shelving books. "Are you familiar with an illustrator named Tim Dougall?" I asked.

She smiled. "Of course. Do you remember when you worked a shift for me so I could go see that documentary in Minneapolis? That's who it was about. Tim Dougall."

"That's why the name seemed familiar," I said. I remembered how much Abigail had looked forward to seeing that documentary.

"Where on earth did you see Tim's name?" she asked. "He's been dead for close to seventeen years now."

"Seventeen years? Are you sure?"

Abigail nodded. "Give or take a year, yes. You can google it if you need the exact date."

"There's something I need to do," I said. "Can you cover for me for about ten minutes?"

"Sure," she said. "Take your time."

I went back up to my office.

Hercules was lying on his back now, jabbing the air with one paw as though he was boxing but not putting much effort into it.

I picked up Ray's CV. If he had taken a class with Tim Dougall, the last possible time he could have done it would have been when he was about sixteen—pretty much the age he looked in that photo of him with Kassie.

"As Alice would say, 'Curiouser and curiouser.'"

Hercules looked a little confused. If he did read, it seemed he hadn't read *Alice's Adventures in Wonderland*.

I checked the CV again and found the name of the art program where Ray claimed to have studied with Dougall. It only took me a minute to get the exact year of the illustrator's death and then I did the math in my head. Ray would have been sixteen. Had he spent a summer studying with the artist? It wasn't impossible. Maybe there was a way to find out.

I looked up the phone number of the art school online, took a deep breath and called. I was rerouted three times before I reached the right department. I explained to the woman on the other end of the phone that I was a researcher for *The Great Northern Baking Showdown* and that I was trying to clarify the background of one of our contestants.

"His name is Ray Nightingale and he was supposed to have taken a summer art course there seventeen years ago. I'm trying to verify the date."

"I'm sorry," she said in a slightly bored monotone. "I can't give out any personal information about any of our students."

Hercules had given up on his quasi-workout and was nosing around the telephone receiver. I nudged him back, which just made him all the more determined to get in the way.

"But I'm not certain Mr. Nightingale *was* a student," I said. "That's what I'm trying to confirm."

"And as I told you, I can't give out any personal information about students."

This wasn't going to work. Hercules butted the receiver again and I moved him back again. He gave a loud meow in protest.

"Was that a cat?" the woman asked.

I glared at Hercules, who glared back at me.

"Yes, that was Hercules. I apologize. He thinks he's a person when it comes to phones. Anyway, thank you for talking to me."

"Not Hercules from the calendar?"

"Umm . . . yes."

"The little tuxedo cat?"

"That's right." The conversation had taken a very strange turn.

"I have that calendar right here in my office," she said. Her voice was suddenly a lot warmer. "My name is Dena, by the way."

"Hello, Dena," I said. "I have that calendar and, as you can hear, that cat right here in *my* office at the moment." The subject of the conversation had turned his back on me in annoyance and was washing his face.

"The calendar makes me smile every time I look at it. I think my favorite photo is the one of them on the circulation desk in the library."

"That's one of my favorites, too," I said. "The photographer, Ruby Blackthorne, is very good at getting them to pose. They are cats after all."

"Dogs come when they're called. Cats take a message and get back to you later."

I laughed. "Dena, you have cats, don't you?"

"Ellery, Agatha and Ngaio."

"And you're a mystery fan," I said. "Ellery Queen, Agatha Christie and Ngaio Marsh."

"Very good," she said. "People usually don't get the Ngaio reference."

"She's one of the Queens of Crime. More people should read her books."

"Yes, they should." I could hear the smile in her voice. "So, you wanted to know if Ray Nightingale was here in what year again?"

I repeated the date. I heard the clicking of computer keys. "Let me just check something else," she said.

I waited.

Silence and then, "Ah, there's the problem. He was here."

So I was wrong.

"But he was kicked out at the end of the first week."

So maybe I wasn't wrong.

"Is that a problem?" Dena asked.

"No," I said slowly. "I don't think it is."

"I'm glad I could be of help."

I thanked Dena for the information and told her there was talk of another calendar. Then we said good-bye.

I leaned back in my chair, closed my eyes and tried to sort out what I knew. Ray had lied—again—about his credentials. Not only did I have to share the information with Marcus, but Maggie and Ruby needed to know as well. Had Kassie known what Ray had done? Was that why she had that photo of the two of them? Was it more than just a walk down memory lane? I was going to have to talk to Ray to find out. One thing I did know was that he was the kind of person who took shortcuts.

I stretched and stood up. Hercules was still washing his face and ignoring me. I leaned over and took his furry black-and-white face in my hands. "I love you, furball," I said. Then I kissed the top of his head. "Two sardines when we get home tonight."

He nuzzled my right hand, his way of saying all was forgiven.

We were out of the library at the end of the day pretty much on time, maybe even a few minutes early. Abigail waved at Hercules and mouthed "Good luck" to me.

We headed across town. I glanced at the cat. He'd

climbed out of the carrier as soon as I'd unzipped the top. He was lying on the seat, head on his paws, a glum expression on his face. Had he figured out where we were going or was I just attributing human feeling to a cat again?

"You know, don't you?" I said. Out of the corner of my eye I saw him give me a look.

He knew.

"It won't take long. All Roma is going to do is look at your leg. No poking at you. No stitches. I promise."

"Mrrr," he grumbled.

"She'll probably have a treat for you."

I looked over at him again. He seemed to be thinking about the treat. "And after Roma is finished I'll take you home for those sardines I promised."

He shook his head, sat up and made a sound like a sigh. I figured that was as good as I could hope for.

The visit with Roma went well. I held on to Hercules while she checked his leg and he protested.

Loudly.

Once she was done she put two little fish crackers on the examining table. I let Hercules go. He used a paw to drag the treats into the middle of the table, away from Roma.

"He's fine," she said to me, pulling off her gloves. "And it went a lot better than last time."

I nodded. "I remember last time."

"Tell Maggie I'm sorry to miss class. David wants a second opinion about a hip replacement surgery on a German shepherd. I'm leaving in a few minutes. If I agree with him, he wants to do the surgery as soon as possible."

David was another vet, a friend of Roma's. He'd helped her on a couple of surgeries and she'd done the same for him.

"I'll tell her," I said. I held up crossed fingers. "Good luck."

Once Hercules was settled on the front seat I checked my watch. There just might be time to tackle Ray if he was at his studio.

I headed for Riverarts. Hercules wasn't paying any attention to where we were going so he didn't object. I pulled into the parking lot and as luck would have it both Ray's and Ruby's cars were there. I slipped into Maggie's allotted spot since I knew she was over at the tai chi studio.

"Do you want to go see Ruby?" I asked Hercules.

He immediately sat up and took a couple of passes at his face with a paw. Then he looked at me, cocking his head to one side. "You look very handsome," I said.

I pulled out my phone and called Ruby's cell. She answered on the third ring. "Hercules and I are in the parking lot," I said. "Could we come in?"

"I'm on my way down," she said.

I rummaged in my bag for a second, picked up the cat, locked the truck and reached the back door of Riverarts just as Ruby reached the bottom of the stairs. She let us in and smiled at Hercules. She was wearing a T-shirt with the sleeves rolled back and a pair of baggy overalls.

"Does Maggie have another interloper down at the store?" she asked.

I shook my head. "No. We just came from seeing Roma. And before you ask, he's fine."

"You had a doctor's appointment?" Ruby said. She made a face. "I hate doctor's appointments. You're so brave."

He preened in my arms. Ruby's words seemed to carry a lot more weight than mine did.

"I've been playing around with a couple of ideas for another calendar. I'd love to hear what you think."

She was still talking to Hercules, I realized, not me.

He murped an okay.

"Actually, could he stay with you for a few minutes?" I asked. "I was hoping I could go talk to Ray."

"Sure," Ruby said. Her hands were in her pockets and she rocked forward and back just a little in her red high tops. She looked like she wanted to say something so I waited for a moment.

"You haven't found anything to clear Elias yet, have you?" she finally asked. "I, uh, I've been trying not to bug you by calling or texting."

I shook my head. "I haven't come across anything that puts Elias in the clear. I'm sorry. I've eliminated some people but I haven't found anything that eliminates him."

She played with one of the several earrings in her right ear. "If someone accused your father of murder you'd know they were wrong, wouldn't you?"

"Yes," I said.

"And it wouldn't just be because he's your dad. It

would be because you know what kind of a person he is. You know him better than just about everyone." She tapped the left side of her chest with a closed fist. "You know what he's like in here."

I nodded. "I do."

"I know Elias that way. He's not my dad, but he's the closest thing I have to one." Her eyes were locked on to my face. "He wouldn't lie to me. If he had killed Kassie he would have told me. I'm not saying he would have told the police, but he would have told me. So I don't mean to put pressure on you—" She stopped abruptly and a tiny smile played at her mouth. "Actually, that's not true. I do want to put pressure on you. Elias didn't do this, which means somebody else did."

Hercules was getting restless and I set him down. He shook himself and moved to sit next to Ruby.

"I wish I had answers for you," I said. "I can tell you this much. I haven't given up. And I know that Marcus hasn't, either."

Her expression grew serious again. "One question. Do you think Ray could have killed Kassie?"

"No, but I do think they had more of a connection than he's admitting to. That's why I need to talk to him."

She sighed. "Okay. I guess I'm going to just have to go with that." She looked at Hercules and tipped her head at the stairs. "Let's go," she said. He didn't give so much as a backward glance to me. I had a feeling even with sardines waiting at home I was going to have a problem getting him back into the truck.

I followed the two of them up the stairs, pushing through the doors to the second floor and walking down the hall toward Ray's studio. His door was part-way open.

I tapped on the door frame and Ray looked up from his easel. "Kathleen, to what do I owe the pleasure? Again." His tone made it clear that me being there wasn't something he was happy about.

I'd had the picture of Ray and Kassie in my messenger bag and I'd fished it out before Hercules and I had gotten out of the truck. Now I pulled it out of my pocket and smoothed out the wrinkles before holding it up. "This," I said.

"You're not still beating that dead horse, are you?"

I took several steps toward him. "How old do you think that photo of the two of you is, Ray? Sixteen years? Seventeen, maybe?"

"Yeah, probably," he said. "What does that have to do with anything?"

"Seventeen years ago you were taking a class from Tim Dougall."

He shrugged. "Maybe. I'm not sure of the date."

I smiled. "I am. I checked."

He was good. He didn't break my gaze. His face didn't flush. "If you say so."

I was still holding the picture. I turned it around so I could take another look. "Why did Kassie have this photo of the two of you?"

He shifted on his stool and looked at the drawing he was working on before he looked at me again. "I already told you I don't know."

"That's a lie," I said. "I think Kassie had that picture of the two of you because it was a way to remind you that you didn't spend a summer studying with Tim Dougall. You got kicked out in the first week. Which means you've been lying on your CV."

He swore and looked up at the ceiling for a moment as though he'd find answers up there. His eyes dropped to mine again. "You can't just stay out of things, can you, Kathleen?"

I was surprised at how angry I suddenly felt. "And you keep lying and cheating, looking for the easy way out. I don't get it. You have talent. Genuine talent. Why do you have to keep lying about who you studied with and who liked your work? You're better than that."

Ray pulled a hand over the back of his neck. "You don't have a clue what it's like to do something creative. I'm not explaining myself to you."

"You knew Kassie was going to be one of the judges, didn't you?" I said. "It was one of the worst-kept secrets in town after the news got out that Elias was going to be filming the show here in Mayville Heights."

He didn't say anything but the way the muscles tightened in his jaw made me think I was onto something.

"You used that connection with her to get on the show, or at least up the odds in your favor."

"You can't prove any of that," he said.

I folded the picture and stuck it back in my pocket. "Kassie saw your CV. It was probably in the information packet on the contestants that the producers put together. You spent that summer hanging out so she knew you'd been kicked out of Dougall's class."

"Yeah, fine, she knew." He wouldn't look me in the

eye. "She was trying to get me to throw the competition for some reason. But I didn't kill her."

I folded my arms over my chest. "Why should I believe you?"

His mouth twisted and pulled to one side. "Because when Kassie was killed I was in bed with Caroline."

16

"Caroline?" I said. I had to have heard him wrong.

"Yes." There was a smugness to Ray's voice that I didn't like. He pulled his phone out of his pocket. "Would you like me to call her?"

"Caroline's married."

He shrugged. "So? Maybe she got tired of being the perfect little earth mother."

"She was at the library that night with Kate Westin," I said. "I talked to them."

He shrugged. "She walked over from my apartment. I don't know where she connected with Kate. And before you ask, after Caroline left I was online playing *World of Warcraft*."

I believed him. It was all too easy to check. I wondered if Marcus knew what Ray had been doing. And who he'd been doing it with.

Ray looked at his drawing again. "Any more questions?" he said.

I nodded. "Just one. Were you going to do it?"

"Do what?" he asked.

"Lose on purpose, the way Kassie wanted you to."

He smiled. "That depends."

"On?"

"On whether she made it worth my while."

I had no more reasons to stay in the room with Ray so I turned around and left. I went out into the stairwell and sat on the top step. Ray truly was reprehensible. I had no problem letting Maggie and Ruby know what I'd learned. It was up to the co-op whether or not he stayed.

I was stunned that Ray had been with Caroline. And not just because she was married. She was warm and nurturing and kind, and in my experience Ray was none of those things.

So far it felt as though all I had learned amounted to nothing more than gossip. Charles had slept with Kassie. Ray had slept with Caroline, and Russell was still sleeping with Stacey. Not to mention that Kassie had tried to blackmail Charles and Ray and undermine Caroline, Stacey and Kate. And she'd threatened Eugenie. The only person she hadn't gone after was Rebecca and that was because Kassie had put a large wager on her. The Baking Showdown had a lot more in common with *The Wild and Wonderful* than I ever would have expected.

I went to Ruby's studio to collect Hercules. They were looking at something on Ruby's laptop.

"Did you get what you needed from Ray?" she asked.

"I think so," I said. "I need to talk to you about Ray.

I don't have time right now. It doesn't have anything to do with Kassie's death."

Her eyes narrowed in curiosity but she didn't ask any questions. "Text me when you have the time."

I nodded. "I will."

"Are you coming to class?"

I reached for Hercules. "I have to take this one home so I might be a bit late."

Ruby waved at him. "Thanks for hanging with me," she said.

"Mrrr," he said in return. Ruby had very rapidly become one of the little tuxedo cat's favorite people.

I drove home, let us into the kitchen and dumped my things on the table. Before I did anything else I got Hercules his two sardines. There was no sign of Owen anywhere.

I ran upstairs, changed and washed my face. Back in the kitchen again, I made a peanut butter and banana sandwich and filled my water bottle. I crouched down next to Hercules. He'd already made short work of one of the sardines. "I'm going to tai chi," I said. "Stay out of trouble while I'm gone." I gave him a scratch on the top of his head and he breathed sardine breath in my face.

"See you later, Owen," I called. After a long pause I got an answering meow. From the sound he was somewhere upstairs. That probably wasn't a good thing.

Maggie had just started the warm-up when I got to class. I changed my shoes and slipped into the circle next to Taylor King.

Maggie worked us hard and my T-shirt was damp with sweat by the time we finished the form at the end of class. I had forgotten my towel so I wiped my flushed face with the edge of my T-shirt. "Roma had to go to Minneapolis to give a second opinion on a surgery," I said to Maggie. "That's why she wasn't here."

"Thanks," she said. "I guessed it was something like that." She stretched one arm up over her head. "Is Hercules okay?"

I smiled. "He got a clean bill of health and celebrated with two sardines."

Maggie smiled. "I think that's how I celebrated the last time the dentist told me I had no cavities." She held up one hand. "No wait. It wasn't two sardines. It was two brownies."

"Hercules would be happy to celebrate with two brownies if I'd let him," I said. I pulled at the neck of my shirt. I was still warm.

"Did you bring your water bottle?" Maggie asked.

I nodded. "It's in my bag. I'll get it in a second. I just . . . I need to talk to you about Ray." I held up my hand. "Not right now. In a day or two when things aren't quite so busy."

"Okay," she said slowly. "You found out something, didn't you?"

"I'm sorry, Mags. I did. I don't mean to be vague, I just don't want to tell you now and then take off before I can explain everything. And it's something Ruby should hear as well."

"So in a day or two the three of us will sit down and you can tell us what you found out."

"Sounds good," I said. "I need to get going." I was hungry. I had wolfed down my makeshift sandwich on the way down the hill but I was pretty sure I'd used all that energy in class. There was chili in my freezer and soup in my fridge and I was going home to have some of one of them.

Rebecca was sitting on the bench under the coat hooks changing her shoes. "I brought you something," she said, gesturing at her canvas tote bag.

"For me or for my two furry roommates?" I asked with a teasing smile.

"For you." She pretended to think about her answer for a moment. "Although . . ."

I laughed. "Next time Roma gets after me about their diet I'm just going to tell her to call you. Don't say you weren't warned."

Rebecca stood up and took a rectangular metal cookie tin from her bag. "I babysat Roma," she said. "I changed her diapers. She doesn't scare me." She smiled and handed me the cookie container.

I eased the lid up on one corner and peered inside. There were two slices of a Swiss roll inside. I looked at Rebecca. "I smell orange and hazelnut and something sweet."

"It's probably the honey," she said. "I was going to make my chocolate raspberry roll, but this was my grandmother's recipe and I thought it might bring me good luck."

"Just based on how delicious this smells, I don't think you need any luck," I said. My stomach growled loudly.

Rebecca laughed. "Thank you for that vote of confidence," she said. "Sometimes I want to pinch myself. I can't believe I made it this far. I can't believe I made it on the show at all."

I closed the lid of the cookie can before I was any more tempted to eat both slices of cake here and now. "What makes you say that?" I asked, setting the container on the bench. "You finished in the top three in the regional qualifier."

Rebecca sat back down and started to tie her shoe. "That was far from a sure thing. In fact, if Dorrie Park hadn't dropped out, there's a very good chance that I wouldn't be on the show right now."

"She's the one who left the contest right before the semifinals."

Rebecca nodded. "Some kind of family emergency. She was a talented baker and extremely creative. She would have placed ahead of me for certain." She held up a hand before I could object. "That's not false modesty on my part, Kathleen. I know my own strengths and weaknesses. Ray, Kate and I were the top three bakers but I have no idea in which order we were ranked. If Dorrie had stayed, who knows how things might have worked out?"

I stepped out of my tai chi shoes and stuffed them in my bag. "Well, they worked out well for you and I hope they worked out for her as well."

"As far I know, they did," Rebecca said. "One of the crew said Dorrie just got back from Paris." She glanced at her watch. "Heavens! I need to get going. Everett is waiting."

"Thank you for the cake," I said.

She got to her feet again and reached for her own bag. "You're welcome. Enjoy."

When I got home Hercules was nowhere to be seen. Owen was in the kitchen sitting at the table. I glared at him and pointed at the floor. "Get down," I said firmly. This was getting to be a habit. I took a step toward him. He made more grumbling sounds than were strictly necessary but he jumped to the floor and went to have a drink.

I hung up my tai chi bag and picked up the things I'd dumped on the table earlier. After I'd washed my hands and splashed water on my face I got myself a bowl of soup and warmed it in the microwave. I was at the table crumbling crackers into my dish when Marcus called.

"I'm sorry," he said. "I'm in the middle of . . . something. I'm not going to make it."

I knew "something" could be a new case, a current case or even an older one that was working its way through the system.

"It's okay," I said. "One question, though. Does Ray Nightingale have an alibi for the night Kassie was killed?"

He hesitated. "Yes."

"He was with Caroline Peters."

"One of them told you," Marcus said.

I was nodding even though he couldn't see me. "Ray did." I hesitated. "And you need to ask more questions about the lorazepam."

"No, I don't."

"Trust me, you do," I said.

"No, Kathleen, I really don't."

I got it that time. He knew about Stacey. I didn't know whether she'd told him herself, or Russell had, or he'd found out some other way.

He knew. Why was I surprised? Marcus was good at his job.

"I'm sorry," he said. "I really have to go."

"Stay safe," I said. "I love you."

I set the phone on the table and went and got one slice of the Swiss roll from Rebecca's flowered tin. It tasted even better than it smelled. The cake, with hints of spices, honey and vanilla, was wrapped around a creamy orange-flavored filling with just a hint of nutmeg. I had a feeling Rebecca was going to be the next episode's Hot Shot of the week as well.

As I licked orange filling from the back of my fork I thought about what Rebecca had told me. How could she *not* have made it on the show? She had described the young woman who had dropped out of the qualifier as being talented and creative. But so was Rebecca.

Curiosity got the better of me. I got up and got my computer. When I got back to the table, Owen was in my chair.

"That's my seat," I said.

"Mrrr," he replied, blinking his golden eyes at me. I suspected that was his way of saying "finders keepers."

I set the laptop on the table, scooped up Owen and set him on my lap once I'd reclaimed my place. It didn't take us long to find an article in the Chronicle about the regional baking contest. I scanned the photo that accompanied the piece. Dorrie—short for Dorian—Park was in the front row between Kate and Rebecca. She looked to be nineteen, maybe twenty. She had black hair twisted into two buns, one on each side of her head, and choppy bangs. The left side of her nose and her left eyebrow were pierced. She wore a black T-shirt under a red-and-black plaid shirt and black Doc Martens. She was looking directly at the camera and while she wasn't smiling it seemed to me there was just a tiny hint of something—arrogance maybe—in her dark eyes.

I leaned against the back of my chair and began to stroke Owen's fur. He laid his head against my chest and looked up at me.

"Rebecca said that if Dorrie hadn't dropped out she might not have made it onto the show."

Owen wrinkled his nose.

"I know, that does sound wrong."

"Mrrr," he agreed.

"It occurs to me that it's also possible that if Dorrie Park hadn't left the contest, *Ray* wouldn't have made it onto the show." Was I too judgmental where Ray was concerned? Too suspicious?

Owen's whiskers twitched. He looked from me to the computer.

Maybe not.

It wasn't hard to find Dorrie Park's social media accounts. They were full of photos from her recent Paris trip. I checked the date of the first photo that had been posted. She'd arrived in Paris less than a week after she'd dropped out of the qualifier.

"Whatever that family emergency was, everything was all right pretty quickly," I said to Owen.

I took a quick look at some of Dorrie's other photos. She was a student at the University of Minnesota Duluth, living in a basement apartment with three other young women. She didn't have a car and she could get pretty creative with ramen. In other words, she seemed like a typical broke student.

"So how did she afford a trip to Paris?" I said.

Owen cocked his head to one side, considering my question, at least from my perspective.

"What if someone gave her the money?"

"Mrrr," Owen said. That made sense. At least to him.

"What if *Ray* gave her the money?"

I didn't trust him. He was an opportunist. I was convinced he had used his past connection with Kassie to help him make it onto the show. So why wouldn't he get rid of the competition? And while it seemed that Ray had an alibi for Kassie's murder, I couldn't help thinking it was possible he'd manipulated that somehow, too.

I decided to send Dorrie Park a message via social media. It was a long shot but I couldn't think of any other way to find out if my suspicions about Ray were correct.

I explained I was a researcher with the show and I had a few questions for her. I added my phone number and crossed my fingers I'd hear back from her.

Owen had gotten bored at some point in the process and jumped off my lap. He was lying on the floor now, fishing under the refrigerator with one paw.

"What are you doing?" I asked.

He didn't answer. He just continued his efforts to reach for something under the fridge.

"Did you lose that frog Marcus got you under there?"

"Mrrr," he said. I didn't know if that was a yes or a no. Mostly it just sounded like aggravation.

The small space under the refrigerator seemed like a tight fit for Ferdinand the Funky Frog, but nonetheless I got one of my extra-long cooking chopsticks, crouched down next to Owen and poked around underneath. I didn't find a catnip frog or even a dusty stinky cracker but I did realize there was a piece of paper under there. After some finessing and a lot of cat commentary I managed to slide the paper out onto the kitchen floor.

"Is this what you were after?" I said to Owen. There was a clump of dust on his paw and I reached over to brush it off.

The page looked to be the image of a check that had been deposited electronically. I picked it up for a closer look. The check was made out to a holding company: Mulberry Hill Holdings. There was something familiar about that name but I couldn't place it. I did recognize who wrote the check. It came from Sullivan Enterprises. Sullivan Enterprises was Sean Sullivan, gym owner and Kassie's father. I looked at the amount. Five hundred thousand dollars. Sean Sullivan had written a check to someone for half a million dollars. The page must have slid under the refrigerator when Owen knocked down some of the papers that had come from Kassie's desk. How had she gotten this? Was Kassie Mulberry Hill Holdings or . . . ?

I got to my feet, picked up my phone and scrolled through the list of contacts. Lita answered on the third ring.

"Hi, Lita," I said. "I'm sorry to bother you at this time of night."

"Kathleen, it's eight thirty," she said, an edge of laughter in her voice. "What time do you think I go to bed?"

"Umm, after eight thirty?"

She did laugh then. "Sometimes after nine. What do you need?"

"Have you ever heard of a company called Mulberry Hill Holdings?" I crossed my fingers.

"Of course. That's one of Elias Braeden's companies."

I gave a small fist pump.

"I think he named it after that piece of land Idris Blackthorne owned out by Wisteria Hill," she said. "Ruby would own it now, I think."

Mulberry Hill. Rebecca had mentioned it when we were talking about Everett's family homestead. That's why the name had seemed familiar to me.

"Thanks, Lita," I said.

"You're welcome," she said. I heard the rumble of Burtis's voice in the background. "Burtis says to tell you he has the house high score at the moment."

"Tell him I said that all good things must come to an end and his end is nigh."

Lita was still laughing when she hung up.

I pulled out a chair and sat down. Owen leapt onto my lap and put two paws on my chest.

"Elias," I said. "He's Mulberry Hill Holdings."

One ear turned sideways and his expression soured a little bit. I stroked his soft fur. There was another dust bunny on his tail and I picked it off. "I can't find anything that points to someone else being Kassie's killer, and there are random things like his fingerprints and the fact that Elias was in the building that suggest he did it. And I don't know what to make of this check."

Ruby was a strong person, but if Elias really had killed Kassie, I didn't see how she would ever get over the betrayal.

And just that quickly I was angry. Angry at Elias for only telling part of the truth or maybe even none of it. Angry that Ruby had put her trust in someone I didn't think deserved it, even if he hadn't killed anyone. Angry at the prevarications and omissions from just about everyone involved with the show.

I set Owen on the floor and grabbed my keys and my wallet. "I'll be back," I told him. I didn't think about whether or not it was a good idea to go confront Elias. I just went.

It wasn't hard to find the man. His fancy SUV was in the parking lot at the community center. I signed in with Thorsten and on a hunch climbed the stairs to the second floor. I didn't see Elias giving up his private workspace. The hallway was dark with just a bit of light spilling out from one open doorway.

I was right. Elias was in the office, talking on his cell phone. "I'm going to have to call you back," he said to the person on the other end of the call when he noticed me standing in the doorway.

I set the image of the check in front of him. He looked at it and the only reaction I saw was a tiny twitch at one corner of his mouth. "Where did you get this?"

I had the urge to say from under my refrigerator, but I resisted the impulse. "Kassie had it."

He leaned back in the chair. "She kept hinting she had something."

"Sean Sullivan gave you half a million dollars."

"He invested half a million dollars in my *company*."

"It's the same thing."

Elias shook his head. "No, it's not. Half a million dollars to me is a gift. Half a million dollars to my company gets him a tiny piece of it. In theory."

I remembered what Eugenie had said to Russell and me: *"I do have more than enough money to relieve Elias of any financial obligation he might have to Sean Sullivan, Kassie's father."* Would she have spent half a million dollars?

He gestured to the chair in front of the desk. "Have a seat, Kathleen."

I sat down, picking up the piece of paper as I did. "Kassie thought this was important. Why?"

"I don't know," he said with a shrug. "You would have to ask her and since she's dead, you can't."

I thought about doing something dramatic like

slapping my hand on the desktop. Instead I stared silently at him for a moment. Then I said, "You're lying." I leaned across the desk. "If it weren't for Ruby, I would take this to the police and wash my hands of you. I would leave you to twist in the wind. But I can't do that. You're the closest thing to a father Ruby has. And that more than anything tells me what a kick in the head life has given her that you . . . you of all people . . . get that honor." I struggled to keep my voice under control and shook the paper at him. "This is just one more thing that makes you look bad. One more thing in a long list. You better be innocent, Elias." My voice cracked. "You damn well better be innocent, because if you're not, you're going to break Ruby's heart."

All the lines on his face had seemed to have gotten deeper. That was the only sign that my words had affected him at all. He cleared his throat. "I didn't kill Kassie, Kathleen. I swear on—"

I cut him off. "Don't go there, Elias," I warned, hoping my voice conveyed how angry I was in that moment.

"The money was for me. Sully made it look like an investment in my company because neither one of us wanted to explain why he'd given me, personally, half a million dollars. He still has several boxers and I'm involved in several TV projects. Optics. You understand that."

"I do."

His face hardened. "What he didn't tell me was that he's being investigated for insider trading, which puts all of his business practices under a microscope."

"Not good for you."

He shook his head. "No."

"So Sean Sullivan paid you five hundred thousand dollars to hire his daughter because she had aspirations of being a TV star, which wasn't exactly on the up-and-up. And then he made that money look like an investment in your company, which also wasn't exactly on the up-and-up."

"Yes."

I folded the piece of paper and put it back in my pocket. "Kassie found out."

"She did. I was having some temporary cash flow problems. I shouldn't have taken the money. That was stupid."

"She must have been angry finding out her father had so little faith in her that he paid you to hire her."

Elias gave a humorless snort of laughter. "You didn't know Kassie. She was going to use that payment to blackmail her father. If he'd pay me half a million dollars so she could do the Baking Showdown, he could pay more than that to get her on some other show."

I wondered what had happened to Kassie to turn her into such a self-absorbed person.

"Do what you want with the information, Kathleen," he said. "I didn't kill Kassie Tremayne. And this is the last time I'm going to say that."

I nodded. Then I got up and walked out.

My hand was shaking as I signed out at the back door. I said good night to Thorsten and walked over to the truck. Some small part of me wanted to believe that Elias wasn't a murderer. But if he hadn't killed Kassie then who had?

Wednesday morning just after we opened, Harry Taylor and his brother, Larry, arrived at the library.

"Do you have something already?" I asked.

"Ever see any of the James Bond movies?" Harry asked.

"I've seen all of them."

He inclined his head in the direction of his brother. "He's Q."

"It wasn't complicated," Larry said with a smile. He handed me a small cardboard box.

I opened the flaps and peered inside. "This is the camera?" I said. The contents looked like a tiny robot spaceman in a white spacesuit with a black-visored helmet.

Larry nodded. "Wi-Fi, night vision, motion detector, 360-degree panoramic view, SD card *and* it will send an alert to my smartphone if anyone is around the gazebo." He looked at me a little uncertainly. "I hope it's okay that the alerts go to my phone. I couldn't have them go to Harry's. All he has is a flip phone."

Harry gave him a look that said this wasn't the first time they'd had a conversation about his phone.

"You could send the alerts to my phone," I said.

Harry shook his head. "I don't think that it's a good idea for you to come down here in the middle of the night to confront whoever has been pulling these stunts. I'm sorry if that seems sexist."

I recognized the size and strength difference between the two of them and me. "No, it's not. But I'd feel a lot better if you'd call the police when you get an alert."

"We can do that," Harry said.

I noticed he'd said "can," not "will." I also knew arguing wouldn't get me anywhere.

Harry and Larry installed the camera just under the back roof edge across from the gazebo. Unless you were looking for it, you couldn't see it from the ground or with a cursory glance at the building.

I was just walking back around the building when I caught sight of Caroline Peters coming up the sidewalk. She saw me and raised a hand in acknowledgment. I waited for her at the bottom of the steps.

"Hi," she said as she reached me. "Ray called me after you two talked last night. I just came from the police department."

I stuffed my hands in my sweater pockets. "I'm glad to hear that," I said.

"I'm sorry I deceived you. I'm sorry I deceived everyone." She played with the knotted bracelet around her left wrist. "No one knew about Ray and me. I wanted to keep it that way. When I left his apartment I was going to walk back to the café and just join everyone else. Then I met Kate." There was a second's pause. "She said, 'So you got tired of working on your bread and decided to come out for a walk, too,' and when I opened my mouth 'Yes' was what came out. I didn't mean to lie. It just happened."

"I believe you," I said. That was the thing about lying. It was surprisingly easy.

"Thank you," she said, and a little of the tension left her body.

I hesitated about whether to say anything else. The fact that I truly liked her won out. That and I didn't trust Ray as far as I could throw him, as Rebecca would say. "Caroline, your life and your marriage are absolutely none of my business," I said. "But Ray Nightingale is not someone worth blowing up your life over."

She pressed her lips together and nodded. I had no way to know if Ray had just been a reckless fling or if she had feelings for him. I hoped it was the former.

"I should go." She looked in the direction of the sidewalk.

I nodded. "Thank you for coming. You didn't have to."

"Yes, I did," she said. "I tell my kids to tell the truth all the time. I tell them when they've made a mistake to admit it. I need to start practicing what I preach." She gave me a small smile and headed toward the sidewalk.

I started up the steps. I realized that Kate didn't have an alibi anymore unless she had some kind of secret romance going on as well. It didn't exactly seem likely, given her soft-spoken, quiet demeanor. Neither did the idea of her being a murderer. So now what?

17

The phone rang Thursday morning before I had even had my first cup of coffee. I glanced at the screen. It was Harry. I knew what that meant.

"Good morning," I said.

"I'm not sure you'll think so when you know where I am," he said.

"You're at the library."

"Larry got an alert about half an hour ago."

I leaned against the counter. "You didn't catch our gazebo guy, did you?"

"No." I imagined Harry pulling off his ball cap and smoothing down what little hair he still had. "Whoever it was disconnected the camera and took the SD card. We've got nothing." I heard him exhale. "Well, almost nothing."

"What did he do this time?"

"There's an inflatable pool in the gazebo—pretty good size, too. It's full of Jell-O. And two squirrels, but

I think they just might be a couple of innocent by-standers."

"What kind of Jell-O?"

"I don't know," Harry said. "It's dark red."

I heard someone else say something.

"Larry says it's black raspberry."

"I'm on my way," I said.

"You sure?" he asked.

I pushed away from the counter. "I'm sure. Do you want coffee?"

"As long as it's not too much trouble," he said. "Aw, hell, even if it is too much trouble."

"It's not," I said. "I'll see you soon."

Owen and Hercules were fed. The litter boxes were clean. All I had to do was brush my teeth and my hair. I pulled my hair into a ponytail, put on some lip gloss and tossed a banana, a corn scone from the freezer, my travel mug and the rest of my makeup into my bag. It looked kind of lumpy.

I stopped at Eric's and got three large coffees. I found Harry and Larry standing by Harry's truck in the parking lot. I handed them each a cup. They both thanked me.

"Let's go see the gazebo," I said, wrapping my hands around my travel mug. Harry glanced at it but didn't say anything.

The pool almost covered the floor of the gazebo.

"I figure fifteen feet in diameter," Harry said. It was filled almost to the top with black raspberry Jell-O. Which had set. The squirrels were gone. I had a feeling that if we didn't get it emptied soon we could become the downtown squirrel hangout.

Part of me admired the resourcefulness of our guilty party. He or she had to be good at chemistry and computers and math. On the other hand, these stunts were costing time and money and I was afraid they might escalate to something dangerous.

I turned to Larry. "So, our offender disconnected the camera?"

He turned to gesture at the building. "I think he spotted the camera and somehow managed to disable the Wi-Fi temporarily." He shrugged. "It's not hard. He probably used a jammer. He did his thing, then he swiped the SD card. The cool thing is—"

Harry glared at him.

Larry's face reddened. "I, uh, mean the interesting thing is it looks like he hacked into the program and got it to send an alert when he was ready to leave."

"To bring us down here on a wild goose chase," Harry said.

"And maybe to show off a little, too," I said.

"You want me to put the camera back up?" Larry asked.

I looked at the building. I looked at the pool. I shook my head. "I appreciate all the work you put in, but I think it's time to bring Marcus in on this."

"It could just be a kid," Larry said.

"A kid that climbed up somehow and got that SD card out of the camera," Harry said. "A kid that could have gotten hurt."

"Harry's right," I said. "The first couple of times it was annoying and yeah, kind of funny, but now . . ." I looked over at the building. "I don't want to get here some morning and find some kid back here with a broken leg or worse."

I thanked Larry again for all his work.

"I'm just going to drive him home and I'll be back to get rid of that." Harry gestured at the gazebo. "You staying here?"

I nodded. "I've got breakfast and there's lots I can do. Come in for a cup of coffee if you'd like one when you get back." Like me, Harry now had a master key and the alarm code to the building.

I got my things from the truck and let myself into the building. It wasn't often I was alone inside. I liked being able to walk around with nothing but silence and thousands of books surrounding me.

By the time Harry came back I'd had my breakfast, brushed my teeth again, touched up my makeup and most importantly made the coffee. I got him a cup and he went to connect the hose so he could empty the pool while I set to work emptying the book drop, which for once was only full of books.

I took an early lunch because once again I needed to make a quick trip to the community center. Eugenie had stepped in to help Elias and since he seemed to be giving her a fair amount of leeway, she and Russell were going to film a quick segment at Wild Rose Bluff. I had mentioned that the library had a reproduction of an original map of the area. Eugenie wanted to use it in her segment.

"I know it's last minute," she'd said on the phone. "I'd be happy to send a production assistant to get it."

"I'll bring it," I said. While the map was just a reproduction, it was old and it wasn't something that usually left the library.

I took the map to the staff photographer, who was all set up to photograph it. The whole process took very little time and I thanked her before I headed for Eugenie's office.

Eugenie was at her desk with her laptop. She looked up when I knocked on the partly open door. "Oh, hello, Kathleen," she said, tucking a strand of her silver hair behind one ear. "I didn't realize what time it was."

"The map has been photographed," I said.

She smiled. "Thank you. May I see it?"

"Of course." I set the portfolio I was carrying down on the desk, removed the map and slipped it out of its protective cardboard cover.

Eugenie leaned over to get a closer look. "The original was all drawn by hand? The detail is spectacular."

"Yes, it was," I said. "And you're right about the detail. The original artist was very talented."

"Thank you for bringing it over," Eugenie said. "This is turning out to be a very busy day. I came in early to help Russell find some clips of Stacey. You know that the two of them are . . . ?" She made a rolling motion with one hand.

I nodded.

"After we finish today he's going to put together a little montage for her."

"You're doing the last part of the filming after lunch?" I asked as I returned the map to its protective cover. Peggy felt more at ease so I wasn't needed for this episode's filming. I had told her to call me if there was any way I could help but I didn't expect to hear from her.

She nodded. "We are. Yesterday went so well." She glanced briefly at the hallway door. "Not to speak ill of the dead, but Peggy has a much better rapport with everyone and she and Richard work very well together."

I slid the map back into the portfolio. "Maybe this will be a new career path for Peggy," I said.

"I don't doubt that she'd do very well on television if she chose to pursue it." Eugenie held up a hand and fluttered her fingers. "And this little birdie will be encouraging her to think about it."

"I'll let you get back to work," I said.

She glanced at the computer and sighed. "I don't mean to be melodramatic but I feel as though I have a bit of a Sisyphean task on my hands."

"What are you doing?" I asked.

She gave me a wry smile. "Elias wasn't happy with the In Memoriam we did for Kassie. He felt it was a little too impersonal, so he asked me to go back through some of the outtakes and other raw camera footage and see if I could find any casual moments of her with the crew or the contestants."

"You can't find anything?" I asked.

Eugenie shook her head. "I can find Kassie interacting with people but they aren't moments that belong in a memorial segment." She slid behind the computer again and hit several keys. "Take a look at this, Kathleen."

I came around the desk and Eugenie turned the computer so I could see the screen.

"This is actually from the day Kassie was killed," she said.

The footage was from the kitchen set. I remembered Rebecca mentioning that they were filming some promos that afternoon.

Kassie was standing in front of Caroline's workstation. Kate was working at her own station in the background, almost out of camera range. I got a glimpse of Ray behind her.

Caroline was angry. It was easy to see by the tension in her body, the rigidity of her shoulders and how she held the whisk she was using more like it was a weapon than a cooking tool. I noticed Kate in the background sneaking little peeks in their direction and even Ray glanced their way more than once. Maybe he did care about Caroline even just a little.

"You're a helicopter parent," Kassie said with the kind of joking tone that people used when they wanted to say something mean but also wanted to be able to say they were just kidding if anyone called them on it.

"I don't want to talk about parenting with you," Caroline said, her words clipped and tight. She kept her eyes down on whatever she was mixing.

"Chemicals are in everything we eat," Kassie continued, "everything we put on our skin. That's just life.

If they were that bad we'd all be dead by now." She either couldn't read Caroline's body language or she didn't care how she was making the other woman feel.

"Brennan reacts to yellow food dye." Caroline's voice was so low I barely caught her words. "He needs to have all-natural, organic ice cream, which I told Oliver's mother."

"Caroline had just found out her husband had to take their youngest to the ER. He had been at a sleepover and had an allergic reaction to something he ate. Ice cream, it seems," Eugenie said softly beside me.

"People like you make me tired," Kassie said. Her voice was dimissive, as though Caroline's concern about her child wasn't warranted. "All-natural." She made air quotes around the words. "You do know those terms are meaningless, don't you? You think those apples you made your pie with were grown only with composted cow dung? Not likely."

"Go away," Caroline said. She still wasn't looking at Kassie.

I wasn't sure if Kassie hadn't heard Caroline speak or had just ignored her.

"I have a friend who had a skincare company and her products were all-natural to keep all of you earth mothers happy. But she wasn't making any money because her line had such a limited shelf life. It looked like she was going to go out of business and the people that worked for her were going to lose their jobs. I told her, you need preservatives, you need stabilizers, that's why your products have no shelf life. Monique came to her senses, those jobs were saved and she even created more jobs when she moved the company headquarters to Saint Barthélemy *and* no harm was done."

She held out both hands and I half expected her to say, "Ta-da!" Instead, Caroline picked up the bowl in front of her and dumped the contents over Kassie's head. A mix of what looked like flour and cocoa coated the younger woman's hair, stuck to her face and floated in a cloud around her. In the background Kate dropped the glass jar she'd been holding and Ray gasped, yanked a pot off a burner and came around the side of his workstation, heading for Caroline I was guessing.

I remembered Rebecca talking about this incident. She'd made the bowl being dumped on Kassie's head sound like an accident.

Eugenie hit pause. "I should have done something sooner. I should have spoken to Elias. Kassie would have been gone and at least she wouldn't be dead."

"It's not your fault," I said. "You had no way of knowing what was going to happen."

She shook her head. "If you make a cake with rancid butter, it doesn't matter how good the quality of the other ingredients. The final result is ruined."

She nudged her glasses up her nose. "Enough of me nattering on. We both have work to do. I'll see you at tomorrow's meeting?"

I nodded. "I'll be there."

I met Kate at the top of the stairs on the way out. She gave me a small, tight smile. "I didn't think you'd be here until tomorrow," she said. She was wearing jeans, a loose T-shirt and a baggy sweater she had wrapped around her body. She looked cold.

"I came to see Eugenie," I said. "I heard you came first in Basics yesterday."

She nodded. "I was lucky. Everyone else was having a bad day." She shifted restlessly from one foot to the other. "Kathleen, I need to apologize to you."

I frowned. "For what?"

"I didn't mean to but I helped Caroline lie the night Kassie . . . died."

"It's okay," I said, switching the nylon portfolio from one hand to the other. It was an awkward size to carry. "You didn't do it deliberately to confuse anyone. There was no harm done."

"Thank you for saying that." Kate brushed the hair from her face. "Ruby told me what you've been doing. Have you managed to find anything to clear Elias?"

"Not yet."

"He made a better choice with Peggy," she said. "Kassie truly was a selfish person." She shrugged. "That kind of thing can get you killed."

18

I couldn't get the video that Eugenie had shown me out of my mind. I kept seeing the look of fury in Caroline's eyes as she dumped the contents of the bowl over Kassie's head. I saw the cloud of flour and cocoa hanging in the air. I could hear Ray gasp and the sound of the jar Kate dropped shattering as it hit the floor. It kept playing on a loop over and over in my head.

I drove home and for once Owen was not sitting on a chair in the kitchen. I went upstairs and changed into comfy yoga pants and a T-shirt for tai chi. When I came back downstairs I found him in the living room peering under the sofa.

"What are you doing?" I said.

Owen jumped at the sound of my voice, smacked his head on the front edge of the couch and yowled.

I went over and kneeled down beside him. "Let me see," I said gently. I didn't think he was hurt. He hadn't hit his head very hard.

He shook his head vigorously.

"Let me see," I repeated, putting one hand on his back.

I felt all over the top of his head, gently probing with my fingers. Owen didn't even wince and it didn't seem like there was any kind of injury under his fur. "You're okay," I said, smoothing his fur. He muttered and gave the sofa the stink eye.

I reached over and felt along the edge of the piece of furniture, just to be sure there were no staples or nails that he could have gotten cut with, but there was nothing but smooth fabric. But it did look like there was something under the couch.

I put an arm around Owen and leaned sideways so I could look underneath. He immediately shifted so my view was blocked. "I'm trying to see what's under there," I said.

He meowed loudly and tried to look injured and pathetic. "You're fine," I said. I gave him a little scratch under his chin. Then I shifted sideways again, and again Owen managed to block my view.

"Oh, for heaven's sake," I said. I was getting exasperated. I turned around, picked up the cat, set him down behind me and crouched close to the floor for a better look under the couch. Two paws stepped on the side of my head.

I squinted up at him. "What is wrong with you?" I snapped in frustration. Before the cat could get any more in my way I swept my arm under the piece of furniture in a wide arc, bringing several items out from underneath.

Owen had climbed off my head. I sat up and looked at my spoils. There was a thumb drive, a small pencil, half a package of gum, a lighter and an orange key chain with a tiny retractable knife shaped like a key. The thumb drive was the one Marcus had been looking for. I had seen the lighter in his SUV. He'd used the key-chain knife a couple of times to open bags of cat food out at Wisteria Hill. He'd asked me about the gum and while he hadn't said anything about a missing pencil I was willing to bet that was his, too.

Owen had forgotten all about his head. He was suddenly engrossed in the area rug in front of the couch.

"Where did all this come from?" I said.

He pretended he hadn't heard me. I stuck my head in front of him and put my face close to his. "All of these things? How did they get under the sofa?"

"Mrrr," he said. He gave me his best innocent face, but just like a person he couldn't quite look me in the eye.

I moved so I was in his range of vision again. "Owen, did you steal Marcus's things?"

He gave me a sulky look.

I shook a finger at him. "We don't take things that don't belong to us."

He muttered under his breath. "And we especially don't take things that could start fires." I wondered how the cat had managed to get in and out of Marcus's SUV on two different occasions to snag the gum and the lighter. At least now Marcus knew about Owen's ability to disappear. I wasn't sure how I could have explained what happened otherwise.

I picked up the thumb drive and the key chain.

There were teeth marks on the package of gum. I didn't think Marcus would want that back. As I reached for it Owen stretched out a paw and pulled the pencil toward him.

I snatched it away from him. "You're walking on thin ice, mister," I said sternly.

He looked down at his feet, puzzled, and then his golden eyes came back to mine.

"It's a figure of speech," I said. I jammed the pencil and everything else into my pants pocket.

I got to my feet and rubbed my forehead with the heel of my hand. Could cats have kleptomania? Did Owen need a kitty therapist? Or maybe I needed one for even asking the question.

I was setting the table when my phone chirped. It was a text from Ruby asking if I could bring Hercules to class. She had an idea for the concept for another calendar. She wanted to pair Owen and Hercules with different artists from the co-op.

Need to see Hercules with one of Maggie's pieces

The idea was a good one, and even better, I was happy to have Ruby focusing on something other than Kassie's murder. I texted back a yes.

I made a big bowl of spaghetti for supper with extra cheese because it had been that kind of day. Owen moped around by my feet. I'd eaten about half of my pasta when my cell rang. I picked it up. I didn't recognize the number on the screen, and I was about to set the phone down when I realized the area code was the one for Duluth. Dorrie Park went to school in Duluth.

"Hello," I said.

"Is this Kathleen Paulson?" the voice on the other end asked, no pleasantries, no preamble.

"It is."

"I'm Dorrie Park. You left me a message about the baking contest."

I nodded even though she couldn't see me. "Yes, I did."

"So you're what? Doing a little more digging into the people who are left on the show so no big secrets come out about the winner?"

"Something like that," I said, shifting sideways in my chair and pulling one leg up underneath me.

"I shoulda guessed this would happen. What'd you want to know?"

I decided not to beat around the bush. "You dropped out right before the semifinals. But you were good enough to make it into the top three. Why did you leave?"

"I had a family emergency."

"You dropped out of the contest for family reasons and less than a week later you were in Paris."

"So?" she said.

I wished we were having this conversation face-to-face. It was impossible to read Dorrie Park from just her voice. "So you were a student working two jobs and suddenly you're posting photos of yourself in front of the Eiffel Tower."

There was silence for a long moment. "Look, I don't

think I did anything wrong, but I don't want to get in trouble."

I rubbed the back of my neck with my free hand. "You're not going to get in trouble. I just want to know whether or not someone offered you money to drop out."

Dorrie made a sound that was halfway between a groan and a sigh. "Fine. Yeah. I needed the money and I didn't really care about taking the cooking course that's part of the prize. So I said yes. That's not really wrong, is it? I mean, it's not against the law or anything?"

"I don't think so," I said. "How much money are we talking about?"

She hesitated once again. "Twenty thousand dollars."

"Twenty thousand dollars?" I repeated. How had Ray gotten his hands on that much money?

"Yeah," Dorrie said. "And she gave it to me in cash so the IRS wouldn't find out."

A loud thumping sound filled my ears—the sound of my own heartbeat. "She?"

"She. Kate. Kate Westin. That's who we're talking about, right?"

"Umm, right." I didn't know what else to say.

"So do you wanna know anything else?" Dorrie asked.

"No," I said. I was trying to make sense of what I'd just found out.

"And just so we're clear, I'm not going to get in any trouble for this?"

"Not from me." That seemed to be enough for her.

"Okay, well, I gotta go."

"Thank you," I said, but Dorrie had ended the call and I wasn't sure she'd heard me.

I set the phone down on the table. It seemed I was wrong about Ray. Or at least about him being the one who had gotten rid of Dorrie Park.

My spaghetti was cold now and my appetite was gone anyway. I pushed the bowl away. I thought about Kate telling me how her modeling career had ended. I remembered the bitterness in her voice and the pain in her eyes. Was that why she'd gotten rid of Dorrie? Did she see winning the Baking Showdown as her only chance at a new career?

Owen was still moping around by my feet.

I reached down and stroked the top of his head. "You're not hurt," I told him. "You don't need stitches. You don't have a concussion. But if you really feel that bad I could arrange an emergency visit . . ."

I didn't finish the sentence and Owen gave me a quizzical look.

A visit to the emergency room. That's what had started the confrontation that had ended with Caroline upending that bowl on Kassie's head. I closed my eyes and tried to picture the video one more time. I tried to focus on every detail, every facial expression, every word, every sound.

And finally I knew who had killed Kassie Tremayne. It made sense. It fit the timeline. It fit the circumstances.

A wave of nausea rolled from my stomach to the back of my throat. I put a hand on my abdomen and took slow, deep breaths until it passed. Then I picked up my phone and called Marcus. All I got was his voice mail. I remembered that he had court tomorrow. He was probably meeting with the prosecuting attorney. "Call me, please, as soon as you can," I told his phone. "I know who killed Kassie." It wasn't until I set my phone on the table that I realized I hadn't told him who the killer was.

I washed my dishes, stopping several times to make sure the ringer on my phone was working. *Where was Marcus?*

I hunted all over the house for Hercules. I finally found him sitting on one of my Adirondack chairs in the backyard. "Want to go see Ruby again?" I asked.

He'd been staring off into the distance but his furry head swiveled in my direction the moment I said Ruby's name.

I gestured with one hand. "C'mon then."

He jumped down and made his way over to the steps.

"I just have to grab my bag and my keys," I said.

He put one paw on the bottom step. I half expected him to start tapping it impatiently.

I was glad to have the distraction of taking Hercules to class with me, but I couldn't help thinking about Kassie's murder. I couldn't see how I could be wrong. There was just one question I didn't have the answer to. I wasn't even sure it mattered, but . . .

I looked at my watch. I had a few minutes. I turned toward the community center.

There was a parking spot close to the back door.

Even more important, Russell's rental car was there. "I won't be very long and then we'll go see Ruby and Maggie," I said to Hercules. "Stay here."

I should have known he'd ignore me. He jumped up onto the dashboard and nonchalantly walked through the windshield. I glanced around to see if anyone had noticed but there was no one around.

I didn't have time to argue. I picked him up and started for the back door.

Harry was at the desk. "Hi, Kathleen," he said. He looked at the cat. "Hello, Hercules."

The cat murped a hello back.

"Is Russell still here?" I asked. "I saw his car outside."

Harry nodded. "He's here. He brought down a piece of strawberry tart about half an hour ago. Stacey's with him. Everyone else is gone."

I thanked him, signed the log and headed up the stairs. This conversation would be easier to have face-to-face.

I found Russell and Stacey in Eugenie's office, just getting ready to leave. He was winding a scarf around her neck and I thought they looked as though they had genuine feelings for each other.

Russell smiled when he saw me. "And you brought Hercules," he said.

Stacey smiled at the cat. "Hello, Hercules," she said. She looked at me. "It's okay, Russell told me I can't pet him."

"What are you doing here?" Russell asked. "Everyone's gone."

"There's something I wanted to ask Stacey."

"What is it?" She looked a little uncertain.

"Did you give Kate one of your pills the day Kassie was killed? I know what happened on the set when you were all filming the promos. I know Caroline dumped a bowl of flour on Kassie and Kate broke a jar."

Her pink cheeks and guilty expression told me yes before she spoke.

"She was so upset she was shaking and she couldn't seem to stand still. I . . . I didn't know what else to do. I gave her two."

I reached out and touched her arm. "Hey, you were just trying to help. It's okay."

"Is that it?" Russell asked.

"It is," I said.

"Let's go, then." He flipped the light switch, closed the door and we started down the hallway.

"Kathleen, we're going over to Fern's," Stacey said. "Would you like to join us?"

"Merow," Hercules said. It seemed he'd forgotten we were meeting Ruby.

"Yes, we know you would," I said, scratching behind his left ear. I smiled at Stacey. "Thank you, but we're going to tai chi."

"I didn't know cats did tai chi," Russell said.

"Are you kidding?" I said with mock surprise. "You should see his Cloud Hands."

My phone rang then. Marcus, finally. "Go ahead," I said. "I need to get this." They headed for the stairs.

But it wasn't Marcus. It was Abigail. "I'm sorry to bother you, Kathleen," she said, "but I'm having trouble with that monitor again, the one closest to the front desk."

"Have a good night," Russell called from the end of the hall.

I waved and he and Stacey were gone. "Whack it with the heel of your hand on the right side right in the middle of the top edge," I said to Abigail.

"Are you sure?" she asked.

"Just try it."

I heard a *thump* and then Abigail exclaimed, "It worked!" She sounded surprised.

"Well, one of these days it won't," I said. "And it probably won't last. I have another cable I can try. I'll see you in a few minutes."

Abigail thanked me and said good-bye.

"I'm going to take you over to Maggie and Ruby and then just run over to the library for a minute," I said to Hercules.

He wasn't listening. Something behind me had caught his attention. The hairs rose on the back of my neck as I turned around.

Kate was pointing a gun at me.

19

Maybe I could bluff.

"Kate, you scared me," I said. "Could you put that down, please?"

She smiled but there was nothing warm about it. "Seeing as how I'm planning on shooting you, no, I can't," she said. She held out her free hand. "Give me your phone."

Bluffing wasn't going to work.

I handed her my cell. She turned it off and put it in her pocket.

I glanced over my shoulder. The stairs were half a hall away. "Harry will hear you if you shoot me."

"I'm not going to shoot you here," she said. "C'mon, I'm smarter than that. After all, I killed Kassie and no one figured out it was me—well, except for you." She was wearing another of her long, loose sweaters and her free arm hugged her midsection. "Besides, at this time of night Harry will have closed the doors at the bottom of the stairs. They're fire doors. You could kill someone up here and no one would hear a thing. Ask me how I know."

"You found out that Kassie was connected to the woman who owned the skincare company that made the mask you had the allergic reaction to," I said.

"Monique Le Clair. They'd been friends since high school. Kassie told my lawyer that she had no idea where Monique was, but I knew that was a lie."

"That morning when you were all filming the promo on the set and Kassie was on Caroline about being a helicopter parent, she mentioned Saint Barthélemy. You finally knew where Monique Le Clair was."

"Eugenie showed you the video this morning. I walked past the door. Neither one of you noticed me." Her eyes narrowed. "How did you figure it out? I knew it was just a matter of time before you did, but what gave me away?"

My mouth was dry. "The glass jar you dropped." Maybe if I kept her talking Harry would wonder what was taking me so long.

Kate frowned. "I don't understand."

"I kept thinking about what happened. Caroline upended the bowl over Kassie's head; the jar slipped out of your hands; Ray pulled a pot off his stove and bolted toward Caroline. I was replaying it over and over in my head and I realized that the sound of the jar hitting the floor came just a fraction of a second before Caroline tipped over that bowl. It was like a storm. You always see the lightning before you hear the thunder because light travels faster than sound."

"She said, '*No harm was done,*'" Kate said. "She was the one who suggested putting chemicals in what was supposed to be a natural product. Kassie and her friend ruined my life and it was like it was nothing. And she was trying to do it again. She was trying to undermine me on the show, for no good reason, just because she liked to stir up trouble."

"The show was your way to get close to Kassie. To find out what she knew. You paid Dorrie Park to drop out of the qualifying competition so you'd be in the top three."

Kate gave a sigh of exasperation. "And she just had to go to Paris and put a whole bunch of photos online. What is wrong with people?" She gestured with the gun and I put my free arm protectively around Hercules as if it could somehow stop a bullet.

Kate noticed the gesture. "I won't hurt him." She seemed almost offended. "I'm not a monster. Kassie was the monster."

"Why didn't you tell Elias, tell everyone?"

She gave a snort of derision. "Like that would do a lot of good. Elias wouldn't have done a thing. Do you know what Kassie's real name is? Do you know who her father is?"

I nodded. "I do."

"Then you know telling Elias, telling everyone, would have been a waste of time. It's not like I had any actual proof."

I glanced over my shoulder again.

"Mr. Taylor isn't coming to rescue you," she said.

"And as far as he's concerned I left a little while ago. I was on the sidewalk when you got here. I had a feeling you'd figured everything out so I came back."

"How did you get back in the building just now without Harry seeing you?" I asked. At some point soon Harry had to wonder why I hadn't come back out.

Kate smiled again. "There's an alarm on the other door now. But not on the windows. Sloppy, don't you think?"

The only thing I could think of was to keep her talking. Maybe she'd have second thoughts about killing me if she had some time to think about what she was planning on doing. "So what happened the night Kassie died?" I said. "I know you'd taken her phone earlier in the day and then pretended to find it."

"Oh, so we're going to do the Miss Marple thing." Kate looked around. "Well, it's not an English country manor house but this will have to do. Yes, I *borrowed* her phone. There wasn't anything useful on it."

"But that's how you knew Kassie had a son."

"I knew that was a mistake as soon as I spoke."

"You went down to Eric's with everyone else." I glanced at the nearest office door. What were the chances it would be unlocked?

"Yes. Then I walked back because I didn't feel like socializing. The thing is, when you're quiet, people don't notice when you're gone."

"Why did you come back here? Why didn't you just go back to where you're staying?"

She brushed a stray wisp of hair off of her face.

"Because I wanted to bake. It's what I do when things or people make me feel crazy. And by the way, I'm not crazy."

"I know that," I said. "You're smart. You can think on your feet. So why did you come here to cook?"

She held up her free hand. "Because the oven in my apartment isn't working right. You know, if it had been, I would have just gone home and Kassie might be alive now. Imagine that." She studied my face for a moment. "How does that saying go? *'For want of a nail, the shoe was lost'*?"

"'*For want of a nail, the shoe was lost; for want of the shoe, the horse was lost; for want of the horse, the rider was lost; for want of the rider, the battle was lost; for want of the battle, the kingdom was lost; and all from the want of a horseshoe nail.'*"

She nodded. "That's it. Benjamin Franklin?"

"He often gets the credit," I said, "but there are variations of the words in both German and French literature that go back hundreds of years before him."

"I knew you would know that." Kate smiled. "For want of an oven a life was lost."

Something was broken inside her.

I shifted Hercules from one arm to the other. His head was cocked to one side now and he seemed to be listening to every word Kate said. "One thing I couldn't figure out was how did you get in that night? I knew there was some confusion when everyone left at the same time and Zach wasn't good at keeping track of people. But how did you get past him the second time?"

"Did you know Elias has a master key so he can use that other door?"

I nodded.

She shrugged. "He should have taken better care of it. Anyone could have copied it."

"Why didn't you show up on the security footage the way Elias did?"

She answered my question with a question. "Did you know there's a basement door into this building? No cameras there. Not then, anyway."

"Somehow you drugged Kassie." It was a detail I hadn't been able to figure out.

"No, I didn't," Kate said. "Not on purpose." Anger flashed in her eyes and the gun jerked in her hand. "Not on purpose. I'd start shaking whenever I thought about what Kassie had done to me. When Stacey first gave me those pills I . . . I didn't want to take them, but I didn't think I would ever be able to stop the shaking if I didn't."

Her hand was starting to tremble a little now. Even though she was holding a gun on me, even though she wanted to kill me, part of me just wanted to wrap my arms around her.

"So what happened?" I asked. "How did Kassie end up taking them?"

"I don't like to swallow pills so I made hot chocolate and I put them in it. Then I realized I'd left my bag in the washroom. I went to get it and when I came back Kassie had my drink. She thought everything was hers. I guess she didn't have the same tolerance for that kind of medication as I do."

I shook my head. "I would have been so angry at her."

She nodded in agreement. "See, you get it, don't you? I told her what she'd done to me. How she ruined my life. Those pills, they were making her sleepy, but she was the same as she always was. She didn't care. She didn't care about anyone but herself."

Hercules leaned his head against my chin. I reminded myself we'd been in worse situations—or close to it. Somehow I was going to figure something out.

"Do you know what Kassie said?" Kate asked. "She said I didn't have what it takes to be a model unless maybe it was walking a runway at the mall. And then she said I was going to be eliminated in the next episode of the show. I said she couldn't do that but I knew she could. She was slurring her words by then and she started to slump forward. She was next to the table and there was a bowl of whipped cream on it. I don't even know where it came from. It was so easy to just put my hand on the back of her head and hold it down. She didn't even struggle." She tugged the front of her sweater a little closer around her body.

Hercules gave a soft mrrr.

"I took the cup with me and I smashed it later and put the pieces in the garbage. Then I just started walking. What had happened didn't even seem real. So I pretended that it wasn't."

"And then you happened to come across Caroline."

Kate nodded. "I was just walking. I wasn't paying attention to where I was going. When I met Caroline I knew where she'd come from. I realized Caroline wanted it to seem like we'd been together and so I just went along with it. I put Kassie and all the bad stuff out of my head the way I always do."

She took a step toward me and she smiled at Hercules. "I like your cat," she said. "Maybe I could keep him when you're gone."

She reached out to take him and the gun dipped toward the floor. I started to tell her not to, but the words died on my lips.

Hercules yowled and slashed one paw at Kate. His claws caught the back of her hand and drew blood.

She yelped, grabbed her hand, and the gun hit the floor, skittering along the tile.

Hercules launched himself out of my arms.

"Run!" I yelled and we both bolted down the corridor and around the corner. We made it out to the main hallway and I realized the mistake I'd made. I should have gone the other way, past Kate, toward Harry and safety.

It was too late now. I pulled an office door a tiny bit ajar and hoped that would distract Kate for a few seconds.

Hercules was all the way at the end of the hallway. I could just barely make him out. We needed to get to the other set of doors, the one with the alarm. I realized the best way to do that was to go through the kitchen. I could feel my way there in the almost total darkness.

I felt my way past more offices, all of them locked. We made it to the kitchen and I worked my way around the room. The door that led to the back corridor that would take me to the main doors was blocked—probably for security reasons.

Hercules rubbed against my ankle. I knew Kate wasn't very far behind us. We had to find somewhere to hide.

I pictured the layout of the kitchen. There was a closet on the left side of the room. It was filled with supplies like birthday candles, muffin cups and parchment paper but it was too small for me to fit inside. So was the pantry cupboard stacked with flour and sugar and other supplies at the other end of the long counter.

I felt a bubble of panic expanding in my chest. Standing in the middle of the room the way I was made me an easy target.

I bent down and picked up Hercules. He nuzzled my neck. I looked around. I could just make out the table where I'd found Kassie's body. A stack of what looked to be folded tablecloths was at one end. Part of the table extended into a small alcove. It was better than nothing. At least I'd be out of sight when Kate opened the door. I scrambled onto the table and pressed myself into the back corner.

I knew Kate was coming. I could hear her opening office doors. She was methodical, careful. That bought me a little time.

What I needed was a distraction, something else like Hercules attacking so we could run back the way we came in. What my mother, when she was on stage, called smoke and mirrors.

There was a recycling bin next to me, pushed against the end wall of the alcove.

Smoke and mirrors.

I had an idea. I felt around inside the plastic bin and found a glass mayonnaise jar. That would work. I patted my pocket. I still had Marcus's gum along with his lighter. I set Hercules on the table. "Stay here," I whispered. I slid along the tabletop, leaned over and managed, somehow, to open the pantry door and grab the side of a bag of flour. At least that's what I hoped it was. I teetered on the edge of the table and almost lost my grip on the bag. I stuck my foot out to brace myself against the counter but I'd misjudged where I was and instead I hit the edge of the bottom cupboard. My foot turned in and a sharp pain sliced through my ankle. I bit down hard on my tongue to keep from making any noise. Somehow I managed to roll onto my side still clutching the flour, then righted myself and crawled back to my corner.

I tried to breathe through the pain. I kept one arm hooked around the bag of flour. This wasn't good.

Hercules crawled onto my lap.

I still needed one more thing. I should have climbed down and gotten the flour. I should have slipped over to the other cupboard first. I swiped a hand over my face. I wasn't going to give up now.

"I need you to get me a birthday candle," I whispered to Hercules. "They're in the other closet."

Did he know what a birthday candle was? I was certain he knew what birthday cake was. I reminded myself that Hercules was smart, smarter than the average cat because he wasn't an average cat. I set him on the table beside me. He jumped silently to the floor.

I fished a piece of gum out of my pocket and started chewing. I wasn't going to think about the possibility that this wasn't going to work. I also had Marcus's tiny key-chain knife in my pocket. I used it to open the top of the flour and make a slit about a third of the way down the front of the bag. As soon as I picked it up the flour would go everywhere. Which was exactly what I wanted.

Flour and some other carbohydrates can explode if they're hanging in the air as dust. All I needed to do was ignite that dust and I should be able to make enough of an explosion to distract and maybe momentarily blind Kate.

I felt Hercules land on the table beside me. He bumped my arm with his head and spit two small birthday candles into my lap. I pressed my face next to his. "Good job," I whispered.

I managed to reach the stack of tablecloths. I pulled one off the top of the pile. Then I got to work.

I used the gum to fix the birthday candle inside the jar. The flour, which was a special organic brand, had a foil liner between the two layers of the bag. I'd noticed that when Rebecca was using it. I tore off enough to cover the top of the jar. I figured I had maybe fifteen seconds maximum after I covered the opening to throw the jar and have it break before the candle went out. I lit it now with the stolen lighter and hid the jar by my leg. The pain in my ankle had subsided to a steady throbbing ache. As long as it would hold me we were good.

I held Hercules with one arm and arranged the tablecloth over the two of us. I gripped the flour sack with my other arm. I let my legs hang over the edge of the table and I waited. I didn't have to wait long.

I'd estimated that I had less than ten seconds for Kate to find the light switch. I hoped it was enough time.

She stepped into the kitchen and I swung the flour bag in a huge, satisfying arc, sending flour everywhere. It hung like a cloud of dust in the air. I jammed the scrap of foil on the jar and threw it toward the flour cloud with every ounce of strength I had.

Kate yelled something. The jar smashed on the floor. There was a second's pause, maybe less than that, and the flour ignited and exploded.

I jumped from the table, sucking in a breath as my foot hit the floor. I pulled the linen cloth farther over my head and ran through the sparks to the door. I dropped the tablecloth in the hall and kept moving. Pain shot up my leg with every step but I kept on going.

I ran headlong into Harry as I came around the last corner. He caught me by the shoulders. His ball cap was skewed sideways and I could see the concern etched in the lines on his face.

"We have to get out of here," I said. For all I knew, Kate and her gun could be right behind me.

I took one limping step and Harry put his arm

around my shoulders. I leaned against him and he half dragged me down the corridor and down the stairs.

"What happened?" he said.

Police cars with sirens screaming and lights flashing were pulling into the lot as we came out the door. We were safe.

"I made a bomb," I said.

Marcus skidded to a stop right in front of us. I set Hercules on the hood of his SUV and leaned against the front bumper to catch my breath. Marcus got out of the car, leaving the driver's door wide open.

"Are you all right?" he said.

I nodded. "Yes."

Hercules meowed loudly.

"Him too," I said.

Marcus shifted his gaze to Harry. "What about you?"

"I'm fine," Harry said. His eyes flicked to me and his head bent slightly in my direction. "I think she may have hit her head. She said she made a bomb."

"Kate killed Kassie," I said. Hercules was leaning against me and I put my arm around him.

"I know," Marcus said. He gestured to a couple of police officers and they made their way into the building. He put a hand on my shoulder. "Elias figured out that she had to have copied his key. He got here early this morning and she was in the kitchen. He called me. Then Maggie called and said you hadn't shown up for tai chi. I listened to your message and I was worried. Right after that Abigail called to say you didn't make it to the library, either. When she told me where you were I knew you were in trouble."

I held up my free hand. "How did she know where I was?"

"She heard Russell Perry talking to you."

He reached up and tucked a strand of hair behind my ear. "What happened?"

"Kate had a gun," I said. "She tried to kill us but Hercules and I made a flour bomb."

The cat meowed his acknowledgment.

Marcus frowned. "You know how to make a bomb?"

"I'm a librarian," I said. "I know all sorts of things."

20

Things were a blur after that. Kate was brought out in handcuffs. Even though she'd held me at gunpoint, all I felt was sad. She was lost and broken and part of that was because of Kassie.

"You need to be checked out by the paramedics," Marcus said.

I waved away his words. "I'm fine."

He looked down at my leg. The ankle was so swollen the top of my shoe was cutting into the skin of my foot. "Yeah, you look fine," he said with an eye roll.

One of the paramedics was walking toward me.

"Hi, Ric," I said.

He smiled. "Hi, Kathleen. You know, when I heard the words 'flour bomb' I had a feeling I might see you." He caught sight of Hercules. "And you," he said. He reached into his back pocket and pulled out half a piece of beef jerky.

The cat's eyes lit up.

Ric gestured at Marcus's SUV. "How about we put

him in the car and then you can sit on the driver's seat
and I can get a look at that ankle?"

"That works for me," I said. I picked up Hercules and
hobbled around the car door, holding on with one hand
while Marcus hovered. I set Hercules on the driver's seat
and he hopped over to the passenger side. Ric leaned
around me and handed him the piece of beef jerky. He
murped a thank-you and began happily chewing.

I dropped sideways onto the driver's seat with my
legs sticking out the open door. Ric crouched at my
feet and began feeling my ankle with gentle pressure.

I looked at Marcus. "Go do police stuff. I'm fine," I
said.

Ric looked up at him. "Go ahead," he said. "I've got
this. She's not going anywhere with that ankle."

Marcus caught my hand and gave it a squeeze. "I'll
be back," he said.

In the end, Ric decided my ankle was likely just
badly sprained. "You really should have it x-rayed just
to be safe," he said.

I pulled a hand back through my hair and flakes of
flour floated down around me. "Tomorrow, I promise," I said. "I just want to go home and have a shower."

"First thing tomorrow." He pointed a finger at me
for emphasis. "I know where the library is. I *will* come
find you."

I made an X on my chest. "First thing tomorrow
I'll go."

Ric wrapped my ankle, then he checked my lungs
and the small burn on the back of my hand. Marcus
came back as he was finishing the dressing on my hand.

"She's good to go," Ric said. "She needs to get that ankle x-rayed in the morning." He shot me a look. "First thing in the morning. And that dressing will need to be changed. Otherwise she's fine." He smiled at me. "Kathleen, as my grandmother would say, you're as tough as a boiled owl. I'm glad you're all right."

Marcus helped me into the backseat since Hercules was settled on the passenger side and didn't seem in any rush to move.

"Don't you need to stay here?" I asked.

He leaned down and kissed my forehead. "I need to get you home," he said. "Right now that's the only thing that matters."

Maggie pulled up in front of the house as we turned into the driveway. Rebecca was with her. Marcus helped me out of the SUV. Hercules got out on his own. "Are you all right?" Rebecca asked.

"I'm fine, really," I said. "Ric checked me out. I have a little burn on my hand and I sprained my ankle. That's all."

"That's enough," Maggie said, leaning down to hug me.

"Thank you for calling Marcus." I suddenly had a lump in my throat, thinking about what might have happened if she and Abigail hadn't guessed that something was wrong.

"I knew something wasn't right when you didn't answer your phone."

"Kate took my phone," I said to Marcus.

"I'll find it," he said.

We made our way to the back door, Hercules leading

the way, Marcus with one arm around me and the other holding my hand, and both Maggie and Rebecca close by. He eased me onto a kitchen chair. "I have to go back to the crime scene for a while," he said, leaning over me. "But I will be back." He kissed me. I put a hand on his chest for a moment before he straightened up.

He looked at Maggie and Rebecca. "Don't let her do anything."

Rebecca reached over and patted his arm. "Don't worry, dear," she said. "We've got this."

And they did. They fed me tea and toast and Maggie got me in and out of the shower and somehow managed to wash my hair without flooding the bathroom. Once I had my pajamas on she helped me into the bedroom. Rebecca came in with another cup of tea for me, trailed by both cats. They smelled like fish. I decided to pretend I hadn't noticed.

I wasn't tired, but Rebecca insisted I at least stretch out on the bed. Maggie sat cross-legged at my feet. Rebecca took the chair. Owen and Hercules sprawled on the floor.

"That poor child," Rebecca said.

"This means Elias is in the clear," Maggie said. "Ruby will be happy."

"That's one good thing, at least," I agreed.

It was pretty much the only good thing as far as the show was concerned. The revival of *The Great Northern Baking Showdown* was over. At least for now. Sunday afternoon Rebecca and Everett threw a farewell party on the set for the cast and crew.

"Thank you for everything you did for Elias," Ruby

said, taking both my hands in hers. She glanced at Marcus. "Both of you."

"I'm just glad that Kate didn't hurt anyone else," I said.

"What's going to happen to her?" Ruby asked.

"She's in jail for now. A judge will order a psychiatric evaluation," Marcus said. "I don't think there will be a trial."

Ruby nodded. "I'm glad. I don't mean what she did was okay but she isn't a bad person. She just got knocked down one too many times."

Over the course of the afternoon I talked to everyone. Russell and Stacey were going to continue their relationship. The way they looked at each other made my heart smile. Richard sent his regards to my mother, of course. Caroline promised to send me the recipe for her banana pancakes and I promised the stinky cracker recipe in return. She and Ray stayed away from each other the entire afternoon and I crossed my fingers that relationship had run its course.

Ray had resigned from the co-op. To his credit he had come clean with Ruby and Maggie and the other members before I said anything. He wished me well and I returned the sentiment. I was never going to know for sure, but I still suspected he'd used the serendipity of Kassie being one of the judges on the show to help secure himself a place, not that it had ended up benefitting him. I wasn't sure if Ray had learned anything from all of this. I hoped he had.

Charles had already left. He was auditioning for another cooking show. I hoped things worked out for him.

Marcus was talking to Everett, and Eugenie came to join me. "I'm very happy you're all right," she said. "I've very much enjoyed getting to know you."

"I feel the same way," I said. "Now that this show is over, what are your plans?"

She smiled. "I already have another job on a show that's quite similar to this one. I had to turn down their offer before because I'd made a commitment here. Luckily, they were still interested." She pushed her glasses up her nose. "You could have the job as my researcher if you'd like it. I'm sure the library would give you a leave of absence. We worked very well together."

"We did work very well together," I said. "And your offer is hugely flattering but I have to say no. Mayville Heights is where my heart is. I don't want to be anywhere else."

"I understand," Eugenie said. "If you change your mind let me know." She made her way over to Elias.

Rebecca came up behind me. "I heard what Eugenie said. The board would give you a leave of absence, you know." She bumped me with her hip. "I have an in. Are you sure you don't want the job? It's a wonderful opportunity, and it could lead to better things."

I looked around the space at all of the people I cared about. Susan and Eric, Abigail, Mary and Ruby. The Taylors. Burtis and Lita. Everett. Rebecca standing there beside me. Roma and Eddie. Maggie and Brady. Marcus.

I put my arm around Rebecca and smiled. "There isn't anything better than this."

ACKNOWLEDGMENTS

The first Magical Cats mystery was published almost ten years ago and here we are with an even dozen books in the series. This would never have happened without so many wonderful, supportive readers. Thank you all for sharing your love for Owen, Hercules and Kathleen.

My agent, Kim Lionetti, is part advocate, part den mother. I'm deeply grateful she's on my team. Thanks, Kim! Thanks goes as well to my editor, Jessica Wade, who makes every book better and lets me get the credit for her hard work.

This book and all the books in the series have benefitted from the talents of many, many people behind the scenes at Berkley. Thank you, everyone!

And last, but never least, thanks to Patrick and Lauren. Love you both!

If you love Sofie Kelly's
Magical Cats Mysteries, read on for an
excerpt of the first book in Sofie Ryan's
New York Times bestselling
Second Chance Cat Mysteries . . .

THE WHOLE CAT AND CABOODLE

Available wherever books are sold.

Elvis was sitting in the middle of my desk when I opened the door to my office. The cat, not the King of Rock and Roll, although the cat had an air of entitlement about him sometimes, as though he thought he was royalty. He had one jet-black paw on top of a small cardboard box—my new business cards, I was hoping.

"How did you get in here?" I asked.

His ears twitched but he didn't look at me. His green eyes were fixed on the vintage Wonder Woman lunch box in my hand. I was having an early lunch, and Elvis seemed to want one as well.

"No," I said firmly. I dropped onto the retro red womb chair I'd brought up from the shop downstairs, kicked off my sneakers and propped my feet on the matching footstool. The chair was so comfortable. To me, the round shape was like being cupped in a soft, warm giant hand. I knew the chair had to go back down to the shop, but I was still trying to figure out a way to keep it for myself.

Before I could get my sandwich out of the yellow vinyl lunch box, the big black cat landed on my lap. He wiggled his back end, curled his tail around his feet and looked from the bag to me.

"No," I said again. Like that was going to stop him.

He tipped his head to one side and gave me a pitiful look made all the sadder because he had a fairly awesome scar cutting across the bridge of his nose.

I took my sandwich out of the lunch can. It was roast beef on a hard roll with mustard, tomatoes and dill pickles. The cat's whiskers quivered. "One bite," I said sternly. "Cats eat cat food. People eat people food. Do you want to end up looking like the real Elvis in his chunky days?"

He shook his head, as if to say, "Don't be ridiculous."

I pulled a tiny bit of meat out of the roll and held it out. Elvis ate it from my hand, licked two of my fingers and then made a rumbly noise in his throat that sounded a lot like a sigh of satisfaction. He jumped over to the footstool, settled himself next to my feet and began to wash his face. After a couple of passes over his fur with one paw he paused and looked at me, eyes narrowed—his way of saying, "Are you going to eat that or what?"

I ate.

By the time I'd finished my sandwich Elvis had finished his meticulous grooming of his face, paws and chest. I patted my legs. "C'mon over," I said.

He swiped a paw at my jeans. There was no way he was going to hop onto my lap if he thought he might get a crumb on his inky black fur. I made an elaborate show of brushing off both legs. "Better?" I asked.

Elvis meowed his approval and walked his way up my legs, poking my thighs with his front paws—no claws, thankfully—and wiggling his back end until he was comfortable.

I reached for the box on my desk, keeping one hand on the cat. I'd guessed correctly. My new business cards were inside. I pulled one out and Elvis leaned sideways for a look. The cards were thick brown recycled card stock, with SECOND CHANCE, THE REPURPOSE SHOP, angled across the top in heavy red letters, and SARAH GRAYSON and my contact information, all in black, in the bottom right corner.

Second Chance was a cross between an antiques store and a thrift shop. We sold furniture and housewares—many things repurposed from their original use, like the tub chair that in its previous life had actually been a tub. As for the name, the business was sort of a second chance—for the cat and for me. We'd been open only a few months and I was amazed at how busy we already were.

The shop was in a redbrick building from the late 1800s on Mill Street, in downtown North Harbor, Maine, just where the street curved and began to climb uphill. We were about a twenty-minute walk from the harbor front and easily accessed from the highway—the best of both worlds. My grandmother held the mortgage on the property and I wanted to pay her back as quickly as I could.

"What do you think?" I said, scratching behind Elvis's right ear. He made a murping sound, cat-speak for "good," and lifted his chin. I switched to stroking the fur on his chest.

He started to purr, eyes closed. It sounded a lot like there was a gas-powered generator running in the room.

"Mac and I went to look at the Harrington house," I said to him. "I have to put together an offer, but there are some pieces I want to buy, and you're definitely going with me next time." Eighty-year-old Mabel Harrington was on a cruise with her new beau, a ninety-one-year-old retired doctor with a bad toupee and lots of money. They were moving to Florida when the cruise was over.

One green eye winked open and fixed on my face. Elvis's unofficial job at Second Chance was rodent wrangler.

"Given all the squeaks and scrambling sounds I heard when I poked my head through the trapdoor to the attic, I'm pretty sure the place is the hotel for some kind of mouse convention."

Elvis straightened up, opened his other eye, and licked his lips. Chasing mice, birds, bats and the occasional bug was his idea of a very good time.

I'd had Elvis for about four months. As far as I could find out, the cat had spent several weeks on his own, scrounging around downtown North Harbor.

The town sits on the midcoast of Maine. "Where the hills touch the sea" is the way it's been described for the past 250 years. North Harbor stretches from the

Swift Hills in the north to the Atlantic Ocean in the south. It was settled by Alexander Swift in the late 1760s. It's full of beautiful historic buildings, award-winning restaurants and quirky little shops. Where else could you buy a blueberry muffin, a rare book and fishing gear all on the same street?

The town's population is about thirteen thousand, but that more than triples in the summer with tourists and summer residents. It grew by one black cat one evening in late May. Elvis just appeared at The Black Bear. Sam, who owns the pub, and his pickup band, The Hairy Bananas—long story on the name—were doing their Elvis Presley medley when Sam noticed a black cat sitting just inside the front door. He swore the cat stayed put through the entire set and left only when they launched into their version of the Stones' "Satisfaction."

The cat was back the next morning, in the narrow alley beside the shop, watching Sam as he took a pile of cardboard boxes to the recycling bin. "Hey, Elvis. Want some breakfast?" Sam had asked after tossing the last flattened box in the bin. To his surprise, the cat walked up to him and meowed a loud yes.

He showed up at the pub about every third day for the next couple of weeks. The cat clearly wasn't wild—he didn't run from people—but no one seemed to know whom Elvis (the name had stuck) belonged to. The scar on his nose wasn't new; neither were a couple of others on his back, hidden by his fur. Then someone remembered a guy in a van who had stayed two nights at the campgrounds up on Mount Batten. He'd had a cat with him. It was black. Or black and white. Or possibly gray. But it definitely had had a scar on its nose. Or it had been missing an ear. Or maybe part of its tail.

Elvis was still perched on my lap, staring off into space, thinking about stalking rodents out at the old Harrington house, I was guessing.

I glanced over at the carton sitting on the walnut sideboard that I used for storage in the office. The fact that it was still there meant that Arthur Fenety hadn't come in while Mac and I had been gone. I was glad. I was hoping I'd be at the shop when Fenety came back for the silver tea service that was packed in the box.

A couple of days prior he had brought the tea set into my shop. Fenety had a charming story about the ornate pieces that he said had belonged to his mother. A bit too charming for my taste, like the man himself. Arthur Fenety was somewhere in his seventies, tall with a full head of white hair, a matching mustache and an engaging smile to go with his polished demeanor. He could have gotten a lot more for the tea set at an antiques store or an auction. Something about the whole transaction felt off.

Elvis had been sitting on the counter by the cash register and Fenety had reached over to stroke his fur. The cat didn't so much as twitch a whisker, but his ears had flattened and he'd looked at the older man with his green eyes half-lidded, pupils narrowed. He was the picture of skepticism.

The day after he'd brought the pieces in, Fenety had called to ask if he could buy them back. The more I thought about it, the more suspicious the whole thing felt. The tea set hadn't been on the list of stolen items from the most recent police update, but I still had a niggling feeling about it and Arthur Fenety.

"Time to do some work," I said to Elvis. "Let's go downstairs and see what's happening in the store."

Sofie Kelly is a *New York Times* bestselling author and mixed-media artist who lives on the East Coast with her husband and daughter. She writes the *New York Times* bestselling Magical Cats Mysteries (*The Cats Came Back, A Tale of Two Kitties, Paws and Effect*) and, as Sofie Ryan, writes the *New York Times* bestselling Second Chance Cat Mysteries (*No Escape Claws, The Fast and the Furriest, Telling Tails*).

CONNECT ONLINE

SofieKelly.com